Moments at McBride

Shannon Everhart

First Edition

PAGE PUBLISHING, INC.
Conneaut Lake, PA

First originally published by Page Publishing 2020

ISBN 978-1-6624-1731-3 (pbk)
ISBN 978-1-6624-3714-4 (hc)
ISBN 978-1-6624-1732-0 (digital)

Printed in the United States of America

For my mother, Patricia Taylor.

Of all the seasons, my favorite season has
been Fishing Season with you.

Thank you for all that you taught me, for believing
in me, and for showing me how hard someone can
truly fight when they believe in something.

Rest in peace Momma.

Acknowledgements

Photography—
Mr. Foto, Located in Scottsburg, Indiana
812-752-7673

Hair—
Hair Today, Located in New Albany, Indiana
812-944-3696

Chapter 1

"I KEEP HAVING that same dream over and over again where I watch the nurses take my sister down a long hallway. She looks back at me with tears running down her face, and all I can do is stand there. I keep thinking I need to run to her and undo the straps to set her free, but I don't. I'm too afraid of my mother and what will happen if I do, so I just let her go. The next thing I know we are in a dark room, and a very tall man dressed in a white lab coat is telling us something went wrong during my sister's procedure and Laura survived, but there were complications. My mother grabs my hand, and we run past him to Laura's room in the ICU. As we burst through the door to her room, the nurses are standing around the hospital bed working on my sister but move aside when we run in. I see my sister's face and its different shades of blue and black. Her head is so swollen that I can barely recognize her. Her right eye is dangling down her face completely free of its eye socket, and I scream at the horror of it all. Then I wake up scared, I'm covered in sweat and crying," I tell my therapist, who sits across from me.

"So the medicine I gave you last time isn't helping with the dreams?" she asks me.

"Well, they weren't occurring as often, but the last couple of weeks, they've been happening almost every night," I tell her.

"Do you think that it's a result of the new job you're getting ready to start? You know I warned you that a position as an orderly in a mental hospital was not the best idea for you considering everything you've been though, Jenny," she scolds me.

"I know you did, and it may not be, but all I can think about is everything my sister went through and then her having died in that place. It haunts me because I think I should have done more for her at the time, and if I had known what they were going to do to her, I would have. I just didn't understand what a lobotomy was. Since I can't change any of that or what happened to her, I would like to have a chance to help others that are like her. It's the right thing to do."

"Jenny, you were six. It wasn't your place to do anything for your sister. You had a mother, and she should have done more, but back then they didn't even understand mental illness like they do today. A lot has changed in the last twenty years, and lobotomies aren't even performed anymore. Now there are medications and advanced therapy people with schizophrenia can take or participate in. We've gone over all of this before, so the fact that you're going through it all again tells me that you should really rethink taking on this new job."

"Oh, Patty, you've been more to me than my therapist over the last ten years. You were a mother to me when I needed you, and you've been my very best friend for a long time. I'm thankful you got me a job at McBride Mental Hospital because it's going to be the very thing to get me past all of this. I really believe it will."

"For your sake, I hope it does, Jenny. I really hope that when you get in there and see that it's nothing like the mental hospitals they closed down years ago for mistreatment of their patients, you will feel much better about all of this. Just remember you can't save everybody. The patients you'll be tending to are not your sister or your friends. It will be a career, a job, and nothing more. My nephew Blake has been an orderly there for six years now, and he'll be there to show you the ropes. Please listen to him. Do what he tells you to do. I know you have the education and the physical strength for this, but it's the mental aspect of it I'm worried about for you. I've only told Blake that you're a friend in need of a job, so he doesn't know about what happened to your sister. It's your choice to tell him or not to tell him, but he's a smart, hardworking man, and I think you'll do well to listen to him."

"I will, I promise. I really appreciate the job and, well, everything over the last ten years. For a while I didn't know if we'd ever get to this point, but I'm ready now. The bad thing about all of it is that I'm going to miss you so much when I move," I confess.

"I'll miss you too, Jenny. If you get up there and need to talk about anything, you give me a call. Pekin, Indiana, is a long way from Lawrence, Kansas, but if it gets bad, I'll visit."

"Thank you so very much, for everything. I promise I'll keep in touch. I do have to go, though. My flight leaves in two hours, and I still have to go back to my apartment and pick up my bags."

I walked over and gave Patty a big hug as she stood up, knowing it would be a long time before we saw each other again. When we pulled apart, she looked just as sad as I felt. After I left, I caught a cab downtown and stopped by my apartment. I took one last look around at the large, empty space, relishing the fact that this was real. I was really going to start living my life after all these years. The excitement I had felt when I first went to Indiana to accept the orderly position at McBride couldn't even compare to the high I was feeling now. I smiled, reached down, and picked up my two suitcases I had left there, then headed downstairs to the cab. On the ride to the airport, I thought about what it would be like living in Indiana. I had only been there once before, when Patty had first told me she got me a position as an orderly at McBride Mental Hospital in the middle of nowhere Indiana. She went out there with me to help find me a place to live, see the hospital, and take a tour of the area so that when I did move there permanently, I would know where everything was.

I happened to find a house for rent about five miles from the hospital. It was an old two-story farmhouse. The woman that rented the place to me said that her mom and dad lived there for years but retired to Florida when they got older and left the property to her. She already had a house of her own with her husband and three kids, so she used the old farmhouse as extra income and kept it rented out. It was a cozy little house with big tall windows, hardwood floors, and a fireplace in the living room. There were no close neighbors, and a short walk through the back field led you to a pond, where you could go swimming. As soon as I saw it, I fell in love with it. I gave the woman my deposit along with the first month's rent and let her know I'd be back in a month to get moved in. Once I got back to Kansas, I sold everything I owned and pocketed the money I made off it so that I could buy new once I got moved. Of course, now that I knew there were no stores in Pekin, no shopping malls, or no cities anywhere close to where I'd be living, this might be a bigger challenge than I thought it would be.

I checked my two suitcases at the airport as I made my way through to my plane. Once I found my seat and got settled in, I took out a book and started to read. I always felt sick on planes, and this time was no different. I felt my stomach knot up and my mouth watered as I fought back the urge to throw up in my lap. I'd just concentrate hard on my book, and after we'd get in the air, I'd feel better, I told myself. I was just starting the second chapter when a man walked up beside me and started putting his things in the overhead compartment. I couldn't help but stare. He was gorgeous. Tall, powerfully built, tan skin, dark hair, and yes, even a nice bulge protruding from the front of his jeans, which I happened to notice considering it was eye level with me. I brought my eyes back up to see the man staring back at me. I instantly flushed and returned my eyes back to my book.

He sat down in the seat next to me and then turned to me and said, "Hi there."

"Hi," I squeaked back, too embarrassed now to really say anything to him.

"My names Robert Shaw," he said, extending his hand out to shake mine.

"I'm Jenny Allen," I replied back, putting my hand in his. His hand was rough, calloused, and when he gripped mine, I felt all my nerve endings suddenly wake up and pay attention. His hand was so big it swallowed my tiny one, but I liked the strong feel of it. I looked back up into his beautiful green eyes. They were so bright they sparkled in the light. My mouth went dry, and my heartbeat picked up. I forgot all about the book I had been reading and felt totally mesmerized by this dreamy-looking man sitting before me.

"Excuse me for being so forward, but you are so beautiful," he said in a deep, husky voice befitting a man his size.

"Thank you," I replied, embarrassed, and I wanted to look away. With everything in me, I wanted to look away, but something held me perfectly still, and I couldn't tear my eyes away from his. He was stunning, and I was utterly thrown by the sight of him.

His lips parted. He suddenly looked lost as he took a sharp intake of breath, and we continued to just stare into each other's eyes. Then out of nowhere a flight attendant came up to us and broke the spell we both seemed to be under as she asked, "Can I get you anything?"

I pulled my hand away, and Robert finally turned to face her.

"Yes, I'd like a Coke, please," he responded, then turning back to me, he asked, "Jenny, is there anything you want?"

I was lost for a moment in his deep voice and that Southern drawl he had. It wasn't thick like someone from the deep South might have, but it was definitely there, making every word that came out of his mouth perfect. I finally answered, "I'll take a 7 Up and some crackers if you have it, please." As I spoke, I finally took my first good look at the flight attendant. She had this idiotic grin plastered across her face, and even though I was the one speaking, she never took her eyes off Robert. She was tall, skinny, a platinum blond with long hair down to the middle of her back and completely beautiful. Of course she was—she was a flight attendant. *Did they come any other way?* I thought to myself.

Robert seemed to notice her staring too and looked back up to her to say, "That's all. Thank you." Then he gave the woman a polite smile.

"No problem. I'll be right back," she answered sweetly and walked away, shaking her hips as hard as she could.

I couldn't help but smirk at the situation, but then wondered if that's how I had looked staring at him. The thought was like getting dowsed with ice water, so I picked my book back up to start reading it, only to hear Robert speak again.

"So, Jenny Allen, what has you traveling to Indiana?"

The way his voice wrapped around my name, and his Southern drawl accented it, made me blush like he had whispered a dirty secret to me. I put my book back down on my lap and mentally scolded myself for thinking all these obnoxious thoughts about a man I'd just met. I was more practical than that. I composed myself and answered. "Well, Robert Shaw, I'm moving there to start a new job." We both smiled.

"Wow, that's life changing," he said, surprised.

"Yeah, that's kind of the outcome I'm looking for. What about you, why are you going to Indiana?" I asked.

"Oh, I was born and raised a Hoosier. I've been out here visiting my aunt and uncle. I got word that he'd been in the hospital and it was pretty serious, so I got on the first flight to Kansas I could, to be with them."

"Is he okay?" I asked.

"Yeah, he'll be okay. I was glad for my aunt's sake. All they have is each other. They've been married forty-five years and are still completely in love. It always amazes me that they've stuck it out with one another as long as they have. If you could meet them, you'd understand what I mean. I think their favorite thing to do is fight with each other, but they always find their way back to make up. It's an amazing kind of love," Robert said with total admiration for them.

"It sounds very sweet. Are your parents still married?" I asked, trying to stay with the topic. I was never good at small talk even with close friends, let alone strangers.

"Oh, no. My mom left when I was a kid. Tired of the farming life, so she met a man and moved to the big city of Louisville with him. My dad raised me all on his own, and the two of us worked the farm together. When he passed away a few years ago, leaving everything to me, I had to step up and start taking care of it. I've been taking care of that place all my life, it seems," he said, smiling, but the smile was weak and laced with sadness. "Anyways, that's what I'm going back to. Can't leave the critters for long, you know."

"Critters?" I asked. "What are critters?"

"Oh, you know, normal farm critters. I have cows, sheep, horses, pigs, chickens, and a few geese on the property," he said, smiling at me like I'd missed a joke of some sort.

"Sounds like you keep busy," I said, amazed at the life he had to go back to.

"Yeah, some people wouldn't consider farming a way to make a good living, but if you do it right and really invest in it, you can do pretty good, although it is time-consuming."

Before we could say anything else, platinum blond returned with our drinks and the crackers. She smiled again just as wide as she could, showing off all her perfectly white teeth at Robert. He took the Coke from her and placed it in his cupholder then passed me my 7Up and crackers. I watched his shirt shift over his bulging muscles and knew he had to be perfectly sculpted underneath those clothes. I had to resist the urge to daydream about touching those muscles.

"If there's anything else I can do for you, please don't hesitate to ask," blondie said to Robert as she ran the tips of her fake fingernails down his arm.

He pulled back and said, "Thank you," then turned his attention back to me, clearly brushing her off. She let out a small huff and walked away.

"I think you made her mad," I said with a smile.

"I'm not too worried about it. I'm sure she'll get over it," he said back, acting irritated.

"Not your type?" I asked. I couldn't resist.

"Her?" he asked skeptically. "She's pretty, don't get me wrong, but definitely not the type for me."

I giggled and said, "Well, you probably have someone waiting at home for you anyway."

"No, not for a long time now," he said, looking at the back of the seat in front of him, lost in thought. "It's just me and the critters," he said then took a quick drink of his Coke. "What about you, Jenny, did you break someone's heart when you decided to leave home?"

"No, it was just me back in Kansas," I replied.

"That's surprising," he said.

"Why is that surprising?" I asked.

"You're very beautiful, and you seem very sweet. It's just hard to believe you didn't have a boyfriend or husband catering to you."

I blushed at his compliment and couldn't look him in the eyes. "No, there's no one," I whispered, staring at my lap.

Robert took his large hand and placed it under my chin, gently pulling my face up so that I was looking into those green eyes again. They were the brightest, greenest eyes I had ever seen, stealing my breath as I gazed into them.

"I hope I didn't upset you by saying that. It's just the truth, Jenny. I know we just met, but I can already tell you're something special," he said, and he didn't smile. He just stared back into my eyes as I stared into his.

"I'm not upset. Thank you for saying that," I said, barely above a whisper.

He dropped his hand, but he didn't look away. Now he was smiling as a big flirty grin stretched across his face before he said to me, "Well, Jenny, since there's no one back home to get all jealous, I'm probably going to flirt with you all the way to Indiana."

"I thought you already were," I said, smiling back at him, and I surprised myself by my bold comment.

"Well, I'm a little rusty at the whole flirting thing, but I'm going to give it my best shot," he said, and a wicked flash gleamed in his eyes.

"Oh, I bet you can flirt very well," I wanted to say, but my nerves got the best of me, so I just replied "Okay" in a soft, shy tone.

He smiled a sexy smirk back at me when he saw my cheeks blazing then turned back to his Coke.

I opened up my 7Up and took a drink to back away from the moment. He had me so nervous, and my stomach was already in knots from being on a plane. I had never met a man that had this much effect on me. My heart was beating fast, my breaths were uneven, and my palms were sweating. *That's attractive*, I sarcastically thought to myself as I tried to discretely wipe them on my jeans, hoping Robert hadn't noticed.

Robert had me coming across so shy and girly, which wasn't me at all, but I couldn't help myself as a dozen emotions blazed inside of me. Of all the people to sit next to me on this plane, why'd it have to be Robert? He seemed like a great guy, and he was a great view to have on the long ride to Indiana, but he made me too nervous. I was not good with men. I never had been. Men hadn't even been on my radar growing up. I'd only ever been focused on my education, my therapy, my healing, after what I'd been through with my family, and now my career. Robert seemed like the perfect distraction to take my focus off what I was really moving toward, and I couldn't let that happen. As much as I liked his attention, and wanted to flirt back with him, I knew I had to keep my eye on the prize, which was my new job, home, and life in Indiana.

I decided to be nice and courteous to Robert, but I'd have to draw a line at that so he knew I was a serious woman. I was not going to be someone for him to take advantage of with those beautiful green eyes or bulging muscles.

I was staring out my window biting down on a cracker when I heard a voice over the intercom letting the passengers know to get seated and buckle up, that the plane would be taking off in five minutes. My stomach immediately lurched into my throat, and I felt my head spin. I pulled on my seat belt and tightened it as far as it would go around me. I gripped both my armrests as tightly as I could then put my head back, closing my eyes. "Just keep your breathing slow and even," Patty had comforted me last time we were on the plane together. "Keep telling yourself that everything is just fine, and keep taking those deep, even breaths. In through the nose and out through the mouth," she had cooed at me. Oh, I wished she was here to comfort me now.

"Are you okay?" I heard Robert ask from beside me. His voice had worry in it.

"Mm-hmm," I answered, not opening my eyes while I concentrated on telling myself, *In through the nose and out through the mouth.*

"Don't like flying, do you?" he asked.

I didn't speak in fear that I might throw up, so I shook my head no. The plane started to move, and the jerking sensation startled me so much so that I jumped in my seat.

"Oh, you really are scared," Robert said to me.

I just nodded. I couldn't speak until we were in the air. The takeoffs and landings were the worst part for me.

"Jenny, I want you to take deep, relaxing breaths and listen to my voice. I'm right here next to you, and I won't let anything happen to you. You are perfectly safe and secure. The pilot is very skilled at flying the plane, which gets serviced regularly and will get us back to Indiana safely. You have nothing to fear and nothing to worry about," Robert cooed at me, and I felt him take my hand in his. "Do you trust me, Jenny?" he asked in a soft, low voice.

I thought about that for a minute and realized even though I had just met Robert, I did trust him. There was something about him that just screamed overprotective man, and I liked that about him. I didn't want to speak, but I made myself reply quickly, without breaking the rhythm I had going with my breathing, "Yes."

"Good, I'm glad that you do, because I promise I am right here for you. Just squeeze my hand if you get scared and know that I won't let anything happen to you, Jenny."

I could hear that Robert was still talking but his words were becoming background noise as my mind was telling my body what to do. "Remember to breathe, don't pass out, and definitely don't throw up." The commands were getting harder to follow. I felt my mind willing me to do the right thing while my body complained and strained to do the opposite. I gripped my armrest and Robert's hand so tight that my knuckles turned white as I felt the plane take off, but he never made me let go. My nerves were getting the best of me, and I started humming to myself.

"Are you humming?" Robert asked me, a little amused.

I just nodded and kept humming the "Star-Spangled Banner." It's the only thing that popped into my mind, so I just went with it. As we got higher and higher into the sky, my humming became louder and louder. Then I realized I wasn't the only one humming. I popped one eye open to squint at Robert. He was staring at me, humming along with the tune. When he saw I was looking at him, he let out the biggest smile and gave my hand a little squeeze. I welcomed the comforting contact, closed my eye tight again, and kept humming away until I felt the plane level out. It wasn't until I heard the intercom again letting us know we were free to move around that I let my grip on the armrest and Robert's hand loosen a little.

"We're okay now," Robert said in a low, soothing voice. "You can open your eyes."

I opened my eyes slowly, looking around and taking in the scene. People were up moving, and flight attendants were busying themselves down the aisles. I took in a long, deep breath, held it, and then let it go. When I noticed Robert still had my hand in his, I looked down at our hands then up to Robert. He was looking back at me, concern etched across his handsome face.

"Thank you for that," I whispered.

"No problem. I'm just glad you're okay," he said, giving me a small smile.

"Yeah, I'm okay now." I smiled back.

"That's good. You had me worried there for a minute, sweet girl," he said, and at first I was swooning over Robert's words, but that feeling quickly left as I suddenly hurled all over Robert's lap.

Chapter 2

I stepped out of the airport bathroom to find Robert sitting on a nearby bench with all our bags looking tired and worn out. I gave him an apologetic smile as he looked up at me. He smiled back and stood up as I crossed over to him.

"You gonna be all right?" he asked me for the millionth time.

I hadn't stopped throwing up the entire flight here, and as soon as we landed, I had to run to the bathroom to throw up again. He was turning out to be a pretty sweet guy taking care of me.

"Yeah, I think so," I said weakly. My voice was almost completely gone now. "You know, I can still get a cab or rent a car. I'd feel horrible if I threw up in your truck."

"I'm not letting you do that," he scolded me. "You're in no shape to drive, and a cab would be too expensive. Besides, if you threw up in my truck, that just means we'd match," he said, smiling at me. I grimaced at his words, reliving the horror and complete embarrassment of getting sick all over him on the plane. Thank goodness we had both changed clothes.

He saw my sour expression and asked "Too soon?" but laughed as he said it. I nodded.

"Well, I've got the bags. You just follow me, and we'll get out of here," he said, leading the way out of the airport.

When we got into the parking lot, he stopped next to a large white truck with rails along the sides and a dual cab. It was pretty impressive as trucks went, I thought. He unlocked his door and put our bags in the back seat. He hit the unlock button so I could open up my door, but I had to practically jump into the seat because the truck was so tall and the motion made me have to lean out the door to throw up all over the pavement. Robert rushed around the truck to stand beside me and placed a hand on my shoulder to help steady me.

"Careful now," he said. "We don't want you falling out."

I couldn't respond. I just heaved again until my body had nothing left to give. I wiped my mouth on my shirt sleeve and leaned back into my seat. Robert stepped closer to me, careful not to step in the mess I had left on the ground, and slowly pulled my seat belt over me, buckling me in. He opened up his glove box and took out a red bandana. I looked up at him.

"Here, it's clean," he said, handing it to me. "You keep it in case you need it."

"Thank you," I whispered to him as I took it, thankful not to have to use my shirt sleeve again. As I took the bandana, our fingers brushed, and I couldn't help but look up at him. A strong current of electricity shot through my entire body, and I felt a slow heat rise in my cheeks. He smiled back at me, but only pity showed on his face. That look told me everything I was feeling was completely one-sided. I sighed and watched as he closed my door and got in the driver's side of the truck. After about ten minutes of driving, which was about how long it took us to get on the highway from the airport, Robert asked me, "So where am I taking you, Jen?"

As bad as I felt, hearing my name like that on his lips could still send flutters through my heart. How crazy was that? I grinned to myself knowing I was completely hopeless then answered, "I have the address on a piece of paper the landlord gave me. Hold on and I'll get it for you." I pulled the note out of my purse and handed it to Robert. He looked at the address written across the paper, scowling at it, but he didn't say anything.

"What?" I asked him.

"Have you been out to the house yet?" he asked.

"Yeah, I looked at it before I gave the lady my first month's rent," I answered. "Is there something wrong with the house?"

"Oh, no, it's a fine house. It's been there for years. It's just that it's near the mental hospital. Actually, it's just a few miles from it. Not sure if that's a good place for a young woman to be living on her own so close to that much crazy."

"Oh," I snickered back.

"Why's that funny?" he asked, noticing my amused expression.

"My new job I told you I was starting, well, it's as an orderly at that hospital you're talking about."

"What?" he snapped back in shock. "Are you serious?"

"Yeah, I'm serious," I croaked, my voice breaking on me.

"Jenny, I have a friend that works there. He tells me about all kinds of crazy shit that goes on up there. Sometimes the patients get out of hand and have to be restrained. He said one time that one of the patients went into this fit where he thought he was a zombie and started trying to bite everyone. When he came at my friend, he literally had to knock him out to keep the guy from latching onto his neck. As small as you are, those patients would take you down in a heartbeat. I don't want to see you get hurt."

"I understand your concern, Robert, but I've been taking self-defense and kickboxing classes for years. I've taken down guys twice my size. I lift weights, work out, jog, and keep myself fit. I'm a lot tougher than I look, especially how I look tonight. I've interned at mental hospitals, and I've had the education to teach me how to effectively handle the mentally ill, and it's not always with brute force. Mind over matter, you know," I said defensively, but the conviction of my words was lost with the tone of my voice. I sounded so fragile and weak with all the throwing up I had been doing. I knew there would be no way he'd take me seriously, but then he surprised me.

"Wow, I'm impressed, Jen. You really kickbox?"

"For five years now," I said with pride and found myself grinning like an idiot at his compliment.

"I know you aren't supposed to ask a woman her age, but if you don't mind, can I ask how old you are?"

"I'm twenty-six. How old are you?" I challenged back.

"I'll be twenty-eight next month," he said.

"Since you know where the house is, how long until we get there?" I asked changing the subject.

"It'll be a couple hours until we're there. You should lay back and try to sleep for a while. Maybe you'll feel better," he said sweetly.

"Okay. Thank you for everything tonight," I said, getting comfortable in my seat. Robert reached into the seat behind us and pulled a flannel jacket up to me, throwing it across me. I welcomed its warmth and snuggled up into it. It was warm with a cotton lining in it that was fluffy and made me think of marshmallows.

"Hey, Jenny," he said softly.

"Yes?" I whispered back, already starting to doze off.

"I'm serious about being worried over your new job. I'm only twenty minutes from your house, so if you ever need anything, I hope you'll call. I don't want something to happen to you," Robert said softly but very seriously, worry wrapped around every word.

"I will," I sort of moaned back, letting sleep take me over.

When Robert nudged my arm to wake me up, it was a couple hours later, but to me felt like I had only managed about five minutes of sleep. My eyes were so heavy, and I didn't want to move. My stomach instantly felt queasy again, and my head pounded. I felt the truck slow down, and even though I didn't want to, I opened my eyes to peer out the window. We were turning into my driveway. Even in the dark, the view was amazing. There were nothing but open fields surrounding my quaint, little farmhouse with its inviting wraparound porch, and at this hour you could see hundreds of fireflies dancing in the fields around my home. I couldn't imagine anything more peaceful or serene.

"You awake, Jenny?" Robert asked me.

"Yeah," I responded, but my voice was so uneven I could hardly get it out. I cleared my throat, but that just made me feel like I might hurl again, so I decided I'd just deal with the raspy voice.

He pulled up in front of my door and turned off the truck. I unbuckled my seat belt and started to reach for my door, but before I could get to it, Robert was already at my side pulling it open. To my surprise, he reached his hand out for me to help me out of the truck, making all my nerves tingle. I smiled up at him, and he smiled back, helping me move slowly out of the truck. We walked hand in hand to the porch, and I thought, well, maybe I could see this going somewhere after all. This was the first time I had ever taken an interest in a guy, so I knew I had myself a little more invested in this than I should be. I relished the physical contact with Robert, and the effect it had on my body was unreal. I didn't want to ever let go of his hand, but that contact lasted mere seconds because when we reached the mailbox next to my front door, he let go and stepped back, letting me go ahead of him. No one had ever held my hand before, and I felt giddy all over despite the nausea that was trying its best to overcome all the other feelings in my body. I let go of his hand and opened the lid to the mailbox to find it empty.

"Shit!" I said at the mailbox.

"What's wrong?" Robert asked.

"My landlord knew I was getting in tonight and said she'd have the keys waiting on me in the mailbox, but they aren't there," I growled in frustration, and Robert looked at me quizzically.

"You could just call her and have her run them over to you. I'm sure if she's a nice lady, she'll understand the situation," he suggested.

"At two in the morning, I doubt she'll answer her phone. Plus, she lives in Indianapolis. It would be hours before she could get here," I said.

"Damn, that's no good," Robert said, moving past me to make sure the front door was locked. When he found that it was, he started around the side of the house. "I'll be right back, I'm going to check the back door," he called over his shoulder at me just as he disappeared around the house. A minute later he was back shaking his head to let me know he'd had no luck getting in.

"Oh, screw it," I said, pissed off at the situation. "If you don't mind taking me, I'll just stay the night at a hotel and call her tomorrow to bring me the keys."

He stood in front of me looking at his cowboy boots, pondering over something before he finally said, "Like you said, its two in the morning, town will be closed down for the night, your landlord is two hours away, and you don't feel good. Why don't you just come home with me and give your landlord a call in the morning after you've rested and the sun is up?"

I studied him for a moment, and he never looked up at me while he waited for my response.

"Umm..." I trailed off, considering his offer. "You have been so nice and sweet to me this entire evening, but I really don't know you, and I'm not sure how I'd feel just going home with you. Besides, if you're expecting, umm, *THAT*, then..." I trailed off again, looking for the right words.

"Oh, no!" Robert burst out. "That's not what this is about at all." His eyes widened at my suggestion. "I have a guest bedroom you can have, and there's even an extra bathroom you can have all to yourself. I'll be all the way over on the other side of the house."

I went to reply when I felt the bile rise up into my throat again. I pushed him aside as I rushed to the edge of the porch. I grabbed the railing and wretched over the side into the grass. I felt Robert lean over me and pull my hair out of my face as I wretched again. When I finally stopped, I felt so weak I just sank to my knees. Robert let go of my hair and wrapped his big arms around me, letting me fall back against him as we both sat on the porch together. I leaned my head against his broad chest as his arms engulfed me and the heat from his body combined with the cool night air helped to soothe the nausea.

"This is so embarrassing," I said into his chest.

"Don't think anything of it," he said, brushing his cheek across the top of my head.

We sat there for a long time not speaking. I heard the crickets making their crickety noise and cows mooing in the distance and the soft breeze blowing across the fields surrounding us. If I didn't feel so bad, I swear this could've been a scene straight out of a movie.

"Do you think you can walk?" Robert asked me gently.

"Oh, Robert," I moaned. "Just leave me here." I knew I wouldn't be able to stand even if I tried.

"I wouldn't do that," he said, soft but serious. Then he stood up, taking me with him, one arm wrapped around my back and the other going under my legs, lifting me like I weighed no more than a small child. I squealed a little and wrapped my arms around his neck.

"Whoever did this to you needs his ass kicked," he said with anger flooding his voice as he very gently placed me in the passenger seat of his truck.

"Did what?" I whispered back, watching him pull my seat belt over me and buckling me in.

"Get you pregnant then just let you leave and have to go through this by yourself," he said, closing my door.

My head popped up, and I was fully awake now. I watched him walk around the front of his truck and get into the driver's side. When he put his own seat belt on and started the truck, he finally noticed me sitting upright staring at him.

"Excuse me, sir?" I said with anger in my voice too.

"What?" he asked, taken aback at my reaction.

"You see a girl sick to her stomach and you automatically think she got herself knocked up? What a guy thing to assume," I spat at him.

"Aren't you?" he asked me with an edge to his voice.

"No, I'm not. Planes make me sick. Not usually this sick, so I might have a virus, but I'm certainly not pregnant."

"Jenny, you could tell me if you were. I've only seen women this sick when they were pregnant. I would understand."

"Gotten many girls pregnant?" I asked him, raising my eyebrows expectantly.

"That's not what I'm saying, Jenny. Look, I'm sorry if I'm wrong, but I was just going by what I've seen with other women."

"Well, for your information, it would be impossible for this to be pregnancy related."

"What do you mean?" he asked, not getting my meaning.

"Nothing. Just forget it," I muttered, looking out my window now so I didn't have to look at him. Why did I always let my temper get the better of me? I shouldn't have said that.

"Jenny, what do you mean it wouldn't be pregnancy related?" he asked again.

I huffed in exasperation. "Not that it's really your business, but I'm a virgin, Robert, okay? Are you happy now? I'm not knocked up,

I'm just sick. Sicker than I've ever been in my life, actually." I almost yelled it at him then turned my face back to my window.

He was silent for a long time as he turned his truck around and started driving down the road in the direction we had come from.

When he finally spoke again, all the anger had left his voice and he was speaking softly to me now. "Jenny, I'm really sorry. I didn't mean to be such an ass. I shouldn't just have assumed that you slept around. I wouldn't have expected this considering your age, but it's a lot better answer than the one I was coming up with. I think it's sweet you're still a virgin and you shouldn't be embarrassed by that. I just hope you can forgive me for being so stupid," he said, looking out the front windshield.

I was so mad I literally felt like my blood was boiling until he sounded so damn sincere. Why did he have to be so nice? As much as I wanted to stay mad at him for making me admit something I really didn't want to, I couldn't stay mad. I let out a long sigh and turned to him.

"You're forgiven as long as it's never brought up again," I said, half smiling at him.

He glanced over at me. "It's a deal," he said, smiling back.

Chapter 3

I'm RUNNING so fast that I can hardly breathe. The hallway I'm in is never ending. Just long white walls, tile floor, and overhead florescent lighting is all there is. No doors, no windows, and no way out. My heart is beating so hard I feel like it's going to explode, but I can't stop running. If I do, she'll die. I finally see a door up ahead. I'm still running, but it doesn't get any closer to me. I hear a scream come from behind the door, and I know it's her. I run harder and faster, determined with everything in me to get to her. Finally, the door starts to inch closer and closer as I slowly make my way there, even though this is the fastest I've ever ran in my life. I eventually reach the door and burst through it, hearing the screams of a young girl getting louder and louder. When I run in, I'm no longer my adult self. I'm six years old again, small and weak. My sister, Laura, is still sixteen, looking beautiful and healthy just like I remember, but she lays strapped to a hospital bed. Her skin has grown over her restraints from lying there so long, and blood covers her wrists and ankles where she has struggled so hard to get out of bed. I suddenly hear an older woman scream, and I jerk my head over to see who is in the corner of the room with us. It's our mother. She stands there glaring at Laura, watching her struggle to get free from her bed and the restraints holding her to it. My sister begs her to be set free, but my mother begins yelling at her to stop talking and stop moving. Laura starts to cry, and our mother stalks toward her, telling Laura to shut up, shut up, or she'll get the doctor, and she won't want that.

Laura goes silent, but the tears continue to stream down her cheeks. I want to run to her, to get in between her and our mother, but I can't move my feet. I look down and see restraints on both of my ankles that are chained to the hospital floor. I'm trapped here, just like my sister. Then I hear Laura talking, and I look back over at her. She's still crying and in a whispered voice begs our mother to let her go. She begs our mother to take the restraints off her and let her be free of this horrible place. She promises to be different, to be a good girl, to be the girl my mother wants her to be, but my mother just glares at Laura with a look of disgust on her face. Then suddenly Laura lets out this shrill of terror, and I have to cover my ears it's so loud and piercing. At the same time, I see my mother's arm come down in a hard blow to Laura's chest. Laura goes quiet, and in seconds her arms that were at a strain against the leather straps across her wrists go limp. When my mother pulls her arm away from Laura's chest, there's a scalpel left there sticking out of Laura's heart. Blood runs everywhere, spilling over Laura's dead body and onto the bed. I scream at my mother, but she doesn't look at me, and when I look back at my sister, I see the Laura that came out of surgery. Her face is black and swollen again as one eye dangles down her face.

I let out a high-pitched scream then suddenly woke up in a cold sweat. I was confused when I first opened my eyes. I was crying, and my heart was beating wildly. I had no idea where I was. Sunshine streamed in through the window across from the bed I was lying in, but nothing looked familiar. Tears streamed down my face as I struggled to catch my breath. My head was all fuzzy, and it was hard to pull my thoughts together. Just then the bedroom door slammed open and in ran a man. At first I had to think about who it was, then as my eyes focused, I realized it was Robert. He looked panicked and rushed over to the bed.

"Jenny, what happened? Are you okay?" he asked, pulling me into his embrace before I could answer. I wasn't sure if I was okay this time. I was so sick last night I forgot to take the medicine Patty gave me, so of course I wasn't okay. *Think, Jenny,* I scolded myself. *Just calm down and think. What happened last night?* I ask myself. *Robert drove you home from the airport, and you were sick. The keys weren't in the mailbox, so you couldn't get into your house, and Robert brought you home with him because there were no hotels open that late. You are in Robert's guest room, so quit scaring the crap out of the man.*

"Jenny, you need to calm down. You need to slow your breathing down before you pass out. God, your heart is beating so damn fast. Jenny, are you listening to me? I'm going to take slow even breaths, and I want you to try and match mine. Just breathe with me, Jenny," he said, still holding me tight. I leaned against his hard, shirtless body and could feel him take a long, deep breath in, and his chest rose against me. He held it then slowly let it out as I felt his chest lower. He did this several times before the rhythm of his breathing started helping me to calm myself. I started to match my breathing with his, and as I did, my heartbeat finally started to slow down to its normal pace. "That's good, Jenny. That's really good. Just keep going. Feel me breathe, and breathe with me. You're okay, sweet girl," Robert cooed. He sounded like Patty did that day on the plane when I panicked and she had to calm me down. I smiled a little at his words and the tone he was using with me. He was so sweet. "Is that a smile I see?" he asked me. "Are you feeling better now?" I didn't say anything, not sure if I could really talk yet, so I just nodded.

"You scared me. I was on the other side of the house, and I heard you let out this horrible scream all the way over there, so I came running. I didn't know what was wrong or what had happened. Was it a bad dream?"

"Yes," I answered, but I wasn't going to offer up any details about it. That was how I lost friends back home. Part of the reason I lived alone and my only friend was my therapist was because once people knew my back story, they suddenly felt so sorry for me. Then instead of considering me a friend, I became a charity case. Eventually they would get tired of the drama that always seemed to follow me around, and the phone calls to hang out would come less and less. What really bothered me the most were the looks I always got after my friends knew. Looks of pity for the feeble girl who needed to be babied all the time. I was sick of that image and the looks I got. That was when I started getting in shape, working out, and learning to kickbox. I wasn't a fragile little girl anymore, and there was no way I came all the way to Indiana just to have those same looks given to me all over again.

"You wanna talk about it?" Robert asked me tentatively.

"No, it's okay," I said and pulled out of his embrace and turned to face him. In my now-calm state, looking at Robert, I suddenly realized that he was not wearing a T-shirt and a T-shirt was all I had on. I pulled the blankets up around me so the bottom half of me was definitely covered up, and then I looked at Robert. He wasn't checking me out. He was just sitting there looking at me with this puzzled and concerned expression across his face. He was probably trying to figure out what just happened. I couldn't help but check him out, though. He was a fine-looking man, and now that I got to see him with his shirt off, it only got better. He had smooth, lightly browned skin from the sun. Not a fake tan like you saw in the cities from all the tanning beds. He was broad, lean, and very muscular. His chest muscles were so defined, and his finely sculptured abs were nothing to laugh at. I saw a tribal tattoo that wrapped around his right bicep, which was huge. I couldn't help wondering if he lifted weights or if it was just the farm work he did that made both of his arms and, well, all his body, so firm and exquisite. Before my brain even registered what my hand was doing, I had reached out and was running a finger lightly across his tribal tattoo. When he smirked at me, I realized what I had done and quickly pulled my hand back, feeling my cheeks flush with embarrassment.

"Do you like it?" he asked, still grinning at me.

"Yeah, it's nice," I said, not looking him in the eyes. "Have you had it long?"

He thought for a moment then answered, "Dad's been gone five years, so I got it about four years ago now."

"Is it something for your dad?" I asked, wondering.

"No, it was actually something me and my best friend did together about a year after dad died. My dad would never have approved of a tattoo," he said and half chuckled as he looked over at his arm. "No, after my dad died I went through a rough spell where I did a lot of things my dad never would've approved of. My best friend, that I grew up with, was right by my side every day through it all. One night we decided we would get matching tattoos since we're practically brothers, just something to signify that bond between us. He's the one I mentioned works at the hospital you're going to start at."

"Wow, so you two are really close then. It must be nice to have someone like that," I said.

"We were," he said sadly.

"You aren't anymore?" I asked.

"No, not for a while now. When my run of doing crazy shit I didn't need to be doing was over, which was a couple of years ago, I pulled away from everyone that was still doing the crazy shit I was trying to avoid. My best friend, Blake, who I thought would always be on the same page as me, didn't understand and didn't want to stop. He's still into shit even now that he really needs to cut out of his life. Hell, we're pushing thirty years old, and he still acts like he just turned twenty. It caused us to drift apart, so we rarely talk or see each other anymore."

"That's sad that you don't have him in your life any more since you lost your dad, now him," I said and put my hand on Robert's arm partly to comfort him and partly to feel his soft skin on mine once more. Man, I needed help.

"What's sad is you screaming over a nightmare. Are you sure you don't want to talk about it?" he asked me, clearly changing the subject on purpose.

"No, I don't, but thank you for being there for me when I woke up," I told him and finally took my hand back.

"How are you feeling this morning, your stomach, I mean?" he asked.

"Actually it feels better. I don't feel sick at all this morning," I said, but I no more than got the words out of my mouth when a long, low rumble came from inside my stomach.

Robert laughed out loud at my new noises then asked, "Are you sure about that?"

I flushed with embarrassment and answered, "Yeah, I just think I'm running on E."

"Well, in that case, I'll meet you in the kitchen in thirty minutes. I have to go finish getting dressed, and you can help yourself to the shower or whatever you need and then we'll sit down to a nice breakfast. Whatever you feel like eating," he said, walking out of the room.

I smiled at him as he walked out of the door, and then when I heard his footsteps getting further down the hall, I jumped up and quietly shut the bedroom door. Once I had it shut tight, I ran over to my suitcase, took out my cosmetic bag and the cutest outfit I could find, and then ran to the bathroom. In less than thirty minutes, I had taken my shower, blow-dried and fixed my hair, brushed my teeth, applied a little makeup since I was still pale from being sick, and got dressed. I looked at myself in the bathroom mirror to make sure I looked okay before heading to the kitchen. I was wearing my blue jean capris that hugged my butt in a most flattering way, my favorite pink tank top, and a pair of white flip flops. The tank top showed off my biceps, which I happened to be very proud of. They weren't as big or as muscular as Robert's, of course, but I had lifted a lot weights and punched a lot of bags to get the decent-sized muscles I had in my arms. I left my hair down so it flowed down my back and had just a hint of pink lip gloss on to give me some color. I looked down at my feet and was thankful I took the time to paint my toenails before I left Kansas. I looked like a totally different person compared to the sick, pasty green mess I was the night before. I have never been a vain person, and in fact, I rarely even thought of my appearance. I took care of myself, but I never got into primping the way some of my friends always had in college. Looking at myself now, I couldn't help but think, *Yeah, I'm totally cute today.*

I was putting all my things back in my suitcase when I realized I didn't know where his kitchen was. I opened the bedroom door and peered down the hallway. No Robert anywhere. I stepped out and shut the bedroom door behind me. I felt like I was sneaking around in his house, like I wasn't supposed to be here. The hallway let out into a large living room with a fabulous fireplace made of large stones. The walls were a light-tan color, which really stood out against the shining hardwood floors. Everything in the room was arranged with purpose. Each piece of furniture and each little knick-knack had its own designated spot. Someone had really put a lot of thought into this room when they were putting it together. It looked like something you'd see in a *Homes* magazine. Simple and country but still beautiful. I was standing there taking it all in when Robert appeared.

"Hey there," he said, letting his eyes roam over me. "I was just coming to get you." He was talking to me but never met my eyes. I blushed furiously, worried what he might be thinking and found I couldn't look him in the eyes either.

"You were?" I asked shyly.

His eyes met mine when I finally looked up again, and he said, "Yeah, I cooked us breakfast. I figured that loud rumble earlier meant you were starving, so I cooked us up something good."

"You cook?" I asked, completely surprised.

"Yeah, I had to learn with mom taking off when I was a kid. Dad was never that great at it."

"He was a great decorator, though. This living room is gorgeous," I said, taking another look around.

"You think so?" he asked, taking a look around as well.

"Yeah, it looks like it's right out of a magazine," I said.

"It might be," he said with a little sarcasm in his tone. I just gave him a confused look, then he continued, "My ex lived here for a little while after dad died. She's the one that decorated it, and she's not one for original ideas, so it probably is something she saw in a magazine."

"Oh," I said with a bitter tone and instantly hated the room.

Robert grinned at my remark then motioned for me to join him. I walked across the living room and followed him into the kitchen which was huge, but we didn't stop there. We walked through the room and into the dining room, which sat right off the kitchen. As we walked into the formal dining room, my breath caught, and I stopped in my tracks. In front of me was a large banquet-style table made of a grainy, stained wood, which looked old but filled with character. The table itself was gorgeous and could sit at least ten people, but that wasn't what caught my attention. It was the food spread across the table that made me stop and appreciate the scene. Bacon, scrambled eggs, sausage patties, biscuits, gravy, fried potatoes, freshly sliced watermelon, milk, orange juice, homemade jam, butter, and various other condiments lined the table. My mouth dropped open, my eyes had to be as big as saucers, and I think I even drooled a little.

"Please tell me this is okay," Robert asked, gesturing at the spread laid before us.

"Oh my gosh, Robert. Did you cook all this while I was in the shower?" I asked, still mesmerized.

"Well, some of it I had done early this morning, but yeah, I finished up while you were in the shower. Is something wrong?" he asked, still unsure of what he'd done for me.

"No, nothing at all. I'm just so surprised. I haven't had a meal like this since I was a child," I said, taking a seat at the table across from Robert.

"That's too bad. Help yourself to anything you want. There's more than plenty here," he said, starting to fill his own plate.

I didn't know where to start. It all looked so good, and I was starving after everything I had been through last night. I was not one to overeat or even eat this kind of food, but I was making an exception today. I started piling everything onto my plate, not skipping out on anything. I heard a chuckle, and I looked up to see Robert looking at my plate.

"What?" I asked defensively.

"Nothing really. I've just never seen a girl eat this much before unless she was, you know…" he said teasingly with a big grin spread across his face.

"Don't even say it," I said to him, pointing my fork at him.

"Oh, I'm not, because you're not, so obviously you're just really hungry," he said and chuckled again.

"Yes, I am. I'm starving after last night," I said, starting to eat. I was too hungry to be embarrassed right now. I savored the first bite, letting the flavor fill my mouth. Not only did it look good, but it tasted good.

"You said that you haven't had a home-cooked meal since you were little. What's up with that? Didn't your mom or dad cook?" Robert asked then stuffed his mouth with some bacon.

I swallowed and sighed before I answered, "I don't have any family. I had a mother, if that's what you want to call her, when I was little, but she wasn't really the motherly type, so no, she didn't cook. My dad passed away when I was three, so I don't really remember him, and I had an older sister, but we lost her when I was six. My mom and I were never close, and I left home at eighteen. I heard from a cousin that I kept in contact with that my mom passed away during my senior year of college. It's just been me ever since, and I don't cook like this. I'm more of a fruit and yogurt eater at breakfast time."

"I'm really sorry you've had to go through so much. Did you go to your mom's funeral or help plan it or anything? You said you heard from a cousin that she passed away," Robert asked between bites.

"I had to meet with her lawyer about the will, but no, I didn't go to the funeral. I had no desire to see her. On top of everything she had put me through, I didn't find out until she died that my dad had left a lot of money to me and my sister when he passed away. Since my sister had already passed away as well, all of it went to me. My mother never told me that and had spent a portion of it without anyone knowing. Just one more thing she kept from me," I told him then took a bite of my biscuit and gravy. Robert's plate was half-empty already, and I thought I better quit talking so much and start eating. I didn't want to be left sitting here by myself in his home with a plate full of food in front of me.

"I can't begin to understand what you've been through, but if you ever need to just sit down and talk about it, we can. I may not always know the right thing to say, but I'm a good listener," he said, finishing off his last bite of food.

"Oh, I think that's enough drama, don't you? I mean, since we met, I've been sick or screaming or telling you about my messed-up family. I think we need more laughter instead of all this drama," I said smiling.

"Well, no matter if you're sick, crying, upset, or have a little bit of gravy on the side of your mouth, you're still completely beautiful," he responded and smiled at my complete embarrassment. I rushed to wipe the gravy off my mouth and felt my cheeks blazing. I was very careful with the last couple of bites I had left to take after that.

After we both finished eating we put up the leftovers and washed the dishes together. While I was drying a plate, Robert asked what my plans were for the rest of the day, which I hadn't even thought about yet. Being with Robert sort of wiped out everything else. I wasn't quite sure if that was a good thing or a bad thing yet. I told him I wasn't sure, but I knew I had to get ahold of my landlord for the keys to my house, get unpacked, go shopping for furniture and food, then somehow find a car for sale. I had no transportation right now other than Robert and his big white truck.

"I think I can help with all of that," Robert said to me as we went out back to lounge on his porch swing.

"How are you going to do that?" I asked him, looking across the large open pasture behind his home.

"You can use my phone to call your landlord and have someone bring the keys to you. While we are waiting on that, we can go up to Salem and speak to my uncle Ron about a car. He has his own car lot, and I'll talk him into giving you a really good deal. Then we can have lunch, run by your house for your keys, head down to Clarksville to buy some furniture, and stop for groceries on the way back. There are a few places in Salem we could get you some furniture, but those few stores aren't going to give you much of a selection and the prices will be ridiculous. Clarksville will be our best bet to find you something nice for a good price. Then tomorrow you can repay my generosity by helping me do a few things around the farm."

"Is it really generosity when I'll need to repay the favor?" I asked, smiling over at him.

He looked down at me frowning. "I wasn't serious. You don't have to come up tomorrow if you don't want to."

I flashed him a big silly grin. "I wasn't being serious either, Robert. Besides I'd love to come up tomorrow. You haven't shown me all your critters yet, and I am dying to see a sheep."

He laughed at me and said, "Well, I think I could arrange a meeting." I nudged his arm, he nudged me back, and we both laughed.

I knew I should be getting up to call my landlord now, but I couldn't make myself move. I sat there taking in the scenery. Robert's place was so beautiful, green, and alive. The fresh air on the breeze that swept across my skin was amazing. I was so relaxed that I could close my eyes and sleep all day out here on this swing of his. The atmosphere, the noises from the farm, and the presence Robert had about him all blended together, enveloping me. This could become very addictive very fast. I closed my eyes, took a deep breath in, and took in all the outside smells that came with farm life, and then I let it out slowly with a long, satisfying sigh. I couldn't remember ever feeling this full and content. I felt something brush across my hand, and I looked down to see Robert's hand moving over to take mine. I let him. I had no reason not to. I watched as my hand disappeared under his, and then I turned it over to let our fingers intertwine with each other's. There were no sweaty palms this time, no wildly beating heart. This was just a simple feeling of pleasure and contentment that I cherished it in all its simplicity. This was all so new to me and the first time in my life that I was actually starting to feel hope and happiness. I was looking forward to what this move was already bringing into my life, and I would pray tonight in the privacy of my own home that this lasted. Neither of us spoke as I laid my head over to rest it on Robert's shoulder. We sat together in silence for a long time, both of us wishing this moment could last forever.

The rest of the weekend went by faster than I would've liked for it to. Spending time with Robert made the time fly by while every second had me wishing I had a magic button to push that could slow things down. I wanted to stay in that magic bubble I'd been in since meeting him on the plane, but that wasn't how the real world worked. Sunday night had been a bittersweet goodbye as Robert left me to spend my first night alone in my new house. The one thing I hadn't expected was that after just meeting me, he'd entrusted me with the keys to his dad's old Ford truck. I knew it was older than I was, but it looked as if it had spent its life inside of a garage. The old red two-door truck that Robert referred to as Ol' Red had a lot of sentimental value, but since I hadn't been able to go see his uncle Ron for a car of my own, this was how I would be getting back and forth to work the next few days.

Chapter 4

Monday morning came with it a list of aches in my neck and my back, and looking in the mirror, I knew there was no concealing the dark circles under my eyes. I'd been plagued with nightmares about my sister all damn night, and no matter how many times I'd woken up, they were still waiting on me when I went back to sleep. My only consolation today was the good-morning text from Robert I'd woken up to find waiting for me on my phone. I smiled just thinking about the little heart emoji he'd stuck on the end. Even though Robert hadn't been happy about this from the moment he'd heard I'd be working at the local mental hospital, he was still considerate enough to make sure he sent me wishes for a good day. Making myself as presentable as I could, I dabbed the concealer over my dark circles and headed out the door.

There were so many trees and shrubs that I couldn't see its size at first. The maroon-colored bricks towered over the trees near the building, and even though there were no outstanding features to the structure, the enormous building was still beautiful even in its simplicity. I drove slowly down the paved drive, admiring the park-like setting the vast lawn provided, and noticed there wasn't one person outside. Up ahead of me, the lane divided, and I remembered that the voice from the intercom that had buzzed me through the large wrought-iron gate had instructed me to stay left and enter in the front door of the hospital where the plaque outside said Main Office. I turned left, and when I reached the large privately owned hospital,

I parked in front of the double doors where the plaque was hanging. I climbed out of the truck and walked down a stone path lined with dark hedges. I took a deep breath before opening the door, feeling myself becoming more anxious now that I was actually here. The time had passed so fast since I had come here for my interview, and now I was starting my first day at McBride Mental Hospital. This was what I had been working toward for years, and now the day had come. I was excited even though I was nervous and couldn't wait to jump in and get my feet wet.

I walked into the main lobby, which was brightly lit and felt warm compared to the cool spring morning air I'd just left behind me. Directly to my left was the office with an open window and a counter, which I walked up to. There were notices and awards cluttering the office walls and a newspaper article framed up in the center. The words were too small to read except for the title, which read, "McBride Mental Hospital Awarded State Recognition for Superior Treatment of Patients." That brought a smile to my face, and I was even more excited to be here now. There were four desks behind the counter, one of which was manned by an older lady with short gray hair in tight curls against her head. She was wearing a brown twill skirt that touched her ankles, a matching jacket, and a soft-pink shirt, accompanied by a name tag, which read Diane on it. She looked up at me and asked "Can I help you?" as she stood up and walked over to me.

"I'm Jenny Allen," I informed her and saw the immediate awareness light in her eyes. So I was expected. A topic of gossip no doubt since I was to be the only female orderly on the staff. That was sure to be noticed.

"Of course," she said smiling, and I watched the wrinkles on her face shift as the corners of her mouth drew up. "Mr. McBride is expecting you," she said and walked through a side door that connected the office to the lobby. When she reached me, I could tell how short she was, and I towered over her. "My name is Diane. It's nice to meet you, Jenny."

"It's nice to meet you too," I said, returning her smile.

"If you'll follow me, I'll take you to Mr. McBride's office," she said and started walking.

We walked down a long hallway with light-blue walls and white-tiled floors. Diane's short black dress shoes clicked against the floor with every step she took, and I was thankful to have my flats on. We stopped in front of a large wooden door with a brass nameplate on the front of it that read Thomas McBride on it. Diane knocked loudly before opening it and peering into the office.

"Tom, I have Jenny Allen to see you," she said, and I suddenly felt like I was entering the principal's office as Diane ushered me through the door and into his office.

Sitting behind an oversized mahogany desk was a good-looking older man with black hair that was starting to turn gray at the edges. His beard and mustache were trimmed short to look tidy and professional. I watched as his brown eyes lit up when he smiled at me. Diane left the room, shutting the door behind me, and I walked over to the desk as Mr. McBride stood, holding a hand out for me to shake. I took it, and after a quick shake, we both took our seats.

"It's nice to see you again, Ms. Allen," he said, adjusting himself into his chair.

"Thank you, sir. It's nice to see you too," I said, still feeling nervous.

"Oh, no need for that. Everyone around here either calls me Tom or Thomas. We don't get into all the formalities," he said, giving me a big smile, trying to make me feel more comfortable.

"Well, in that case, you can call me Jenny," I said, trying to follow his lead.

"Very well, Jenny. I'm pleased to have you as a new addition to our orderly staff. I've known Patty for a lot of years, and she speaks very highly of you. When she assured me you were more than qualified for the position, I couldn't say no. I do have to ask you, however, if you are aware that you will be the only female orderly in the hospital?"

"Yes, I'm aware. Can I ask why that is?"

"Well, Jenny, I guess I've just never met a woman with the strength or the desire to take on such a responsibility before. Our orderlies do their best here to take care of patients and be there for them, but there are just some that can't abide by the rules that we have here. That causes incidents to happen, and unfortunately, there has been more than one orderly who's been attacked in the hospital by an unruly patient. It's even more common on the fifth floor, where we house our more complicated patients. That type of work doesn't appeal to most women."

"I definitely understand that. I've interned at one other hospital before, and although its size was nowhere near the size of this one, they still had the same problems with the patients there. There were also no female orderlies there either," I responded.

"While we're on the subject of patients, there is something I need to discuss with you," Tom said, and I watched as his entire demeanor went from open and friendly to serious and stern.

"Okay," I said, unsure of where this was going.

"Everyone here gets the same lecture from me when they enter into employment at my facility, from the janitorial staff to the therapists, and everyone in between. We have a wide variety of mental health illnesses at this hospital ranging from mild cases of substance abuse and eating disorders to extreme cases of paranoia and schizophrenia. My outlook on the patients carrying these burdens is this: I don't care what the patient has, what they are doing at the time, or how they came to be at this facility. Once they are admitted into my hospital, they are to be treated with nothing but kindness, respect, and understanding. As an orderly, you are going to be a top advocator of this treatment. Other staff members will follow your lead because they know it's your responsibility to effectively handle the patients and their odd and sometimes violent behavior. How you choose to do that will mean the difference between a paycheck from me or an unemployment check from the state. Is that understood?"

I watched Tom as he stared at me, waiting for an answer, and I suddenly felt like a child being scolded for stealing a cookie from the cookie jar before supper.

"Yes, I understand," I answered as my voice cracked under the pressure of his stare.

"Good. My son is a patient here. I'm not sure if you knew that or not. His name is William, and he was just moved over to this building from our juvenile center, when he turned eighteen a few months ago. He was diagnosed with schizophrenia when he was little. While William was institutionalized, I researched all about the illness he had and what it meant for him and our family. I lobbied for better treatment, facilities, and for the rights of mental health patients just like William, hoping that what I was doing was making a difference not just for William but for all those dealing with a mental illness. I made enemies during my crusade, and they got their revenge by mistreating my son and even went as far as performing a lobotomy on him without my consent. He was only ten years old. Do you know what a lobotomy is, Jenny?"

"Yes, Tom, I do," I replied quietly as a single tear fell down my cheek.

"Since that horrible procedure, he's just been an empty shell, just a shadow of his former self. He's not the William I knew before it happened. After that, I pulled together all my assets, and with the help of some private investors, I was able to build this hospital. William was one of the first patients to be brought in. I may not be able to make a difference in the world, but I can make a difference for anyone who can find their way here. I make it a priority to have my son treated well and without prejudice. I also want every single patient, and every single employee for that matter, that walks into my hospital treated just as well as William. I take this responsibility very seriously, and I will fire anyone who doesn't. Do you understand that, Jenny?"

I was so overwhelmed with his words that I knew I had made the right choice by working here. Everything he was saying and all that he stood for were exactly why I should be here. We had both been through so much, lost so much, and still had this hope and idea despite everything, that the world could be a better place, even if it was just a small postage stamp in the middle of nowhere that we had an effect on. It was still worth trying and fighting for.

"Yes, I understand, Tom, and you need to understand something too," I said and watched him furrow his eyebrows, probably anticipating some sort of argument from me. "I more than appreciate you sharing with me what you've gone through with William. I know, from experience, how hard that is to do. It's hard to gauge how someone will react to you once you share such a dramatic part of your life with them. I normally don't share, I just stayed closed off to everyone, but I want you to understand why I want to work for you and that I more than relate to where you're coming from. When I was a little girl, I had an older sister. Her name was Laura, and there were ten years between us. I remember being envious of Laura and how beautiful she was. I wanted to be just like her. She could've been a model; she was so pretty. She was tall, skinny, gorgeous, with green eyes and long red hair. There wasn't anything about her looks that you could consider a flaw. I remember seeing a scrapbook once that my mother had kept. It was newspaper articles that my mother had cut out and pasted onto the pages. Articles about Laura. Beauty contests she had entered and won. Awards she had won at both school and sporting events. She was my parents' pride and joy. Laura never let it get to her, though. She wasn't stuck-up or preppy like you would've expected her to be. She had the biggest heart and was so sweet to everyone she met, but especially with me. It didn't matter what Laura had going on, she would put everything off to spend time with me. I couldn't have asked for a better big sister than her.

"Things eventually changed, however, and Laura was diagnosed with schizophrenia. My mom and dad took Laura to every doctor and every treatment facility they could to try to find her help. No one could do anything for her, and a couple years later my dad died of a heart attack. My mom always blamed it on Laura, saying the stress she caused them both killed him. I never agreed with that, but I was so little that it didn't matter what I thought. My mom was never the same with Laura after dad died and, at some point, had her locked away in an asylum. I didn't see Laura much after that, but the few times I can remember visiting her, she was always worse than the last time I had seen her. When Laura was sixteen and I was six, I seen her one last time, after her lobotomy. They had cut all of her beautiful hair off to the scalp, and something had gone wrong during the procedure, causing Laura's right eye to break free from the eye socket.

That image of her, laying in her hospital bed like that, still gives me nightmares to this day," I finished telling him. I had to stop talking about it. My hands were becoming shaky, and I didn't want to lose it in Tom's office.

"Oh my god, Jenny," Tom broke in, and as I looked up at him, I saw the expression of shock and disgust on his face.

"Yes, it definitely left its mark on me. Not long after that, Laura died in that awful place. My relationship with my mother was never the same, and I left home at eighteen. Laura is my reason, my cause, for working hard my entire life to get to this point now. That's why I understand what you've been through with William and why, when I heard about your efforts here in Indiana with this hospital, that I had to come work for you. I spoke with Patty, and that's when she got in touch with you for me. This is where I need to be, helping people like my sister and your son, trying to give them a better life. The life they deserve."

"That is so amazing," Tom said, staring at me.

"What's amazing?" I asked, confused.

"You have been through so much, yet here you are, prospering and moving ahead with your life. You're a fighter, Jenny, and I can tell you have a good heart. I'll have to let Patty know she did well when she said you'd be a good fit here. I think we can do great things together for the patients here, Jenny," he said, smiling.

"Thank you so much," I said, surprised at his sincere compliment.

"Once you get settled here, I'd like for you to meet William. I think he would really love you," Tom said, and it caught me off guard.

"Of course. I'd love to meet him," I said, touched that he'd offered.

"Great. Now we have to get down to the details of your job. After all, that's why you're here," Tom said with a light chuckle and sifted through some paperwork on his desk.

The next hour was spent going over the ins and outs of my position, my daily duties, and other employees that I would need to get familiar with. I needed to get with the head nurse for my uniforms and stop by the first-floor security booth to get a badge so that I would be able to get around the building since all wards were locked down to keep patients separated.

"Have you met Blake Jaxson yet?" Tom asked.

"No, not yet," I responded.

"That's surprising. He's Patty's nephew," Tom said, smiling.

"Oh, okay. I'm sorry. With all of the other names you've been listing off, his didn't stand out to me. Now that you say that, it clicks for me. We haven't met, though," I confessed.

"He will be here this morning to retrieve you. You will be his shadow this week, and I want you to do exactly what he says when he says it. He will report back to me at the end of the week with your progress, and if we both feel like you're ready, then you will be a permanent orderly on the fifth floor, the forensic psychiatry unit, partnered with him and another orderly, Zack Bennett. With your previous experience, are you aware of the types of patients that we house in that unit?"

"The dangerous ones," I answered, putting it simply so that he knew I understood.

"Yes, those who are court ordered to be here, deemed criminally insane, patients who are on suicide watch, and any other overly active patients that the docs feel need watched more closely or time to cool down in one of the padded cells. We only have those on the fifth floor. There is usually quite a diverse collection of patients up there. Do you feel that will be a problem for you? On the phone, you didn't seem to think so, but we didn't get to speak in much detail about it."

"No, I'm sure I'll be fine," I told him, and I meant it. I wasn't intimidated.

"Patty made me aware of your self-defense training, kickboxing classes, and weight lifting, which is all impressive, by the way. We have a personal trainer on staff, an indoor pool, a gym, and a weight room. I expect you to keep up your fitness level while employed here. All the orderlies working here need to stay fit to keep up with some of the patients we have coming through the doors."

"That's not a problem at all," I said, looking forward to having access to the facilities he named off.

"I'm going to walk you over to the employee lounge, and you can work on getting your paperwork filled out until Blake comes over there to get you. If you ever need anything, please feel free to come see me. Not only am I everyone's boss, but I'm also the human resources department, and the only free therapist in the building," he said with a laugh.

We both stood up then, and I followed him out of the office and back into the hallway I had come down with Diane earlier. As we walked, it occurred to me a question I should have asked.

"Hey, Tom, who do I report to during the week? Is it you?"

"Since you're a first-shift orderly, you'll report to Blake. He has the most seniority among the orderly staff members, and if he's out for any reason, then you can go to Kelly Johnson, our head nurse. If you can't find her, then come see me. After you get your schedule down, you probably won't need to see any of us. As of right now, you'll come in at five forty-five in the mornings, go to the hand-of meeting in the lounge, then start your day. The afternoon hand-off meetings are at five forty-five as well, and you'll leave at six o'clock. It's pretty basic," he explained.

"Sounds good," I said as we entered the employee lounge.

When we walked into the lounge, I gasped in surprise. I was taken aback by the stylish surroundings, which made the room feel like more of an up-to-date hotel lobby than an employee break room. Everything was sleek and modern. There were gorgeous metal black dining sets for the employees to sit at. There was a large flat-screen TV with a gaming system and DVD player hooked up to it. In front of the TV sat a very expensive-looking couch, table, and lamp. As I walked further into the room, a row of vending machines on the far wall caught my eye, and I was shocked to see them open and a man rummaging through one, helping himself to some chips. I looked up at Tom, waiting for him to yell at the guy.

"Everything is free in here," Tom said, smiling when he seen my shocked expression. "It's my pleasure to provide you all with anything you need while you're here. So whenever you're in the lounge, please help yourself."

"Wow, that's really nice of you," I said, completely surprised by his generosity.

"You're welcome, Jenny," Tom said gesturing for me to take a seat at the table in front of him, and when I did, he handed me a stack of papers to fill out. I looked at them and then up to Tom.

"You can go ahead and work on these until Blake is able to make his way down here. He has to wait for someone to go up and relieve him before he can come down."

"Okay, thank you," I said and watched Tom go, waving at some of the employees in the lounge as he left.

I received small smiles from some of the other employees in the lounge, but no one offered to talk to me or come over, so I spent my time concentrating on the paperwork in front of me. I had a lot of it filled out when I got to a section labeled Emergency Contact and realized the only person I knew in Indiana was Robert. I grabbed my phone and sent him a quick text.

Me: "Hey, at orientation. Okay to put you as emergency contact?"

Robert: Hey there, sweet girl. Really missing you today. Yes, it's okay."

Me: "Thanks! Miss you too."

I smiled at his text before putting my phone down and continuing with my paperwork. I wrote Robert's name and phone number down, hoping there'd never be a time where my emergency contact would have to be called for me. Finishing up the last page in the stack a few minutes later, I felt the table shift a little, and I looked up to see a tall, broad, very muscular man with short black hair, baby-blue eyes, and one hell of a smile looking over at me.

"Jenny Allen?" he asked.

"Yes," I answered hesitantly, still staring at him. I couldn't look away. He had a bad-boy model look about him, even in his white orderly uniform. His full lips and sexy smirk caught my eye, and I could feel a deep blush rising in my cheeks under his intense stare.

"Aunt Patty said you were pretty, but man, she did not do you justice," he said, grinning wickedly as he raked his eyes over me.

"You're Blake," I said, my tone flat as I tried to keep cool.

"Yep, that's me," he answered, his eyes still at chest level.

"Excuse me," I said with an edge to my voice. He took his time meeting my eyes with his, and the look on his face was so damn cocky. He knew I had caught him checking me out, and he just didn't care. Patty never told me what an arrogant ass her nephew is. My facial expression had to let him know I wasn't happy, but he didn't act affected at all.

"You have your paperwork done?" he asked, snatching it up before I could answer.

"You tell me," I said bitterly, and he smirked, but never looked up.

"What the hell?" he mumbled, more at my paperwork than at me.

"What is it?" I asked, afraid that I had messed up one of the forms.

Blake looked at me suspiciously and asked, "How do you know Robert Shaw?"

"Why? Do you know Robert?" I asked back, already knowing the answer.

"You must not know him very well," he said with a sarcastic laugh.

"I haven't known him long," I admitted.

"Then why is he your emergency contact?" Blake asked skeptically.

"He's the only person I know in Indiana."

"Are you the guy's family or something?" he asked, still holding my papers hostage.

"No," I said a little more defensively than I meant to.

"So…" he asked, raising his eyebrows as he drew out the word.

"We're dating," I said, feeling aggravated that I had to explain any of this to him.

Blake stared at me for a moment with a weird look on his face as he studied me. He finally said, with a harsh tone to his voice, "Robert doesn't date."

"Well, I guess he does now," I snapped.

Blake made a noise, huffing at me as he tossed my paperwork back across the table.

I scrambled to grab it all before it slid to the floor and couldn't believe I was going to have to work with this asshole.

"You ready to start?" Blake asked, standing up from the table.

"Start?" I asked and stood up next to him, realizing he was almost an entire foot taller than me.

"Start your tour. You need to know the hospital, the staff, and the patients to be able to do your job well. We'll start with a tour, then we'll go up to the fifth floor, where you'll meet the patients you'll be seeing every day," he said, leading the way out of the lounge.

Several women sitting in the lounge waved and said hi to Blake as we walked out, and it felt like junior high all over again. Blake was the football star that all the girls noticed. I couldn't help but roll my eyes.

"Ladies first," Blake said, gesturing for me to walk out of the door first and into the hallway.

I was steps ahead of him when it dawned on me why he'd let me go first, and I turned around to see him staring at me.

"Anyone every tell you you're an ass?" I stopped and asked him.

A smug grin stretched across his face as he said, "I've been called worse."

I couldn't help but laugh at his unexpected response, and we walked side by side from then on as I got my tour of McBride Mental Hospital.

Chapter 5

The next hour was a whirlwind of names, faces, and places around the hospital that I was sure I wouldn't remember. I knew the first and the fifth floors were the two main floors I'd be spending my time on, so that's where I paid the most attention. No matter where we went in the hospital, people took notice of Blake's presence. He was definitely someone that stood out.

As we were passing the computer labs, library, and other amenities Tom had put in on the first floor for patients and staff to use, we got bombarded by patients and staff members. It was their scheduled activities time, Blake told me over his shoulder as we continued on through the crowd. I trailed behind Blake, taking in all the faces that passed us. Some of the patients smiled at me as we passed them, some of them ignored me all together, but it was the ones who were giving me hateful glares that made me nervous.

"Don't worry about them," Blake said, glancing back at me to see I had a nervous expression.

"I'm not," I lied.

"Sure, sweetheart," he said half-heartedly.

"They don't look very happy that I'm here," I said and avoided eye contact with them.

Blake turned and, seeing me stare at my feet, asked, "What are you doing?"

"Walking," I answered.

"Why are you staring at the floor?" he asked, sounding irritated with me.

"I don't know," I said, not wanting to tell him the truth.

"Well, don't. When you don't look at the patients, they know you're intimidated by them, which makes you a target. Most of the patients will ignore you all together unless they know they can get to you, then they'll try to. Plus, if a patient is in front of you, who has somehow gotten ahold of something he isn't supposed to have, like a letter opener, you want to be able to see that coming. You don't want to be counting the fucking tiles on the floor when he tries to stab you with that letter opener. See the problem, princess?" he snapped.

"You don't have to be so shitty about it," I snapped back.

Blake grabbed my arm and pulled me into the empty cafeteria.

"Look, princess, I don't know where you worked at before, but you're in the big leagues now. Orderlies that work here, who don't do their job right, get hurt or get others hurt, and I don't have time for that shit. I thought having a female orderly on staff was just asking for trouble, but both Patty and Tom insisted you could handle the job. I trust their judgment, so here I am escorting our new princess through the halls, but don't waste my fucking time. If you don't think you can handle this place or the patients in it, tell me now before an entire week goes by," he said, still gripping my arm and staring me straight in the eyes.

I tore my arm out of his grip and took a step closer to him so that we were only a couple inches apart and said low and deliberate, "I can handle it."

He lowered his head down so that his eyes were level with mine and said just as low and menacing as I had, "Then act like it."

I stared into his cold blue eyes that were the color of ice and thought how much I'd love to smack to him across his sexy mouth, but I held back. I wanted this job, and I was prepared for this. I knew there wasn't going to be one male orderly happy about me being here. I was just going to have to push through and keep moving forward. I stepped back a couple inches from Blake and asked, "You know today is my first day, right? You think you could cut me just a little bit of slack today?"

Blake smirked, just slightly, in a condescending way before saying in a harsh tone, "Slack can get you killed on the fifth floor, so no, I'm not cutting you any slack. Now get yourself together."

"What do you mean?" I asked, mad as hell at his attitude with me. Dammit, why did he have to be so hot? It was distracting, and I was determined to stay pissed off at his smug ass.

Blake straightened his stance then said, "We have fifteen patients up there right now. Two are on suicide watch from the other floors. The other thirteen are all permanent residents on our floor. They're all men and all a hell of a lot bigger than you are, cupcake. You need to walk onto that floor like you own the place or they'll have you for breakfast. Most of those men have been to jail, prison, or committed some heinous act to land themselves here. That's who we have on our floor. This isn't sunshine and rainbows, and if that's what you're looking for, you better ask to go to another floor now. If you think you have what it takes to help control these men who aren't going to take it lightly having to answer to a woman, then grow a backbone, quit looking at the damn floor, and let's go."

"So you're telling me to go up there and intimidate these men into seeing me as an authority figure, but when I interned back in Kansas, you weren't supposed to intimidate the patients," I replied and suddenly questioned everything I'd been taught.

"It's like this, the patients here, dealing with mental illness, are usually only a threat to themselves, if they're a threat at all. That's not the patients on the fifth floor. In our ward, the patients are known for their rage and act out violently. They all have dangerous disorders and are prone to acting out both verbally and physically. Intimidation is one of the only defenses we have up there. When we walk in, you play that card, do what I tell you to do, and always be paying attention to everything going on around you. Falling out of sync with the ward's rhythm is an invitation for chaos," Blake said, looking down at me with a scowl on his face.

"Okay, I've got it," I said, never breaking eye contact.

"Good. Follow me," he said, turning and leading the way to the elevator.

When we stepped off the elevator and onto the fifth floor, we were met by another security booth and two men wearing navy-blue security uniforms.

"Hey, guys," Blake said to the two men. "This is the new orderly I told you about."

Both of the guards looked me over top to bottom, and I suddenly felt like a piece of meat. A rush of heat spread into my cheeks, and I turned away from their stares to hide my blush.

"I thought you were just kidding about bringing a woman up here," one of the guards said.

"Yeah, well, this was Tom's decision, not mine," Blake said with obvious objections to it, which only made the heat I felt turn from embarrassment to anger as they sat there talking about me like I wasn't even in the room.

"I'm standing right here. You don't have to talk like I can't hear every word you're saying," I spat at them both.

"I'm sorry," the older of the two guards spoke up. "It's just an unusual situation, is all. We don't mean to be rude."

"Jenny, this is Wayne and Richard," Blake spoke up. "Guys, this is Jenny Allen."

Both men nodded and smiled politely at they were introduced to me, and I gave them a weak smile in return. I wasn't ready to play nice just yet.

"Jerry is the third guard on duty for this floor, and you'll meet him in a minute. He's covering for me while I show you around," Blake said, and I nodded. "I'll send Jerry out in a few minutes," he told the other two guards, who smiled and returned their attention back to the monitors in front of them.

Blake scanned his badge over a strip next to the double doors, which led onto the fifth-floor ward, and I followed him in, feeling nervous, but trying hard not to let it show. I half expected to walk into the ward finding patients in cells or, at the very least, in handcuffs. That was not what I found. There was a large commons area in the middle of the large space with a couch, several chairs, a TV, and a couple of card tables. Two men, one wearing a white orderly uniform and one wearing the same navy-blue security uniform I had just seen, slowly walked around the room keeping an eye on all of the patients sitting around. I quickly counted them all in my head and saw there were twelve black uniforms. Black signified a patient was a resident on the fifth floor, so if it ever happened that a patient was somehow able to wander onto the wrong floor, staff members could easily identify the patient was in the wrong place. For our floor, patients wore black. This color also alerted others that the patient should be under close observation and was a high-risk patient, Blake told me in the elevator on the way up to the ward. Other floors had their own colors. The fourth floor, just below us, had blue uniforms for their patients. They housed the long-term patients with severe illnesses that kept them from functioning normally in society. The third floor used gray uniforms and mainly housed substance abuse patients. The second floor used yellow, and those patients were mostly voluntarily admitted, and that floor was referred to as the open unit because yellow uniforms gave patients more freedom to come and go between the first and second floors. There were no patients on the first floor. It had counseling centers, the cafeteria, employee lounge, activities areas, and administrative offices. Our patients weren't down there much and stayed under close observation, so the chances that they would be found on any other floor were low, but it was still a backup safety strategy.

The orderly on the other side of the commons area walked up to us. He was young with short spiked hair, dark-blue eyes, and although he wasn't muscular, he still looked fit and in shape.

"Zack, this is the new orderly I was telling you about," Blake told him as he approached us. "Jenny, this is Zack. Zack, this is Jenny Allen."

Zack smiled, stuck out his hand to me, and said, "Nice to meet you, Jenny."

I took it and as we shook hands replied, "Thanks, you too."

"Fuck her, you prick!" one of the patients at a nearby table yelled at Zack, and it startled me. We all turned to see who had said it, and the man busted out in a high-pitched laughter that sounded manic.

"That's enough," the security guard snapped as he hit the chair the patient was sitting in.

The patient quickly stopped laughing, and I was pretty sure he had called the guard an asshole under his breath, but no one seemed to pay any attention to it.

Before I could say anything about it, Blake asked Zack, "Any problems while I was downstairs?"

"Dave's in his room. He had an episode when one of the other patients told him you were going to bring some girl up here. They did it just to get him going, and it worked," Zack reported.

"What happened?" Blake asked, concerned.

"He has it in his head that Cheryl was coming up with you, coming to get him, I think. He tried breaking through the doors of the ward and got all the other patients worked up. Jerry got him in his room and calmed down while I was dealing with everyone else out here. I just got everyone settled back down a few minutes before you got back," Zack told him and looked around at the still room, checking for any signs of trouble.

"Come on, Jenny, you should go ahead and get meeting Dave out of the way. Maybe if he sees you aren't Cheryl, he'll stay calm," Blake said, giving Zack a nod and turning to head down one of the hallways off the commons area. I got a polite smile from Zack and followed Blake from the room.

"Who's Cheryl?" I asked, but Blake didn't answer right away.

When we were out of earshot of the other patients, he finally said, "David Hall has been here for six months. He has an extreme delusional disorder, so basically everything is one big conspiracy theory in his life, all the damn time. Less than a year ago, he killed his wife, Cheryl, swearing to everyone that his wife had left him and the Cheryl he killed in the kitchen of his home was a drone. I don't have any other details than that, but I guess, for whatever reason, he now thinks the real Cheryl is here even though in real life she's dead. Dave's never hurt anyone since he's been here, but he does have frequent outbursts. The docs have been treating him, but even with his daily therapy sessions and the medications he's on, so far it's not helping." He stopped in front of a large metal door with a small window in the center of it. I read the nameplate on the wall beside the door. It said David Hall and had two stars beside it.

Blake was quietly peering in the window of the door when I asked, "What are the stars for?"

He backed away from the window and said, "It's a four-star system to assess the risk level of the patient. One star, and you don't have too much to worry about. Dave has two stars because he's prone to frequent outbursts. Three stars tell you the patient is at high risk for acting out violently, and if the patient has four stars, for the highest risk level, you better be ready to deal with some messed-up shit. It's always best to have a guard close by when dealing with four-star patient. Now, stand off to the side while I go in and talk to Dave. I'll come back out and get you in just a minute."

I nodded, moved back so that Dave couldn't see me from his room, and watched Blake as he went in and closed the door behind him. Once the door was closed, I walked around a little in the hallway but stayed close to Dave's room. I noticed all the other rooms around his were empty. All those patients were in the commons area, and I glanced that way about the time that Blake opened the door to Dave's room and motioned for me to come in. I walked in, and sitting on the bed, staring up at me with sad eyes, was a man in his mid- to late twenties with light-brown hair, the start of a beard and mustache, and a lanky, thin body. He really looked like a nice man, I thought. Weird to see him in such a place as this.

"Dave, this is Jenny. She's the new orderly that we hired to help me and Zack out," Blake said, and I stepped a little closer. He didn't say anything, so I gave him a small wave and smiled sweetly at him.

Dave finally looked over at Blake, after studying me, and asked, "If she's an orderly, why is she wearing dress clothes instead of scrubs?"

"This is her first day, Dave. We haven't given her any uniforms yet," Blake answered, his tone level and patient.

Dave looked back at me, turning his head slowly to glare at me. When he didn't speak, I took the initiative to say hi first. "Hi, Dave. It's very nice to meet you," I offered, trying to sound sweet.

Dave never spoke, and in a flash, he was lunging for me. I stepped back right before Dave could get his hands on me. I stumbled a little, and my back hit the wall behind me, hard, but I didn't fall. I looked back up, surprised that Blake already had Dave and was pinning his arms behind his back to hold him in place. Dave kicked his legs back, trying to throw Blake off him, and the two men fell forward, hitting the floor with a thud. Dave continued struggling and kicking, knocking over a nearby table, and in seconds, Zack and Jerry were shoving me aside to get into the room. It took the three of them to hold Dave down, restraining him belly down on the floor. Jerry and Zack had his arms, while Blake sat on Dave's legs. I watched as Zack pulled out a syringe from the pocket of his uniform and injected a calming drug into Dave's arm. Dave let out a piercing shriek, and his eyes blazed hatred up at me. I gasped, but before I could turn away, his look faded under heavy lids as the calming drug started to work. Everything had happened so fast that I was still processing what had just happened. The three men hauled an unconscious Dave off the floor and laid him in his bed with a huff. We all left the room, and Blake closed the door behind us.

"Thanks for the help, princess," Blake said coldly.

Zack and Jerry quickly turned around and headed back to the commons area with the other patients, not wanting to witness the ass chewing I was about to get no doubt.

"I'm sorry," I said, still processing it all in my mind.

"Did you freeze or what?" Blake asked, clearly pissed at me.

"I don't know. I guess I didn't realize you needed my help," I said, feeling ashamed.

"It took three of us to restrain him, and that never clued you in? Look, if you froze or you were scared, just tell me. I can't help you if you aren't honest with me," Blake said, still out of breath from wrestling with Dave.

"I'm not scared," I said a little more harshly than I meant to.

"Then wake up. You've got to be alert and on your toes, cupcake. I'm telling you now, even if you are gorgeous, you freeze up again, and I'll have Tom kick you off this floor so fast you won't know what happened," Blake said, and I glared up at him, hatred showing in my eyes.

The rest of the day was uneventful compared to the morning's drama, but every time I turned around, Blake was scolding me like a child. I couldn't do anything right as far as he was concerned, and

I wasn't sure if he was acting that way because I was a woman or because he was just that big of an asshole. By the end of the day, I was so upset with him, and at myself, I couldn't think straight. At 5:30 p.m., which was right before we needed to go to the hand-off meeting with second shift, Blake looked at me and told me to go on home. I couldn't believe he was dismissing me early. I couldn't even respond to him. I was so shocked and hurt, so I left, letting the guards know on my way out that I was done for the day. I moped the entire ride down in the elevator, replaying the day in my head. I was questioning my every move and wondering where I had gone wrong. I was convinced I hadn't. I was smart and accomplished, and I knew what the hell I was doing. It was that stupid asshole, Blake, that was causing all the problems. He had made it a priority all day to point out every little thing he thought I was doing wrong, and every time he called me one of his pet names, like cupcake, sweetheart, or princess, I just wanted to punch him in his sexy mouth. It would figure a guy that good looking would be such a jerk. I huffed in exasperation as the elevator opened and I stepped out into the hallway, running face-first into an older lady with brown hair, wearing a nurse's uniform. We hit so hard we both stumbled back and almost fell.

"I'm so sorry," she told me as she pulled herself together.

"It was my fault, don't worry about it," I muttered, starting to walk off.

"Are you Ms. Allen?" she asked before I could go.

I turned to face her and replied, "Yes, I'm Jenny Allen."

"I'm Kelly Johnson. I was just coming up to your floor to get you," she said, smiling, and I thought, *Oh great, what kind of trouble am I in now?*

"We need to get you your uniforms before you leave today. Do you have a minute so that we could do that before your shift ends?" she asked, and I was relieved that it was something so simple.

"Sure," I said, following her to a laundry facility located at the rear of the gym.

I stared in awe at the impressive facilities set up in this part of the hospital. On our way back to the laundry room, we passed the indoor pool, gym with basketball court, weight center, and locker rooms. I couldn't wait to use it all. In the back of the room were big bins filled to the top with different uniforms. On the front of each bin were labels that read Orderly, Nurse, Doctor, and Patient. Kelly lead me over to the bin labeled Orderly, which was stacked high with white uniforms. Kelly studied me and then rummaged through the bin and grabbed a top, holding it up to me.

"I'd guess you to be a small. What do you think?" she asked.

I eyeballed the shirt and answered, "Yeah, that should work." She pulled out enough tops and pants to get me through a workweek and handed them all to me.

"Thanks," I mumbled as I took them from her.

"Just turn them in at the end of the week, come in here, and pick out enough sets for the next week. They're always in here," she said, smiling wide, and I could tell she was waiting for me to return her smile, but I couldn't. I couldn't shake off the bad mood I was in.

"Okay," I said and turned to walk away.

"Jenny," she said hesitantly.

"Yeah?" I asked, half turning to look back at her.

"How was your first day?" she asked, sounding genuinely concerned.

"Fine," I told her, but couldn't meet her eyes.

"I bet it's hard, being the only female orderly," she said, still trying to read my face.

"A little," I answered and let out a long sigh, glad that someone got it.

"Do you want to talk about it?" she prompted.

"No, I'm not big on talking about my feelings," I said, sounding a little harsher than I meant to.

"I know I'm the head nurse, and not an orderly, but if anyone ever treats you unfairly, you can come talk to me or even go to Tom. Either of us would be understanding and try to help," she said, sounding sweet and sincere.

I really looked at her then. She had long wavy brown hair, wrinkles starting to form at the corners of her soft brown eyes, and she had a kind, motherly face that went with her protective, motherly personality. When our eyes met, she gave me a sweet, reassuring smile that made me feel like I could confide in her if I ever needed to, but I wasn't going to do that today.

"I appreciate it, but that's okay. I just need to go home and run off some of this frustration," I said, trying to put on a small smile for her, but it felt forced, and I was sure she could tell.

"You know, you can run here if you'd like to. There's also the pool, the weight center, and gym. You are welcome to use any or all of it if you'd like to," she offered.

I thought about it for a moment and said, "It would be nice to get into the weight center."

"You lift weights?" she asked, a little surprised.

"When I can," I said, already feeling slightly better.

"Well, take advantage, and remember, the first day is always the hardest. Tomorrow will be better," she advised me and gave me one last smile before leaving the room.

I nodded politely and watched her go before carrying all my uniforms over to the women's locker room and sticking them in the locker they had assigned me. Once I had it all arranged, I realized I was wearing dress clothes, not something I wanted to work out in. I took them all off and stripped down to my underwear and the black cami I had been wearing under my dress shirt today, put on a pair of the white orderly pants Kelly had given me, then headed out to the weight center. I was glad to see no one was in there when I entered and walked over to the bench in the corner of the room and lay down on it, feeling the cold plastic against the exposed skin of my upper back and shoulders. It felt good. When I put my hands on the bar above me and lifted the weight for the first time, I instantly felt some of the stress of the day melt away. This was what I knew, and this was what was familiar to me. I concentrated and was glad to have an outlet for all the crap that I had been through today. I thought of Dave's outburst, Blake and his bad attitude with me all day, and all the uncomfortable looks I received throughout the day from not just the patients but from the staff members too. It all fueled my anger, and I pushed even harder against the weights on either side of the bar I was holding. Before I knew it, my fifth push had already become my fifteenth, and I was feeling so much better. It wasn't until about twenty minutes later that my mood plummeted, when the ceiling over me was suddenly replaced with Blake's face as he smirked down at me. It caught me so off guard that I almost dropped the bar and the weights it was holding down on my chest. Blake caught it in a huff and put it back on the stand for me.

"I had it," I snapped, sitting up and putting my back to him.

"Never said you didn't, princess," Blake snapped back then asked, "Damn, what is that, like two hundred pounds?"

"Just a little over, actually," I mumbled, wishing he'd just leave me alone.

"Wow, cupcake, I'm impressed," he said, walking around to stand in front of me.

I didn't bother responding.

"I thought I told you to go on home?" he asked, looking down at me.

"I'm leaving right now," I told him, getting up from the bench.

Blake stopped me, putting his hand on my shoulder. "Are you mad at me, princess?" he asked, grinning at me, and that pissed me off even more.

"Is that funny to you?" I asked in a bitter tone.

"A little. Usually women aren't mad at me until after I've slept with them," he said and laughed a little.

"Well, since I'll never sleep with you, I guess I'm just cutting to the chase," I said, glaring up at him, and he instantly dropped his hand from my shoulder.

More seriously, he said, "You can be mad at me all you want, princess, but everything I said to you today was for your own good. If you show up for day two, you better be on you're A game because I won't be taking it easy on you tomorrow."

"Everything you said, huh?" I asked. "Even cupcake, and princess, and the other five hundred names you called me today? That was all for my own good?"

"No, actually, those were just for my own entertainment," Blake answered, and the sexy smirk he taunted girls with returned to his face.

"Well, stop. I don't appreciate it at all," I said as hateful as I could manage so he'd get the point.

"I really get to you, don't I?" he asked, enjoying this all too much.

"Don't flatter yourself, Blake," I spat.

"I hope you get your shit together, cupcake. Things just might get interesting around here working with you every day," he said, giving me his cockiest smile.

I huffed in exasperation at him and turned around, storming to the locker room. I heard Blake laughing behind me, and I could not, for the life of me, understand how Robert could have ever considered Blake a brother. I couldn't stand him, and the two men were polar opposites.

I was glad to find, when I came out of the locker room a few minutes later, that Blake was nowhere to be found. I walked fast to the truck, hoping not to run into him again. As soon as I sat down in the driver's seat, my phone vibrated, and I looked down to see I had a text from Robert. I swiped my finger across the phone screen to open the text and read the message Robert had sent me.

Robert: "Hey, sweet girl, just checking in with you to see if we still have plans for dinner tonight at my place."

Jenny: "I'm so sorry I didn't text you sooner. I'm just now leaving work."

Robert: "That's okay, Jen. What do you want to do?"

Jenny: "Crazy first day, literally! But I still want to get together if you do?"

Robert: "LOL, sure, darlin'. Can't wait to see you."

Jenny: "Same here. See you soon."

Robert: "XOXOXO."

I looked up from my phone, glad that Robert was so sweet and understanding. I felt bad about pushing our plans back, but with the mood I was in tonight, he didn't need to see me like this until I'd had a chance to cool down. I put my phone away, buckled my seat belt, and started the car. Glancing in front of me one last time at the large hospital, a sign caught my attention that read, "Caution: Do not leave keys in vehicles," and I frowned at it. I was so irritated right now that even the signs to this place were bugging me. I pulled out of the parking lot and headed home. On my way there, I passed another sign. This one sat next to the highway that read "Do not pick up hitchhikers." Really? All I wanted to do was get away from that place for the evening, and no matter how far away I got, reminders of my day followed me. I rolled my eyes and cranked up the radio, hoping a good song would put me in a better mood.

A few minutes later I was pulling into his driveway, his father's truck I was driving coming home for the night, and as I got closer, I could see Robert standing there on his porch waiting for me. The smile that was stretched across his beautiful tan face was enough to take my breath away. Even though it had been a day since we'd seen each other, it felt as if it had been a lifetime. As soon as the truck was parked, I jumped out and ran over to him. Robert opened his arms wide and caught me as I practically tackled him. As our arms wrapped around each other, he lifted me so high that my feet left the ground, and we both hugged each other like it was both the first and last hug of our lives.

Chapter 6

ROBERT TOOK MY hand and led me into the house and back to where his kitchen was. Set out on the table was a huge meal he'd cooked me while waiting for me to get off work. "Did you do this yourself?" I asked, knowing my eyes had to be as big as the plates sitting on the large table.

"Of course I did. You need a good, hot meal after your first day at the hospital," he said, pulling my chair out for me to take a seat.

Robert and I sat there eating his home-cooked meal and talking for the next couple of hours while we both told each other about the days we'd had. While Robert had to deal with his tractor breaking down, for the millionth time, he said, his day still sounded much better than mine. For some reason, I didn't even understand why, I didn't tell him about Blake's attitude with me and how shitty he'd been all day. I told him about the hospital and gave him the bare minimum details about meeting Blake, the guy he'd grown up with and, for some reason, considered his closest thing to a brother he had. After we both jumped in and cleaned up, putting the leftovers away and doing the dishes, I had to go home to meet the furniture guys with the last of my furniture for my new house.

"I'll go with you," Robert said, stalking closer as I stood there with my back to his kitchen sink.

"You don't have to," I said, feeling my pulse race as he slowly crept closer and closer. The way he was watching me made me think of a lion in the wild stalking its prey. When he finally reached me, our chests touching with the rise and fall of our uneven breaths, I knew for sure that I was definitely the prey in this scenario.

"But I want to," he whispered, leaning down so that his warm breath danced along my cheek.

"Are you sure?" I mumbled, my question sounding breathy and awkward as I tried to focus on not putting my hands all over him, which was where they desperately wanted to be. The way his tight shirt shifted over his hard muscles with his every movement had me aching to run my fingers over his chiseled chest and bulging biceps.

"I'm positive," he said as his lips brushed over my cheek, then the corner of my lips. My breath caught, and I just knew he was going to kiss me. My entire body tensed up, and I closed my eyes as I waited for what was sure to come.

"Okay then," I said, my voice barely audible over my pounding heart, which was beating so hard that I was sure he could hear it in the otherwise silent room.

His warm breath, which smelled sweet with the honey he'd eaten just a few minutes earlier, disappeared, and the next thing I knew, his voice came from across room. "Just let me grab my keys," he called as I opened my eyes just in time to see him walking out of the kitchen.

I stood there, my hand over my pounding heart, as I stared at the empty doorway wondering what in the hell just happened.

A little while later I followed Robert into the driveway at my house and parked next to his truck. Robert walked up behind me, and I gestured for him to follow me in. The living room, with its tall windows all along the front wall, was lit up by the sunlight and was so welcoming. The original hardwood floors in the place gave the home so much character. We walked through the living room into a large eat-in kitchen. Oak cabinets that had been recently refinished lined the walls. Stainless steel appliances were already in their places, and I was fortunate enough to even have a dishwasher in the kitchen, but that wasn't my favorite thing. My favorite thing about the kitchen was the large island in the middle along with the tan-and-black granite countertops. Sure, it was true that I was no chef. In fact, I was more known for my microwaving skills than my stovetop talents, but I have always pictured myself in a large kitchen with an island cooking magnificent meals for friends and loved ones. I walked into the kitchen and ran my hand along the granite top of the island and looked everything over. It was such a beautiful room I thought. Robert stood in the door way watching me, and I felt his eyes following me around the room. I looked back at him, but he quickly looked away. I turned and walked toward him slowly, deliberately, and watched him look up to watch me back. My eyes never left his as I got closer and closer. When I finally reached him, I didn't stop until our bodies were pressed tightly together. I tentatively placed both my hands on his chest and looked up at him.

"Robert," I whispered seductively.

"Yes," he whispered back as his eyes darkened.

I paused, letting myself go for just a moment, but then said loudly "I love this kitchen!" With a smile and a hard shove, I pushed Robert back. I giggled as he stumbled a little not ready for my push.

"Jenny!" he half-yelled, half-chuckled at me. Then he rushed toward me.

I squealed and took off running toward the back of the house, away from Robert. I heard his loud footsteps on the hardwood floors behind me moving closer as he picked up his pace. When I got into the main bedroom, I ran into the walk-in closet and closed the door behind me. I edged all the way back to the end of the closet, putting my back against the wall. I tried to slow my breathing so he wouldn't hear me. My heart was pounding as I listened to him enter the bedroom. I heard him stop in the middle of the room then head over to the master bathroom. When his footsteps got quieter, I started to inch my way out of the closet, hoping to run back to the front of the house before he could catch me. I wasn't fast enough. I no more got to the closet door when Robert jerked it open and I screamed and ran back to the wall at the end of the closet. I had nowhere to go. I was trapped in here. This really wasn't a good idea I scolded myself.

Reading my thoughts, Robert said, "There's nowhere to go now." I watched him as a cocky grin spread across his face, and he knew he had me, and there was nothing I could do about it.

My entire body pulsed with adrenaline. With each step he took, getting closer to me, my body tingled that much more. My heart was beating fast, and my breaths were ragged and uneven. My sweaty palms were back, and I couldn't manage one coherent thought in my head. When Robert reached me, he didn't touch me. He stood there with his body a couple inches from mine. He suddenly looked lost like he wasn't sure what he should do now. I looked him in the eyes and took one last minute to make up my mind about something that had been plaguing me since we met. With my mind made up, I asked him, "So you have me, what are you going to do with me now?"

I smiled after I said it. I couldn't help it, because I knew what he was going to do. He leaned in, and I leaned in, never breaking eye contact. My breath caught as I prepared myself for my very first kiss. His large hands found my hips, engulfing them, and he pulled me in close. My hands were on his chest again, and I was fully aware of every place my body touched his. He lowered his head down to me, and I could see the want burning in his fiercely green eyes. I wanted this with everything in me. *Kiss me!* I screamed in my head. *Kiss me now!* Right as our lips were about to touch, I closed my eyes then felt his lips on mine. They were soft and sweet as they pressed against mine. He lingered there then pulled back looking at me, wanting me to let him know this was okay. I nodded, and he came back to me more eager this time, pressing his mouth to mine harder, letting the desire pass through his body into mine. I felt a slow heat rise through my body, and it wasn't the usual heat of embarrassment I was familiar with. This was a passionate heat that I had never known before. I let my hands slide the rest of the way up to lock around Robert's neck, and his hands went to the small of my back, pulling me in tight against him. I let out a small moan, and when my lips parted, it allowed his tongue entry into my mouth. It was wet and a completely foreign feeling to me as his tongue and mine ran across each other. The eagerness with which I knew Robert had been feeling took me over as well, and our kissing became more of a necessity than a choice. As we kissed, our hands roamed over each other, and I felt Robert's hard erection press against my belly. I suddenly knew this was getting way out of hand, and I stopped, pulling away. Robert looked at me shocked as he processed what had just happened. I leaned against the back wall of the closet breathing hard, still trying to catch my breath from all the kissing.

"What is it?" he asked, looking at me all confused.

"I just think we need to slow down."

"Was I too rough with you?" he asked.

I laughed. "No, it was perfect, actually. I just don't want to rush into anything."

He stood there, mouth hanging open, staring at me.

"Is that okay?" I asked when he hadn't said anything yet.

"Yeah, of course it is," he said, moving closer, and took my hand. "Jenny, I would never pressure you into something you didn't want to do. I really like you a lot, and I don't want to mess things up. You just surprised me, and I shouldn't have been. You told me you were…" he trailed off, seeing the expression on my face, then said, "the word we do not speak of." He continued smiling at me. "That didn't cross my mind, and I got caught up in the moment. You aren't like other women your age, and that is my absolutely favorite thing about you. You're wonderful in so many different ways, Jenny. Please don't be upset with me."

I stood straight, getting off the wall, and looked him in the eyes. I could tell by his eyes he was being sincere, and I smiled up at him. He smiled back, still holding my hand in his. I put my other hand on his chest, rose up on my tippy toes, then gave him a light kiss on the lips. I lingered there probably a little longer than I should have, then eased back again. This time when I looked up at him, his eyes were still closed, and he had this small satisfied grin on his face. It was really cute.

"Come on, sweet girl," he said, intertwining our fingers together and leading me out of the closet. "You still need to show me the rest of your house."

I smiled and followed him out of the closet and my bedroom, never taking my hand out of his. As we walked through the house, Robert started singing some song I didn't know, and I realized in that moment that he did that a lot.

"How do you know so many songs by heart?" I asked, kind of jealous. I loved to sing along to my favorite songs when I had headphones on, but without the music playing to sing with, I was lost on the lyrics.

"You'll probably laugh when I tell you this, but I used to be in a band," he said.

"What? That's amazing, Robert. When was it?" I asked. I wanted all the details now.

"Last time we played was at my dad's funeral. We did 'Amazing Grace' and some old-time gospel songs for him that I knew he'd love. I couldn't do it any more after that, so I quit going to practice and showing up at gigs. The guys finally just let it go too," Robert said, and you could hear the sadness in his voice.

"I'm sorry," I said, not really knowing what else I could say.

"Don't be sorry. It was another life, Jen," he said, trying to make himself feel better about it, more so than me.

"Were you the lead singer? You'd have to be with that amazing voice," I said, trying to make him feel better.

"Yeah, actually I was. Sometimes I played guitar, but the other guys in the band were much better at playing than I was, so I mostly just did the singing," he said, and although he was looking ahead as we walked through the house, you could see his mind was back in the good old days of hanging with friends and playing music with his band.

"So what was the name of your band?" I asked, genuinely curious.

"Blood Brothers," he said, smiling now.

"Blood Brothers?" I asked, not expecting that.

"Yeah, there were six of us in the band, but me and one guy started the whole thing. We were inseparable at the time. We had grown up together, and he had practically lived with me and dad for a lot of years. We did everything together, even went and got matching tattoos. That was a long time ago, though," he said, trailing off.

"Is that the tattoo I'd seen on your arm?" I asked, remembering the black ink on his skin as he sat in my bedroom shirtless the morning he had comforted me after I'd had a nightmare.

"Yeah, that's it," he said.

"So all this was about you and Blake? Blake that I'm working with at the hospital?" I asked as my mind started putting all the pieces together from a dozen conversations we'd had over the last few days.

"Yep, that's him. Good old Blake," Robert said, but there was a sarcastic edge to his voice as Blake's name spilled out.

"So what happened between the two of you?" I asked, wondering why he kept talking about him in past tense. I could tell they weren't close any more from the way he spoke about him.

"After my dad died, we were both going through a lot. We were hurting, and we didn't know how to really deal with everything, so we started getting into all kinds of trouble, and things really got out of hand. That went on for a couple years, and one day I knew I had reached that point that I had to stop. If I didn't get my life on track again, I was going to either end up dead or in prison, so I told him I was done. He said he understood, but he wasn't at the same point in his life that I was, so we went our separate ways. I talk to him occasionally, and when he's feeling lonely, he'll stop by the farm and hang out with me for a little bit, but he never stays long. We haven't spent any time together in over a year. Thinking about that now, it feels like forever since I saw him last. It's a damn shame too. I worry about him a lot," Robert said, looking like he might cry. I felt so bad for him and all the hurt and sadness that he'd had in his life.

"You have been through so much. I'm really sorry, Robert," I told him, truly sincere about it as my heart ached for him. I knew all too well what Robert was going through.

"I'm okay, Jenny. Don't feel bad for me. I'm just afraid that if you really get to know me that you won't want anything to do with me," he said, glancing at me for the first time.

"Why do you think that?" I asked, knowing that it would have to be pretty bad for me not to want to hang out with him anymore.

"I've done some really bad things that I'm not proud of, and I'm just worried that it might be too much for you to handle."

"Robert, your past is your past. You said that's not who you are now, and I believe you. You've been so great to take care of me and spend time with me this weekend. If it weren't for you, I probably would've already given up on this adventure and moved my sorry butt back home to Kansas. You didn't know me, and you still have been so sweet and kind to me through all this craziness. That tells me right there that you have a big heart. Don't be so hard on yourself," I said, trying to comfort him.

"You have got to be one of the sweetest girls I've ever met, Jenny. I'm glad we sat next to each other on that plane," Robert said, looking right at me this time.

I instantly blushed a million shades of red, and this time it was me that quickly turned away, unable to hold his stare any longer. "Me too," I whispered just loud enough for him to hear.

Without even realizing it, we'd left the house and had been walking through the field behind it. Robert was so easy to get caught up in, and I couldn't imagine how my evening would've gone without seeing him. Working with Blake was going to be a lot harder than I'd anticipated, and he was one person that I wasn't looking forward to seeing when I went back to the hospital in the morning.

"We'd better head back in," I said, looking up into Robert's piercing green eyes. "I don't want to be back here when the rest of the furniture arrives," I explained.

"Of course, my sweet girl," he said, moving a strand of my long hair the wind had blown across my cheek. Tiny sparks of electricity followed the trail of his long fingers as he carefully tucked the hair back behind my ear, and I wondered if his touch would always have that kind of effect of me.

We walked back into the house, and I felt the familiar rush of exhilaration I had the first time I stepped in knowing this was all mine. There was so much open space, yet it felt quaint and cozy. Robert went into the living room to open the front door and wait on the delivery guys while I went through the house opening up every single window. That was one of my favorite things about this house. The tall windows were perfect for letting in a lot of sunlight. With the house being surrounded by fields, you could open up the windows and let the country air flow right through the entire house. I stood in the living room with Robert, breathing in the fresh air and looking around at my house. *My house*, I thought again. I liked that it was all mine and I couldn't stop smiling. Robert saw me standing there in the middle of the room and crossed over to me. He put his hands on my hips and smiled down at me. I put my hands on both of his biceps and laid my head on his chest. I was just tall enough that Robert could lay his chin on top of my head, and that was exactly what he did. My head rose and fell with the movement of his breathing, and I could hear his heart beating loudly. It sounded as if he had run a marathon, which he hadn't, so it startled me, and I looked up at him.

"Your heart is beating so hard," I said, concerned.

He smiled down at me and then said, "It always does that when you're near."

I blushed, and he kissed me. I kissed him back, a small, soft, sweet kiss, then laid my head against his chest again. His heart was beating even harder now, and I smiled at the effect I was having on him.

"So do you know where you want everything when the furniture gets here?" Robert asked.

I pulled out of his embrace and looked around the room. The living room furniture was the last thing to arrive today, and while the rest of the house had been easy to organize, this room left me clueless. "I don't know. I'm more of a visual person, so I won't know exactly where it should all go until I see it in the room."

"That's not a problem. I'll supervise while you move it around the room fifty times," Robert said jokingly.

"Hey!" I said and pushed his arm. He didn't even move. It was like pushing against a brick wall. He smiled broadly, and his green eyes sparkled in the sunlight.

"Okay, I guess I can help a little," he said, teasing me.

"I sure hope so," I said, teasing back.

I left him to go to the restroom, the day having been a complete wash until Robert saved it, that was until I walked in to my master bath and caught a glimpse of the red hair in the mirror that had my feet frozen in place. My face was barely visible in the large mirror, and I could hardly see it without the lights on, but the hair, the deep-dark red as vibrant as a fire engine was hard to miss. I gasped as I reached over and flipped the switch on, casting light over the entire bathroom. I looked back into the mirror and was shocked to see in my reflection staring back at me, my normal, boring brown flowing down my shoulders. What in the hell? I struggled to get my feet moving again, and when they finally did, I got as close to the bathroom mirror as I possibly could. I grabbed the long strands of hair hanging in front of me and held them up to the mirror. They were definitely brown. I stepped back and glared down at them as my mind raced to figure out what I'd just seen in the mirror. Some small voice in the back of my mind said that I'd seen Laura, or Laura's red hair at least, but the notion was so insane that I brushed the though aside. Walking back over to the light switch, I held my breath as I turned the light back off and slowly turned to look in the mirror once more. Staring back at me, overshadowed by the darkness and barely visible in the small room, was me. Just me. My brown hair was there, too, and all I could do was question if I'd even seen the red hair. The practical part of me said it had been something to do with the lack of light in the room and the way my eyes were adjusting having just come out of the sunlight in living room, but a sense of unease had me hurrying to do my business and get the hell out of there.

A little while later the furniture arrived, and the next hour was spent unloading it, putting it in the room that it all belonged in, and just like Robert had said we would, we moved it around about fifty times before I was sure everything was in the right place. I finally gave up when the delivery men started getting attitudes with me about moving it one more time, so I just thanked them for all their hard work and let them get back to the store. Once they were gone, Robert and I flopped on my new couch, taking in the furniture, and enjoying the feel of home that it brought to my new house.

"What do you think?" Robert asked, lying down and putting his head in my lap.

"I think it looks pretty good. Thank you for helping me with everything," I said, running my fingers through his short brown hair. He almost purred, and I giggled.

The next morning while I showered, got dressed, and ate my breakfast, I went over all my training in my head. I reviewed all the moves my restraint training class had taught me and how to effectively wrestle a patient into submission without harming them or yourself. Arm breaks, head locks, and two-man restraint images played through my mind. *Be gentle, but be assertive with the patients*, I told myself. *Remain steady and calm no matter the situation. Always be aware of any slashing hazards, suicide risks, and accelerants the patients might have access to. Remember that there's always sedation if the patient gets out of control, but de-escalation is always the best way to handle the situation.*

Hand-off was at five forty-five this morning, so I needed to be in the employee lounge by five thirty-five, just to make sure I was not late. Make sure to find Blake for job shadowing. Morning rise and shine would be first with the patients, then it was off to breakfast. Baths would be next, followed by an activities hour for those patients that had worked hard to earn those privileges, then we would split up at that point. Blake and I would stay on the ward while Zack and one of the guards go down with those few patients seeking activity time. Lunch would be right after their activities, at which point we would all go down to the cafeteria from the ward. The cafeteria would be closed to all other floors during our designated lunch hour. After lunch, the patients would have downtime in the ward, some time spent in the commons area for a few of the patients, and then counseling sessions will start. At five forty-five, we would go back to the employee lounge for the hand-off meeting, and I'd leave at six to go home. "Damn, girl, you've got this," I told myself in the mirror of Ol' Red as I sat in my driveway preparing to leave for work.

The morning was going great so far, and even the weather was nice. I pulled up to the intercom at the wrought-iron gate and hit the call button next to a small speaker. I would have to continue to do this until someone gave me a code to get in. A bubbly Diane came across the speaker and, after learning it was me, buzzed me through the entrance. I drove slowly, noticing this time that there were little wooden benches dotting the grounds. It was so beautiful here, looking at the building from the outside. It was thinking of what was on the inside of the building that made me shiver. I shouldn't think like that after having a sister who went through so much and knowing these were just troubled people in need of help, but there were patients who had a darkness in them. I'd seen some of them on the fifth floor yesterday. Those were the patients that could scare you, because you knew if they could get to you, they'd tear you apart.

I parked in front of the building and stared up at the enormous sign decorating the front of the building, which read McBride Mental Health Hospital. It was yellow and made you feel sunny to look at it. I stared at it while I took a deep breath, steadying myself for the day, determined to stay focused on the patients I'd be helping and not on Blake with his nasty attitude. I stepped up to the large double doors, straightened out the wrinkles on my white orderly uniform, and walked into the building with confidence. Diane met me at the counter and gave me a key code so that I would no longer need to be buzzed onto the grounds. I tucked it away so that I wouldn't lose the small paper she had written it on. I was pleased to find that she had my badge as well, and I wouldn't have to rely on Blake or other staff members to be able to get around the building now. I thanked her and gave her the brightest smile I could, knowing today was going to turn out to be a good one.

Kelly, the head nurse that had given me my uniforms the day before, was waiting in the hallway, holding a clipboard and a cup of coffee. She greeted me with a warm smile as I walked past her into the lounge. White lab coats, clipboards, and cups of coffee were everywhere. I barely glanced at the people with them and found my way to the back of the room, taking a seat with my back to the wall, where I could watch everyone that entered. Kelly and Tom were the last two in the room, and I could see Blake sitting a couple tables over. He hadn't spoke to me this morning, but I could hear him talking with Zack and a couple other first shift employees I didn't quite know yet.

"So are you headed out right after work Friday?" Zack asked Blake excitedly.

"Yeah, more than likely," he answered.

"That's if your shadow doesn't slow you down and make you late," one of the other guys at the table joked, and they all chuckled except for Blake, who didn't seem amused.

"Well, we'll see how today goes," Blake said dryly.

"Yesterday wasn't so bad. I bet she does even better today," Zack replied.

"If you say so," Blake said, seeming uninterested in the conversation.

"You have any challenges lined up for Friday yet?" one of the other guys asked Blake.

"No, not yet. Just going to see who all comes out for it," Blake answered.

"I talked to Eric, and he said Chase will be there. He's wanting a rematch with you," Zack said.

"When did you talk to Eric?" Blake asked, interested now.

"I was headed out to Brandon's house last night when Eric called my cell," Zack said.

"Is Eric backing him up after the shit Chase pulled last time?" Blake asked.

"That was fucking dirty, the way he did you," the other guy said to Blake.

"No shit," Zack replied. To Blake, he said, "No, he was warning me. He wanted me to let you know Chase was going to be there. That way, if you didn't want to put up with his stupid ass, you would know not to go out there."

"And basically say to everyone that I'm a coward? No thanks," Blake said and laughed.

"That's not being a coward. That's just playing it smart, man. If he wasn't scared to take you to the floor with your back turned last time, no telling how far he'd go this time," Zack told him.

"We'll just see if he actually shows up. Either way, I'm not sitting at home," Blake said, irritated.

"Hey, at least you have something to look forward to now. Beating his ass would make for a great Friday night. You'll probably need it after babysitting all week," the other guy said, nudging Blake in the side.

"No shit," Blake said, and before anyone else could say more, Kelly cleared her throat and the hand-off meeting began.

Chapter 7

Everyone was crammed into the small room, including the therapists that I hadn't met yet. I heard about problems that occurred the night before and activities scheduled throughout the day. I couldn't concentrate on any of it, though. I kept wondering what was going on Friday night that Blake and the other guys were going to and whose ass Blake was going to beat. It was going to irritate me all day if I didn't find out more. Was Blake some sort of maniac that I needed to worry about pissing off? Who was this Eric guy they kept referring to, and wasn't Blake a little old to be getting into fights? I knew out of all of them, Zack would be the most likely to tell me what was going on. He had been nice to me all day yesterday, despite Blake's best efforts to make me look like an incompetent ass. If I found a chance to talk to him today, I'd see if he could tell me what was happening Friday night. Before I knew it, the meeting was over, and we were being dismissed to our wards. Clipboards switched hands, and people started filing out of the room. I followed behind them until Blake stepped in front of me, stopping me in my tracks.

"Well, princess, are you ready for day two?" Blake asked.

"Bring it on," I said, feeling the confidence I had brought with me today backing me up.

Blake just looked at me, unmoved by my enthusiasm, and said, "Come on then. We have an hour, then we have to start getting the patients up and moving."

Before we could reach the elevators, I heard someone yell my name, and I turned around to see Kara making her way through the crowd and up to where I was standing with Blake.

"Jenny!" Kara squealed, giving me a big hug.

"Kara," I said, giving her a hug back, not really believing it was her.

"I'm so sorry I didn't come find you yesterday," she said, pulling back and standing upright.

"I'm so confused right now. I haven't seen you in over a year," I said, looking her over. Not much had changed about her since I'd worked with her last. Her light-blond hair was still long, and her looks could still give the most beautiful fifties pinup girls a run for their money. She had a classic look about her that defied timelines and made every girl envious.

Kara laughed. "I bet you are. Right after your internship ended and you left the Kansas City Mental Health facility last year, my grandma got sick and I moved out here to live with her. I've been living with her and working here at the hospital," she said, looking around the large hall we were standing in.

"I can't believe you're here. This is amazing," I said, feeling ecstatic to know another person in the state.

"I can't believe you're here," she said, laughing. "I heard you were starting in one of our meetings, and I wanted to come find you, but I got so busy yesterday. Then I saw you in the meeting this morning and wanted to come check on you before I head up to my floor. Everything going okay so far?" she asked, glancing down at her watch.

I looked over at Blake, who looked completely confused. He had no idea I had friends working here, but then again, neither had I. "It's going good so far," I lied, not daring to hold any sort of eye contact with Blake as I said it.

"Great!" she said, and turning to Blake, she said, "You better take good care of her, Blake. If you don't, you'll have me to answer to."

"I might like answering to you, cupcake. You're a hell of a lot prettier than my boss," Blake said and ran his hand down Kara's arm.

Kara blushed and let out a giggle, not minding at all that he was flirting with her.

"Will we be able to hang out soon?" Kara asked, returning her attention to me.

"I'm not sure," I stammered out, not knowing for sure what my week was going to turn out to be like. "But I'll try to make time," I finished quickly, feeling lame.

"You have my number. Text me when you know you're free. I gotta run. Hope today goes good for you," she said and gave me another quick hug before doing a flirty wave at Blake and running off for the stairs.

I didn't say anything, just smiled at her as she disappeared into the sea of white lab coats and different-colored staff scrubs. I looked over at Blake, who was clearly checking out her ass as she ran off, and I couldn't stop myself from rolling my eyes. When she was out of view, Blake finally remembered I was still standing beside him, and he returned his attention to me as we stepped onto an open elevator.

"You know her?" Blake asked once the elevator doors had closed.

"Yeah, that's Kara," I said, thinking it had been pretty obvious that I knew her.

"I know that's Kara. I guess I should've asked how you know her," he said, irritated again.

"I met her during an internship, when I worked at a mental health facility in Kansas," I explained. Blake made a noise like he was surprised, then I thought to ask, "How do you know Kara?"

"You mean other than working with her?" he asked sarcastically.

"Sure," I replied, watching as the numbers above us lit up one by one so that I could ignore his sarcastic tone he always used with me. Today was going to be a good day, I said again inside my head, and forced a smile onto my face.

"I met her a few times when we were at the river doing some cold-water jumping," Blake answered with a devious smile on his face that told me I did not want to know what he was remembering at that moment. I could only imagine what sort of mischievous acts were running through his mind, and I didn't want to go there.

"What's cold-water jumping?" I asked, figuring that was a safe enough topic.

Blake looked at me with his brows pinched together. "You've never been?" he asked, and when I shook my head no, he let out a dry laugh. "If you and Robert are so close, maybe you should have him take you some time."

"Robert goes?" I asked, thinking I'd have to get him to explain it to me some time.

"I don't know if he does anymore, but when we used to go, we'd have a blast. Everyone from town was going back then. There's not as many that show up for it now that we're all getting older," Blake said, and I was surprised. It was the most words he'd said to me without some sort of attitude behind them since we'd met.

"So you go too?" I asked, not really able to picture Blake doing anything fun.

"You really need to get to know Robert better," Blake said with a small laugh.

"Why would me knowing Robert better explain if you go jumping or not?" I asked, confused.

"If you knew Robert better, you wouldn't have to ask me so many questions when we talk," he said, sounding aggravated with me.

"I know Robert well enough that he said he once considered you a brother," I spat at him.

"Oh, so he has mentioned me then?" Blake asked, sounding surprised.

"Yeah, sometimes, but he didn't tell me everything," I said, noticing we were passing the fourth floor.

"Oh yeah, what he leave out?" Blake asked, curious now.

Just as the number 5 lit up and the ding of the elevator signaled we had reached our floor, I replied to Blake as I stepped off the elevator, "How big of an ass you are."

Blake laughed out loud as he followed me off the elevator.

The morning went by in a rush as we went through our routine with the patients. It was awkward when it came time for patients to shower, however, because no one had considered the fact that all of the fifth-floor patients were men and they were bringing a woman orderly up here to work. Blake and Zack instructed me to wait in the hallway and only come in if they yelled for me. Otherwise, they would be in the shower room with the patients as they got ready for the day. I was sure this wouldn't be the only thing to point out the face that I was a woman orderly as the day went on, but as much as I wanted to just be considered an orderly and not a *woman* orderly, I would have to accept the fact that in some cases, such as this one, that fact would have to be obvious. There wasn't anything I could do about it.

When lunchtime came, I figured out that was going to be the hardest part of the day. All our patients, even the ones that were four-star, high-risk patients, would be taken down to the cafeteria together. Our floor would be completely empty at that point. It took all three of us orderlies and two of the three guards to escort the patients downstairs and through the lunch line as they sat down to eat. I couldn't let it show, but the way some of the men from our ward would stare at me scared the hell out of me. I knew there was no way I'd ever be able to handle them on my own if they decided to act out and do something stupid. I understood now why that when our ward came down for lunch, no other wards were allowed to be in the cafeteria at the same time. I watched Zack, Wayne, and Richard take points around the room to keep an eye on the patients. When I found Blake, he was not in a fixed position as the other men were. Blake took his time walking around the room, watching the patients as they ate, and motioned for me to follow behind him. He pointed out and explained to me anything I should be looking for, taking notice of, and out-of-the-norm behavior. I was impressed that it took no effort for him to see everything that was going on in such a large room. As much as I didn't want to admit it, Blake was a smart man. He knew the patients well that he watched over and took care of. I was impressed.

Suddenly an alarm started sounding in the hallway and everyone froze, looking at one another. Some of our patients started yelling and jumping around in their seats, but Blake quickly put an end to it before yelling at Zack to take me and check out what was going on. I ran over to Zack, who was already running into the hallway, not waiting on me to catch up. I ran faster, and once I reached the hall, covered my ears from the deafening alarm sounding overhead. Zack looked around in both directions of the hall before we both found a crowd of people gathered down the hallway to our left. Zack took off, and I did my best to stay right behind him. I didn't know what in the world was happening. We weren't even to the crowd yet when Blake shot past me and Zack yelled up to him, asking who was with the patients. Blake yelled back that other guards had taken over for him, but he never slowed his pace and was able to reach the swarm of people before us. Zack and Blake pushed their way through the mess of people to see what was going on, but I could only stare. Blake, Zack, and another orderly I didn't know were consumed by several patients in blue informs from the fourth floor, and in the middle of everyone were two nurses screaming. I could barely make out their white uniforms through the mass of people surrounding them. I started pushing my way through those standing around to get in there and help out anyway I could. One of the nurses was violently attacked as I approached, and she screamed, but the patient clawing at her like a wild animal took her to the ground while I tried to break through to get to her. Blake and the other orderlies were trying to get the patients around them to the floor to effectively restrain them until help got here, but they were all outnumbered and seemingly overpowered as I shoved my way through, getting pushed around like I was in a pinball machine.

A tall man in a blue uniform grabbed my arms, digging his thumbs into my flesh. I didn't have time to think, just react to it, and I drove my fist up between us the way I had been taught in my self-defense class. I broke his hold on me as I hit his chin hard. He stumbled back, opened and closed his mouth, and I could see his teeth were pink with blood. He came back at me and gave me a hard shove. My feet couldn't keep up on the smooth tiled floors, causing me to stumble, and as I reached out to catch myself on anything I could find, I only found air before pain exploded in my face as my temple smashed against the knee of another patient, then the floor. I stood back up, angry and hurting now. I turned to face the guy that had shoved me down and tackled him to the floor. I had him belly down in seconds with his hands securely behind his back before looking up to find Blake, Zack, and now two other orderlies still wrestling with other patients. Kelly and two more women in nurse's uniforms came running around the corner, and each had syringes in their hands. Kelly saw me in the floor and came running over to me and injected the patient I had restrained with a calming drug. Once I felt the constant struggling stop and the man's body relax, I let go and stood up. Kelly and the two nurses that had ran up were injecting the same drug into the other restrained patients, but the nurse I had seen attacked, along with the man that had grabbed her, were both missing. I started to run down the hall looking in all the open rooms as I went. Someone behind me yelled my name, but I wasn't about to stop. They hadn't seen what I had, and I was scared that the woman who had been attacked was in serious trouble. I passed the library, computer lab, and two classrooms, but they were all open and empty. I ran into the men's and women's bathrooms, but they were empty too. I heard loud footsteps behind me, running fast as they caught up to me, but I kept sprinting down the hall, only to look back and see that Zack had reached me.

"What are you doing, Jenny?" he yelled as he struggled to keep up with me.

"There was a nurse that got attacked by a patient and they're both gone. The nurse and the patient are gone!" I exclaimed, trying to make him understand.

I rounded a corner and heard a scream from up ahead. I slowed down, trying to quiet my breathing and figure out where the scream had come from. Zack stopped too and slowly walked up beside me. We kept our footsteps quiet as we moved silently down the hallway. All I could hear was my pounding heart and the fast breaths Zack and I were both still taking. I heard a loud thud two rooms up, which was one of the old therapist's offices that wasn't in use any more. Zack and I looked at each other, making sure we were both on the same page, and slowly moved up toward the office where the noise had come from. As we got closer, I heard a woman crying and a man grunting loudly. I closed my eyes and prayed that I wasn't going to walk in and find a woman being raped, which was exactly what it sounded like. I hugged the wall with my body as I reached the door, and Zack got against it beside me. I inched next to the open door of the office and held my breath as I quickly peeked around the corner into the open room. Everything that had been on the unused desk had been pushed off into the floor, and the nurse that had been attacked in the hallway had been thrown over the desk, and the man I had seen her with was now standing over her, petting her scratched up face like she was a small animal. He looked down at her, almost lovingly, as one hand held a fingernail file to her throat, jabbing the pointed end into her flesh so hard that blood was slowly trickling from her skin. The other hand stroked her face over and over again as he watched her whimper and squirm beneath him. Tears and blood covered her face, and I felt so bad for her as I watched from the doorway. I turned back to Zack and didn't dare speak a word. I only gestured to show him that they were in there and that the man had a weapon, bringing my hand up to my neck, gesturing in a way to let him know that the patient had a knife to her neck. Zack nodded and seemed to understand what I was trying to tell him.

Just as I was getting ready to turn around and barge into the room, hoping to catch the patient by surprise, Zack's eyes grew wide as he looked past me. I started to turn back to the room just as a sharp pain radiated through my entire body, starting at my hip and working its way through all my nerve endings. I screamed out in pain and surprise before I realized that the patient had stabbed me with the fingernail file. I knew that's what he had done because it was still stuck in my hip as I looked down. Rage and adrenaline took over, and before I could think about it, I hit the patient across the face with a right hook as hard as I could. A hard thud sounded through the empty hall as my hand connected with his face and he stumbled backward into the office. Zack tried to get around me to the patient, but I blocked him and wouldn't let him through the door. The patient was still pulling himself together as he stood there with his back up against a large bookshelf, holding on to the side of his face. I realized now how tall he was, which was towering. His broad shoulders filled his blue uniform to the brim, and his hands looked like catcher's mitts—they were so big and bulky. I glanced over to the nurse, who had ducked down behind the desk and was barely peeking over the top of it as she tried to stay out of the way.

"Stay there," I said roughly, and she nodded in confirmation as she continued to cry.

At the sound of my voice, the man's eyes slowly came up from the floor to focus on me, and an eerie smile crept onto his face as he stared into my eyes. I didn't flinch, only watched as blood flowed from the man's mouth where I had hit him. I was glad to see I had done some damage. He stood up straight, taking his back from the shelves behind him, then took a step forward. Suddenly I remembered my de-escalation training and thought that would be better in this moment, then to try to fight the man to the ground.

"I have another orderly with me and more are on their way. If you slowly lay belly down on the floor, all of this can stop now. You have to show me you aren't going to pursue this any further. Please lay belly down on the floor, sir," I told the patient and kept repeating it, hoping it would sink in, but the more I talked, the closer he seemed to get.

"I hear the guys coming down the hall. Just keep talking to him, Jenny," Zack whispered behind me.

"Sir, if you'll please stay where you are and lay down on the floor, we can avoid any sedation drugs. I know you don't want that, but you have to stop so that we can all calm down. The other orderlies are on their way now. We can hear them coming down the hallway as we speak. Please lay down on the floor," I told him, but he took another step closer to me. I could hear my heart pounding so hard, and I wondered if anyone else could hear it in the room besides me. I tried to keep my breaths slow and even so that the patient standing in front of me wouldn't know how bad I was hurting. He looked as if he were ready to attack me at any moment, and I didn't want him to know how much damage he had already done, even though I was sure the red blood pouring down my white orderly uniform was going to give it away.

Just as I had anticipated he would do, the man suddenly lunged at me, letting out a roar as he did it, and my world went into slow motion. I saw him coming straight at me, I heard the nurse behind the desk scream, then Zack was behind me yelling my name, as if that was going to do any good. I watched as the man ducked his head and charged me like a football player. Then just as he was about to wrap his arms around me and take me down, I side-stepped out of the way, grabbed his shirt by the back of the collar with my left hand, and happened to snatch one of the belt loops of his uniform bottoms with my right hand. Using his momentum against him, I hurled him into the painted concrete blocks of the wall beside me. He slammed against it hard enough that the room actually shook, and with a loud thud, he bounced off the wall and landed hard onto the tiled floor at my feet. I watched for a moment, waiting for him to get back up, but Zack rushed over to him. He looked the man over for injuries and felt for a pulse.

"He's alive, but you knocked him the fuck out, Jenny," Zack said, looking shocked.

The nurse jumped up and ran over to me, throwing her arms around my neck and hugging me hard. "Thank you so much." She cried into my hair. I patted her back and tried comforting her, but her quiet sobs were quickly becoming louder and more hysterical as her entire body rocked with the motion. I looked to Zack for help, and he pulled a chair over from the desk for the lady to sit. He softly pulled the scared woman's arms from around my neck and slowly sat her down in the chair just as Blake, another orderly, and Kelly all came running up to us.

As soon as they walked in the door of the office we were in, they all halted, taking in the scene. A scared, crying, bloody nurse sitting in a desk chair was being comforted by Zack, who was rubbing small soothing circles on her back and telling her it was all going to be all right. Then there was a large man, dressed in a blue uniform, lying motionless on the floor, and finally, there was me. I was leaning against a wall for support, light-headed from the knock to my head, combined with all the blood loss. My left eye was swelling shut from the fall in the hallway earlier, and I could feel blood running down that side of my face, so I must have popped the skin open in the fall somehow. My shirt was turning red from the blood pouring out of my head, and my pants were already crimson from the heavy blood loss where the fingernail file was sticking out from my hip. I was sure I looked like a complete nightmare.

"Princess, are you okay?" Blake asked as he rushed over to me.

"I'm fine," I said, swatting his hand away from my face.

"Kelly, will you have someone look at Jenny?" Blake asked her, but she was already with the injured nurse, trying to check out her injuries and comfort her.

"She needs Kelly, let her be. I said I'm fine," I told Blake before Kelly could answer him.

"You aren't fine, princess. Your eye is already swelling shut and turning black. You have a big gash by your eye too. That should definitely be cleaned up, and you're probably going to need stitches," he informed me as he leaned closer to examine me.

"Check her side," Zack said from across the room.

"What's wrong with your side?" Blake asked so sweetly I thought for a moment that I hadn't heard him right.

I looked down at my side and moved my arm, which had been hanging in front of the wound, and revealed the bloody mess to Blake. His eyes went wide as he inhaled a large intake of air, then looked up at my face.

"What the hell happened to you?" he asked me, but he suddenly sounded so far away.

"What?" I asked, hoping he'd speak up.

"What happened to your side, princess?" he asked again, but I couldn't concentrate on his words. I felt my body lean into him, and his hands grabbed my shoulders.

"Blake," I slurred, trying to tell him something, but I wasn't sure if I had even gotten that much out. I heard him yell something to the person behind him, which I thought might have been Kelly, but I fell asleep before I could be sure.

I felt my eyes flutter open just long enough to realize I had taken a nap on the floor. The bright lights from the ceiling were glaring down onto my face, and it made it hard to focus. Everyone above me looked blurry, and I could hardly see what was going on, so I gave up and let myself fall back asleep. The next time I felt my eyes open, I realized I was in a hospital bed, and at first, I thought I might be dreaming. Why would I be in a hospital bed? I wasn't a patient here. I suddenly felt panicked and looked down to make sure I wasn't strapped to the bed. My heart settled a little when I found that I wasn't. I was just lying there with an IV hooked up to my arm, pumping fluids and pain meds into my body. Monitors beeped around me, and as I looked further out into my room, I could see someone sitting in the chair next to my bed.

"How's my sweet girl?" I heard Robert's deep voice ask, and it made me smile.

"Good, now that you're here," I said, but my words came out sounding like they were in slow motion. Hmm, did they only sound like that to me? I wondered.

Robert smiled and asked, "Do you need anything? I can get the nurse for you if you need her."

"I love your voice," I cooed at Robert, and he chuckled. "What's so funny?" I asked, and I think I scowled at him, but I wasn't for sure.

"Nothin', darlin'. I'm just glad you're okay," he said, and I watched him reach out and take my hand. His skin against my skin was so warm and soft. It felt really nice, and I smiled again.

"How did you get here?" I asked, watching our fingers intertwine.

"Blake called me, and I drove the truck up to the hospital. They just let me back to your room a few minutes ago," he said so soft and sweet, like we were in a library and he couldn't talk above a whisper.

"Blake knows you," I blurted out.

"Yes, and I know Blake too," Robert said, smiling at me like I had said something funny, but I didn't get it.

"You miss him, and I'm pretty sure he misses you too. That means you guys should be friends again," I told him, and no matter how hard I tried to speak plainly, my words still sounded muffled in my head.

"Okay, we'll try," Robert said.

"He's kind of an ass, though," I said, and for whatever reason, I was finding it really easy to blurt out whatever I wanted to say. It was pretty nice.

"Has he been mean to you?" Robert asked, and I noticed the tone of his voice had changed.

"You sound so serious," I said, mimicking the tone of his voice, and it made me laugh.

"Jenny, I really want to know. Has he been mean to you?" Robert asked again.

"No, Blake isn't mean. He's just a crabby ass," I said as I made a face, which Robert apparently thought was funny because he laughed out loud that time.

Wait, that wasn't Robert's laugh. That was someone else's laugh. I looked around and found Blake standing in the doorway of my room. I tried my best to scowl at him, but he only smiled at me. Dammit.

"How's she doing?" Blake asked Robert.

"She seems like she's doing okay, considering everything, but she's so high on pain meds it's hard to tell for sure," Robert reported.

"Hey," I said as sternly as I could manage to the both of them. "Don't talk about me like I'm not here. I'm right here," I said, pointing to my legs in case they hadn't seen them.

"Are you hurting?" Blake asked me, nothing but seriousness in his voice.

I looked down at myself, then up to the ceiling, then at Robert, and finally back at Blake, who was scowling at me as he waited for his answer, and through all those seconds of looking around, I decided nope, I wasn't hurting at all.

"Nope, I'm good," I told Blake then asked, "Are we going back to work?"

"No, you won't be back to work for a couple of days. I already spoke to the doctor, who said he's not releasing you to come back to the ward just yet," Blake informed me.

"Aaahhhh," I whined, and Blake let out a little laugh.

"You're going to have your hands full over the next couple days," Blake told Robert.

"I can handle it," he replied to Blake and was looking at me with such a sweet smile on his handsome face. I tried to smile back, but I was pretty sure I had drooled a little. I wiped my hand across my face and felt the wetness on my chin and decided yep, I drooled. I made sure to wipe it all off before I asked, "Are we going home now?"

"I'm not sure, Jen. I'll have to wait and see what the doc says about it. Do you want me to go ask him real quick?" Robert asked me, unsure what to do since I wouldn't let go of his hand.

I finally let go of it and replied, "Sure." He instantly looked relieved to have something to do.

I watched him walk past the end of my bed and pass by Blake, who was standing there with his hands in his pockets. "Wait!" I yelled, and they both froze.

Looking over at me with quizzical expressions, Robert asked, "What is it?"

I shooed him with my hand as I said, "Closer. Get closer to Blake."

The guys shared a confused expression, but Robert did what I asked, and as I lay there staring at the two of them, two things became very clear to me. "You sure you aren't really brothers?" I asked, looking them over as best as I could through the haze I was in.

They both laughed nervously. "We're sure," Robert answered.

"But you're both so tall," I said, pointing out my first observation, and they were. The two of them, though they looked nothing alike, were easily each a foot taller than me, maybe more. When neither of them said anything, just stood there smiling back at me, I took the opportunity to point out my second observation. "And the two of you are so hot. Like model hot. That's just not natural in real life," I said, and I kind of thought that maybe some of my words had slurred there at the end, but I didn't care. They knew what I meant.

"Okay," Robert said, drawing out the word. "I'm going to talk to the doctor. Good luck in here," he said to Blake, who only laughed.

Shaking his head as he walked over, Blake took Robert's seat next to my bed and smiled up at me.

"What's wrong with me?" I asked, noticing to late that my words were slurred.

"You're high," Blake said, and that was all the answer he was offering up.

"No, Blake. Medically. You know, what happened to put me in this bed?" I tried again.

"You took down a patient that was harming a nurse, got stabbed, hit your head, and pretty much single-handedly saved the day. You have stitches above your eye, which is swollen shut, and you have stitches on your hip where you were stabbed. The docs said you got lucky, though. The fingernail file you were stabbed with didn't go in deep enough to damage any organs. You also have a concussion, but that's nothing to worry about," Blake said as if this was all normal.

"That's all?" I asked, thinking that didn't sound too serious to me.

"Yeah, princess," he said, laughing a little. "That's all."

"Good, I'm glad I'll be going home when Robert gets back in here," I told Blake, confident I was right.

"I don't know about that, princess. The docs might keep you for a little while. You lost a lot of blood today," he told me.

"Nah," I said and drew the word out a little longer than I had intended to, which made Blake smile again. Why was everyone always smiling at me? I wasn't funny.

"Okay, princess," Blake said, trying to appease me, and the way he stared at me was so intense.

We both got quiet after that, and the room suddenly felt like it was spinning, so I laid my head back on my pillow and closed my eyes.

"Are you okay?" I heard Blake ask, and it sounded like he was right next to my face.

I was not sure why, but that suddenly made me think of something I should say, so I popped my eyes back open and raised my head up real quick, which was the wrong thing to do because Blake was right in front of me. Our foreheads hit hard, and we both grabbed our heads and moaned with pain.

"Damn, princess, you could've warned me." Blake said, still holding his head, but he was smiling, so I knew he wasn't mad at me.

The pain didn't bother me, dulled by all the meds I was on, so I kept going, determined not to let the head bump stop me from getting out what I wanted to say. "Blake," I started, and I sounded really loud in my head, so I lowered my voice when he looked up at me. "Blake," I said again, but in a low whisper.

"What is it, princess?" he asked with raised eyebrows.

"This weekend, you're coming over to, you know, my house. You need to be there," I said.

"To your house?" he asked, surprised.

"Yes, to my house, silly," I said and laughed a little because it sounded super funny for me to be calling Blake silly. When he didn't say anything, I continued to explain. "Robert and you need to hang out, and I think it should be at my house. We can eat. I'll cook, and we can use my new plates. They're really pretty," I said and was satisfied that I had gotten all of it out without slurring any of my words. Well, at least I didn't think I had.

"We'll see what's going on. Robert may not even want me there," Blake said and walked close to the bed as I laid my head back down on my pillow.

"He'll want you there. He said you're his brother," I assured him and closed my eyes.

"And you, princess, will you want me there?" Blake asked softly in my ear.

I moaned in agreeance as the fog of painkillers surrounded my brain and then added, "You smell nice."

Blake laughed lightly, and the heated wisp of air from his mouth tickled my ear. I smiled and rubbed it away before letting the medication I was on take me off to dreamland again.

Chapter 8

"JENNY," I HEARD a female voice call from far away.

I looked for its source but only saw blackness. I spun around, looking in every direction, and was irritated to realize someone had turned off all the lights with me still in the room. I stumbled around in the dark, trying to find a light switch, but I couldn't even find a wall. I had no idea where I was, and I couldn't see anything in here.

"Jenny," I heard the voice say again. It sounded closer this time and more urgent now.

"Yes?" I called in response this time. "Who's there?" I asked, but got no reply.

A cold, harsh breeze blew by me, and it seemed to cut through me like ice. I shivered and hugged myself, rubbing my arms to try to warm back up. "Is someone there?" I yelled into the darkness. When I was met with an eerie silence, a voice in the back of my mind told me I should be scared.

"Hello," I said more quietly this time, and even though I never heard anything, I suddenly felt someone at my back. I made myself slowly turn around and jumped when I saw a figure standing there. I almost screamed until, through squinted eyes trying to focus in the dark, I finally made out Laura's face. My sister, with all her perfect features, stood there silent, unmoving, but watching me closely.

"Laura," I said hesitantly, but she still didn't move or speak. There was just enough light now that I could see her standing in front of me still wearing the hospital gown she died in. That upset me, but I did my best to put a small smile on my face and slowly reached out to her. She didn't smile, and she never took her eyes off my face as my hand slowly moved out toward her arm. When my arm was extended all the way out to allow me to touch her on her arm, my hand sliced through the air where her flesh should have been. I stared at her arm and was confused when I couldn't grab it. I dropped my hand and looked back up at Laura. Her mouth moved, but no sound came out.

After another moment, she said quietly, "Danger here."

My heart sank as I realized she was telling me she was in danger.

"No, Laura," I said, trying to comfort her. "You aren't in danger anymore."

Tears threatened to spill from my eyes, but Laura didn't seem to notice. She just stood there scowling at me as if she were mad at me.

"Danger here!" she yelled this time, and it alarmed me so much so that I took a step back from her. My feet slipped in something wet. I looked down, but it was still too dark to see anything. I bent over and swiped a finger through something warm covering the entire area I was standing in. When I stood up, I brought my hand close to my face to examine it and saw that my finger was covered in a dark-crimson-colored blood. My stomach flipped, and I felt nauseous as I looked from my blood-stained finger up to Laura, but she was gone.

"Laura!" I yelled. "Come back!"

I couldn't see her, but I heard her from far away, screaming into the dark the same phrase as she had said to me before, "Danger here!"

Just then a light flicked on in the middle of the darkness surrounding me, and I squinted at it, realizing it was an open room. There was just enough light coming from the door of it to show me a path to walk over. I started moving, trying to get to the room, but the entire floor was a slow-moving river of blood. While it was only an inch or so deep, that still made it so hard to walk across it, that I felt like I was barely moving at all. I went slow, my feet sliding with every step, and I tried hard not to fall.

When I finally reached the door of the lit-up room, I grabbed onto the doorframe, still trying to keep my feet underneath me in all the blood. As I got my feet steady, I stood up straight and looked into the room. It was the office I had been in that day with the patient that had stabbed me. Lying motionless and limp across a huge oak desk was a nurse. A steady stream of blood was running from her neck, which had been cut open from ear to ear. The river of blood covering the floor was from her. I gasped at the horror of it and covered my mouth with my hand, but that wasn't the scariest part of the scene laid out before me. Standing over her, looking down at her lifeless body, was a tall black figure masked in the darkness of the black cloak covering him from head to toe. He, too, was still and motionless like he was frozen there. Empty bookshelves surrounded them, covering the walls of the office, and standing in the far corner of the room was Laura. When she saw that I had noticed her, she spoke again.

"Danger here," she whispered so softly to me that I barely heard her, then she disappeared into thin air right before my eyes.

"Laura!" I called, frantic to talk to her, and just as I yelled her name, movement on the other side of the room caught my attention, so I turned back toward the nurse and cloaked figure.

The dark figure shifted slightly, but turning to him triggered more movement from him, and his head whipped up, allowing him to look straight at me. His cloak, which had been hiding his face from me, fell back to rest on his shoulders, revealing that he had no face. The blank canvas that stared at me was more frightening than if he would've had some horrific-looking face to glare at.

Laura's voice came from the darkness, somewhere behind me, as she said to me in a low and menacing tone, "He'll kill you, Jenny."

Then, as if her words had been a command, the man, with his blank, empty face, lunged at me, causing me to stumble backward into the pitch-black space again.

"Run!" Laura screamed, but it was already too late.

My feet slipped out from under me on the wet blood covering the floor, and I screamed out of fear and terror as I fell flat on my back, hitting my head hard on the floor beneath me. I closed my eyes and grabbed my pounding head just as someone jumped on top of me, gripping my arms tight and pulled them down as if to restrain me. I fought to keep them off me.

"No!" I screamed and tried hard to knock them away. I made myself open my eyes to fight harder, and I was completely shocked into stillness when I focused on Robert's frantic face as he stared down at me. I lay there motionless as I stared into his green eyes, frozen in place. I watched him breathing hard, still holding my arms down, and I couldn't understand what was happening. My mind whirled with thoughts, trying to make sense of what I'd just gone through, but I couldn't get ahold on the situation.

"Jenny, you're okay," he said, but he wouldn't let go of me just yet. "You're still in the hospital, sweet girl."

I looked around the room as noises started to register in my ears. I realized I was still hooked to the heart monitor, which was going wild with an annoying beeping sound, mimicking the panicked beats of my heart.

"Turn on the light," I demanded, still a little scared.

Robert was hesitant to let go of me, but after a moment, he did, reaching over to a light switch by my bed, which illuminated a small overhead light above us. He stood there watching me, trying to gauge if I was alright, and I couldn't stop myself from grabbing my left foot to check the bottom of it for blood. When all I found was a clean white sock, I let it go and tried to wrap my mind around the fact that everything I'd just went through must have been a dream. It all had felt and sounded so real that it was just so hard to believe that was what it had been. I looked back up at Robert, who was still watching me closely, and saw how scared and out of breath he was.

"What's wrong?" I asked. "Why can't you breathe?"

"You had a nightmare, darlin'. You screamed and started thrashing around in your bed. I was afraid you were going to pull your IV out, so I wrestled you back down into your bed and held you still while I called your name over and over again. You were so hard to wake up. You really had me worried," Robert said as he stepped closer to the bed. He looked really freaked out.

"I'm sorry," I said, and before I knew what was happening, big fat tears started streaming down my face. I turned my face away from

Robert, ashamed of myself for crying over a stupid dream. I expected him to tell me to stop being such a baby, or even laugh at me for doing something so stupid, but he didn't do any of that. He didn't say anything at all about it, only crawled into the bed next to me, pulling me into him. I shamefully cried into his broad, muscular chest as his big, protective arms wrapped around me, holding me tight.

"It's okay," he cooed at me. "It was just a bad dream, that's all. I'm here, my sweet girl. I'm here now, and I won't let anything else happen to you. I promise."

I couldn't say anything. I let him hold me as I cried into his gray T-shirt. He kissed the top of my head and I let the tears run their course until sometime later when they had all dried up. Even though I couldn't stop the tears, I knew it would all be okay with Robert there. He had a natural goodness about him that comforted me to my core.

It was a long night after that, but Robert continued to hold me close, even after the crying had stopped. It was late when we finally dozed off again and was glad to see, when I woke up the next time, that the sun had come up and it was morning. I noticed, with Robert in bed with me, there were no more nightmares, and I was thankful. I watched dust particles dancing in the rays of the sunlight streaming through the hospital windows and stretched my body, feeling how sore and stiff it was from lying in one position with Robert all night. I looked over to see Robert had slept with me all night, lying half on the bed with me, and half of him was hanging off into the floor. He was so tall, and his legs were so long, that it was no surprise to find that not all of his body could fit onto the hospital bed with me. I smiled down at him, watching him sleep. He looked so peaceful, and I just couldn't get over how amazingly sexy he was. How lucky was I to have such a great guy, such a good-looking guy, here to watch over me? It was way more to have than I'd ever thought possible.

Before I could swoon over him any longer, the door to my room slowly opened, and in walked a nurse. Her smile quickly turned to a frown when she saw Robert asleep in the bed next to me.

"He's still asleep," I whispered to the nurse.

"He should be asleep in the guest chair," she said bitterly as she walked over to me.

I watched as she checked over my IV, the lines and cables hooked up to me, and then stood there reading the information on the monitor screens that were next to my bed.

"Let's get your blood pressure, then I'll go get your breakfast," she said, grabbing the cuff off the stand next to my heart monitor. I held out my arm for her to put it on me but jumped when Robert let out a loud snore. I looked over at him to see he was still sound asleep, but when I looked back at the nurse, I found her grinning ear to ear. I couldn't help but let out a small giggle, then held my arm back out for her to put the cuff on.

"You need to wake him up so he gets back in the chair. You'll need the room for your bed tray to be brought around so I can put your breakfast on it," she instructed before leaving the room.

I nodded then waited for her to leave the room before nudging Robert a little on his arm. He shifted and slowly opened one eye, peeking up at me. He let out a small whine then shut it again. I laughed and nudged him again.

"Robert, it's time to get up," I said sweetly.

"Nope," he said playfully and smiled, but still didn't open his eyes.

"Hey, sleepyhead, the nurse was just in here and said you better get in the chair. She's bringing me breakfast," I told him.

"There's a price you have to pay to get your bed back all to yourself," he said, eyes still closed.

"Oh really?" I asked, watching him smile wickedly. "What's the price?"

"A kiss," he said and puckered his lips up in an overexaggerated kissing motion that had me laughing out loud at him. "Come on, darlin', kiss me," he said through the pucker, and I laughed so hard that pain shot through both my hip and my head. I stopped laughing and grabbed my hip before I could do any damage.

Robert opened his eyes and was serious when he asked, "Are you okay?"

"I'm fine," I told him as he sat up on the edge of the bed. "It just hurts to laugh like that."

"I'm sorry," he said, and I felt bad for ruining the moment, so I puckered up, sticking my lips out as far as they'd go so that I looked as silly as he had and made kissing noises so he knew I still wanted that kiss. He laughed at my foolishness then leaned over the bed and gave me a funny kiss of his own. The kiss was silly and carefree at first, but soon after our lips touched, we relaxed, and the kiss became real. It was soft and sweet, and my heart melted in the intensity of it.

The nurse came in, and we heard her clear her throat. The kissing stopped, and Robert quickly got in his chair beside the bed, out of the way of our grumpy nurse. She scowled at Robert as she sat my breakfast down on the side table and brought it around in front of me. I hadn't realized how hungry I was until she took the lid from the plate, and I was met with eggs, bacon, toast, and coffee. It smelled wonderful, and I couldn't wait to eat it all as my stomach rumbled. Robert let me eat in peace while he went down to the cafeteria to get some food for himself. Apparently, he hadn't eaten all afternoon, too upset to eat after Blake had called him and he found out what happened to me. I felt really bad and made him go downstairs to eat.

My day was filled with visitors after breakfast. Tom, Kelly, Zack, Kara, and Blake had all stopped in at different times to check on me and make sure I was doing okay. Blake said that Jerry, the guard on our floor, was filling in for me while I was down, but he was nowhere near as pretty as I was, so I'd better get well soon and get back upstairs to the ward. Zack had called me Lil' Firecracker while we were talking, and when I asked him about it, he said that was my new nickname on the floor, and honestly, I kind of liked it. It was a lot better than princess or cupcake, like Blake always called me. I was afraid Tom might have been mad at me for knocking the patient unconscious, but he said he had already taken down a full report from Zack and knew I had tried to talk the patient down, but there was just no getting out of the situation. He was proud of the way I had handled it and said that he already spoke to Blake, and when the doctors released me to come back to work, I'd be a permanent orderly on the fifth floor, if I still wanted the job after this. I assured him I did, even when Robert protested and begged me to quit. There was no way I was giving this up. This was what I had wanted to do all along, and although it was a lot more chaotic here than I had anticipated, I still liked the job and the people here.

My doctor came in that afternoon and, after checking me over one last time, said I was free to go home, but he wanted me to take Thursday off to make sure I healed and didn't pull any stitches free. If I promised to stay on light duty, and no fighting with patients, I could return to work Friday, but he said I had to come by his office some time during the day to be checked one more time. If I was still doing good on Friday, I could return to full duty on Monday. I agreed to his terms and let him know I'd be back in the medical wing on Friday for my checkup, although I really wasn't feeling too bad. I had a slight pinch in my hip and light headache, but that was all, and I was glad to be going home. After the pain meds had been taken away, and my IV removed, my hospital bed had become extremely uncomfortable. I wanted my own bed tonight.

It was getting close to dark when all my visitors disappeared, and the nurse left me to get my discharge papers together. The only two left in the room were Robert and Blake, and I was currently enjoying myself, watching as the two of them stood at the end of my bed, bickering like an old married couple. I sat in silence watching their exchange.

"All I'm saying is that if she's going to continue working here, then I need to rely on you to keep an eye on her while she's here. I can't be here to do that," Robert told Blake.

"I've got around fifteen patients to keep an eye on, and now you're asking me to babysit her too?" Blake asked, irritated with Robert.

"Yes, as a friend, you should be okay with doing that for me," Robert said.

"Are we friends, Robert? This is the most we've talked in how many years?" Blake asked skeptically.

Robert stopped talking and looked hurt for a moment before saying, "I thought we were."

Blake looked sad as he said, "Well, you sure have a funny way of showing it."

"I'm sorry, but I've explained to you that I can't walk your path anymore. It's been that way for a while, and now I really can't because I have Jenny to think of too," Robert said and glanced over at me. I felt heat rise in my cheeks and really didn't want brought into this.

"You just met her. She's some chick, and you're going to throw her into the middle of this?" Blake asked as his temper flared.

"She's not just some chick to me. She's important," Robert said as he and Blake glared into each other's eyes. I didn't know if they were going to start throwing punches or kiss they were so close.

Seconds passed as they continued to stare at each other, then Blake, defeat in his voice, finally broke the silence as he said, "Okay, man. I can't guarantee anything, but I'll try to keep an eye on her while she's here."

"Thank you. I really appreciate it," Robert said quietly.

"Yeah, okay," Blake said, and they both relaxed, stepping back from each other.

I watched them as an awkward and strained silence filled the room and felt I should do something to lighten things up. They couldn't stay mad at each other forever, so I chimed in and said to Robert, "Did Blake tell you he's coming over to my house this weekend to hang out with us?" Both men flipped their heads around to look at me, surprised by what I'd said.

"No," Robert said, and instead of sounding happy about it, like I thought he might be, he sounded kind of irritated.

"I never said that," Blake interjected.

"Sure you did, yesterday, when you were in here. You asked if Robert and I really wanted you to come over, and I said yes, and you said you'd be there," I told him, smiling.

"I didn't know you were serious. I thought that was the painkillers talking, and anyway, I don't remember actually agreeing to come out," Blake said.

"Well, it wasn't, and yes, you did. So we'll see you Saturday evening around five, so I can fix you both dinner," I told him and left no room for debate as I looked to Robert and asked, "Right, Robert?"

He looked at me with an expression of shock on his face but finally smiled and said, "Sure, darlin'. Whatever you want is fine with me."

I smiled back at Robert, then to Blake, I said, "See, he wants you there too. We'll see you Saturday."

Blake sighed, knowing he was outnumbered then said, "All right, I'll be there."

He had to get back to work after that, so we told him bye, and soon after the nurse came in and released me to go home. Robert took me home and informed me, once we were sitting in my living room, that I wasn't going anywhere for the night. I had to heal and get better. I didn't argue with him. I was worn out from being in the hospital the last couple of days, and all I wanted to do was snuggle with Robert on the couch and watch TV. I laid my head on Robert's leg, and he pulled a throw off the back of the couch and covered me up with it as we found something to watch on TV together.

We had been quiet for so long, watching a movie together, that when Robert finally spoke a little while later, it startled me, and I jumped, causing him to laugh before asking me something that I really wasn't ready for.

"Jenny, can I ask you something personal?" he asked sheepishly, knowing he was headed into a touchy subject with me.

"I guess so. What is it?" I asked, feeling nervous before I even heard his question.

"What do you have such bad nightmares about?" he asked hesitantly.

I sighed and thought for moment about how I wanted to answer his question. I didn't really want to tell him anything about them, but I owed him an explanation after scaring him. Finally, I said, "Different things, but mostly about my older sister, Laura."

"If you're dreaming about your sister, then why do you scream out like you do?"

"Laura didn't die in a good way, Robert. I was six when she went, and it was really hard to see, especially at that age. I think I dream about her when something is bothering me or scares me because when she died, it was scary for me. I think my mind just associates all scary or stressful situations with Laura because of what happened to her, and I can't separate them even though I've tried. That's the best way I know how to explain it."

Robert sat there for a long moment, thinking about my words, and I tried to watch what was on the TV in front of us, but I couldn't concentrate on any of it. I knew Robert, and I knew he wasn't going to leave this alone now that he'd started asking questions.

"Can I ask how your sister died?" I heard him ask in a whispered voice above me.

"No," I said and raised up to get off the couch.

"Jenny, I didn't mean to upset you," he offered as I stood.

"It's fine, I'm just going to the bathroom," I told him, lying to get out of the room.

"You really shouldn't be up moving around too much. You could pull the stitches in your hip," he said, standing up next to me.

"It's the bathroom, Robert. If I have to go, then I have to go," I said, looking at him like he was crazy. He couldn't keep me from going to the bathroom.

Before I knew what was happening, Robert had scooped me up in his arms and was carrying me across the house to the bathroom. "What are you doing?" I squealed.

"Keeping you from pulling your stitches out," he said as we reached the bathroom door on the other side of the house.

He put me down very gently in front of the toilet in the main bathroom, and I stood there looking at him like he was nuts. "Go," I exclaimed, waiting for him to leave so I could use the bathroom.

"I'm going," he said, smiling at me, and even though I was aggravated at him, I couldn't help but smile back. He was such a goofball.

I used the bathroom then stood in front of the mirror, looking at my swollen eye and the stiches just above it. It was still hard to open, and the entire area was black. It looked like I had taken one hell of a beating, but all I could remember doing was hitting my head on the floor when I fell outside of the cafeteria. Still, though, it did look pretty cool. I touched a finger to it and winced at the pain. It was pretty tender to the touch even though it was feeling much better from yesterday. I didn't want to go back into the living room with Robert just yet, so I stood there a few more minutes checking out my head. I was afraid he'd ask more questions about Laura, and she was a subject I just didn't want to discuss with him. If Robert wanted to share everything with me about his past, that was fine, but I wasn't ready to do that with him. I liked Robert, way more than I wanted to admit to myself, but telling him everything about myself would just ruin what we already had going for us. It was better to leave the past in the past. A light knock came at the door, and I sighed, knowing Robert had been standing in the hall all this time, waiting on me to come out of the bathroom.

"Are you okay?" Robert asked through the closed door.

I pulled it open and gave him a small smile before answering, "Yeah, I'm fine."

I didn't get more than a couple steps out of the door when Robert grabbed me again, hauling me across the house like a child in his big arms.

"You don't have to do that," I told him, but he only smiled down at me as we reached the living room and he sat me back down on the couch.

"I'm going to fix us something to eat. You set there, and I'll be right back," he instructed me, and I rolled my eyes, annoyed at being babied.

"And don't roll your eyes at me. This is for your own good," he said from the kitchen.

I laughed at the fact he'd been right and tried not to do it again.

The rest of the evening, Robert waited on me hand and foot. I wasn't allowed to do anything but sit on the couch and watch TV, eat when he brought me food, or drink when he brought me my tea. It was pretty annoying because I wasn't used to someone babying me like this. I had always been on my own, taking care of myself, and all this was doing was driving me crazy. I kept insisting that I was able to do things for myself, but Robert wouldn't listen. He would smile his sweet smile at me or give me a kiss on forehead, thinking I was being cute when I'd tell him to stop his antics and let me do things on my own. He acted like one wrong move and I'd bust my stitches open and bleed out everywhere. It was so damn frustrating.

I decided to call it a night when nine o'clock rolled around, and I stood up, ready to tell Robert good night, but he stood up with me, ready for wherever I wanted to go.

"I'm just heading to bed," I told him.

"Okay, let me walk you," he offered, but I told him no.

"I'm going to take a shower and get my things ready for in the morning before I go to bed. You can sit here and relax," I told him, gesturing at the TV that was still on.

"It's fine, I can help, darlin'. Please let me," he almost begged me as I started to walk away.

"What are you going to do that can help me, Robert?" I asked, trying not to show my irritation with him.

He didn't answer. The next thing I knew, he had picked me up again and was carrying me to the master bath on the other side of my bedroom. He gently sat me down on the toilet and reached into the shower, starting the water up for me.

"Really?" I asked, fed up with this foolishness.

"I'm leaving right now. Enjoy your shower," he said and kissed the top of my head before walking out of the bathroom.

I stripped my clothes off and carefully removed the bandages from my hip before climbing into the shower. The hot water pouring over my skin felt amazing, and I didn't want to move. I stood there for a few minutes just soaking in the heat the water provided and had just started washing my hair when I heard the bathroom door open and shut. I jumped and quickly stuck my head out of the shower curtain to find that Robert had brought me clothes in and laid them on the sink. That man was going to drive me crazy before the night was over.

I finished my shower, dried off, and went to get dressed, but when I pulled the shirt off the sink, I saw that it definitely wasn't mine. I pulled it over my head since there wasn't anything else to wear and watched it fall down my body and rest at my knees. The shirt was longer than most of my nightgowns were. It had to be Robert's shirt. There was a pair of boxers sitting there when I looked back at the sink and giggled at the fact that Robert had brought me his shirt and his boxers to wear to bed. I turned to put them on, and a pull at my hip stopped me. I raised Robert's shirt and looked at my stab wound and remembered I needed to wrap it in fresh gauze before I went to bed. I worked tirelessly, trying to wrap the damn thing up like the nurses had at the hospital, but it was no use. When I gave up and looked at it again, I knew that the mess on my hip was as good as it was going to get. I let Robert's shirt fall and giggled in the mirror as the bulge of gauze on my side jutted out like a large tumor on my hip. There was no way I was going to try to pull his boxers over that mess, so I decided I just go without underwear or shorts tonight. His shirt was long enough I didn't have to worry about Robert noticing I had nothing else on.

Chapter 9

I OPENED THE bathroom door and found that Robert had already made my bed and pulled the covers and sheets down for me. It looked like a scene from a hotel. I shook my head and walked over to the bed, but before I could climb onto the bed, Robert entered the room and looked at me with a weird expression on his face.

"What?" I asked, suddenly feeling shy.

"What the hell is under your shirt?" he asked, pointing at my hip.

I looked down, realizing he was pointing at my gauze tumor, and giggled. "It's the gauze on my stab wound. I had to redo it after my shower," I explained.

"Why is it sticking out a foot from your hip?" he asked, laughing as he walked closer to me.

"It's the best I could do from this angle. It's a lot harder than you'd think," I told him.

Robert reached down for the bottom of the shirt I was wearing, and I jumped back, smacking at his hand. He had a shocked expression on his face when I looked back up at him, and he was waiting for me to explain.

"I'm sorry, but I don't have any underwear on under this," I said, feeling myself blush with embarrassment at the confession.

"What happened to the boxers I laid out for you?" he asked, looking around the room for them and found them lying over on the dresser.

"I didn't want to try pulling them up over this mess, so I left them off," I said as I sat down on the bed.

"Can you try, darlin'? I really need to look at your hip. I don't think you're going to be able to sleep like that. It won't be comfortable," he told me, grabbing the boxers and holding them out to me.

I looked at the boxers, and something clicked in my brain that made me decide something I didn't even know I was debating until my mind was made up. I took the boxers from Robert and laid them over on the dresser and walked back to him, knowing he didn't understand what I was doing. Hell, I wasn't even sure what I was doing. My heart was pounding, and I couldn't believe what I was getting ready to do, but I was doing it. I grabbed the bottom of my shirt and started to pull it up when Robert grabbed my wrist, holding my hand in place.

"Whoa, Jenny. What are you doing?" Robert asked, his eyes wide.

"I was going to pull my shirt up and show you my hip. You said you need to look at it."

"You said you weren't wearing any underwear," Robert said, not letting go of my hand.

"I'm not, but I trust you," I said, and I meant it.

Robert reluctantly let go of my hand and stood there with a look on his face that said he wasn't sure about any of this. "Before you do that, let me get the supplies to redo it. I'll be right back."

I sat down on the bed and waited for Robert to come back from the bathroom with everything and felt adrenaline coursing through my veins. No man had ever seen me naked before. I was completely freaking out about the whole thing, but I was determined to follow through with my decision. Robert came back with his hands full, and I lay back on the bed so he could get a good look at the mess of gauze I had on my hip. Robert sat beside me on the bed and stared as I slowly pulled my shirt up to my stomach, giving him a full view of everything from the waist down. Awkward silence filled the room for a few seconds before Robert finally spoke.

"You really made a mess of your hip," he finally said, and I let out the breath I'd been holding and laughed a little.

"Yeah, I know," I told him and felt some of the tension fade away.

Robert went to work taking off the dressings I'd tried putting on my hip in the bathroom, and a few minutes later he had me all cleaned up and new bandages on my hip.

"That should do it," he said, grabbing up the supplies from the bed and heading back to the bathroom.

I looked down at my hip, and it was as neat as it had been at the hospital when the nurses had patched me up. I was impressed that he had done such a good job with it. Robert came back and stared at me from the doorway. I still had my shirt pulled up and was examining my hip.

"Looks good," I told him and dropped my shirt, letting it fall back to my knees.

"Thanks." He said, and I was sure I wasn't the only one feeling how serious it had just become in the room.

I walked over to Robert, who met me halfway, and I put my arms around him, laying my head against his chest. He put his arms around me and rested his chin on the top of my head until I pulled back and looked up at him.

"Robert, would you care to sleep in the bed with me tonight? I know you had said something about sleeping on the couch, but I'd really like to have you in here, if that's okay with you."

Robert looked almost embarrassed when he said, "But you aren't wearing much, Jen."

I laughed and asked, "What's that got to do with it?"

"I don't know how much self-control I'm going to have if I lay down beside you in the bed and you don't have any underwear on," he said, and I watched as he actually blushed.

I smiled ear to ear as I said, "Just because I'm naked doesn't mean I'm going to have sex with you, Robert."

Robert's eyebrows pulled together, and he said, "I don't expect you to, and you aren't naked. That's not what I meant."

"Robert, I want you to sleep with me tonight. Just sleep. That's it. Can you do that, please?" I asked him with my best version of begging, puppy-dog eyes.

He let out a chuckle at my expression and finally caved. "All right, I will."

"Good. You get in bed, and I'll be right back," I told him as I ran into the bathroom once more.

I shut the door behind me and reached into the medicine cabinet. I didn't want to have more nightmares, not tonight, so I pulled out the medicine Patty had prescribed me and took one of the long white pills from the bottle and downed it with a small cup of water. I put the medicine bottle back up in the cabinet and prayed tonight would be a nightmare-free night for me. I walked back out into the bedroom to find that Robert had already gotten in bed, turned out the lights, and turned on the small lamp next to the bed. I turned out the bathroom light and walked over to the bed, standing there as we both stared at each other. I reached down for the bottom of my shirt again and started to pull it up when Robert yelled, "Stop!" I instantly stopped and looked back up at him.

"What are you doing?" he asked quickly.

"I'm taking my shirt off," I told him like it was no big deal.

"Why?" he demanded, looking nervous, and I thought it was cute.

"I want to sleep naked beside you, and the only way to do that is to take off my shirt, Robert."

"Dammit, woman, you're killing me," he said, and I giggled. "We aren't having sex, right?"

"Right," I agreed. "We're just sleeping."

"Then I think you should keep the shirt on," he told me in a pleading tone.

"I'm ready for you to see all of me, Robert. I'm getting naked, and I'm sleeping beside you. You're a grown man. I'm pretty sure you can handle it," I told him.

He sighed and buried his face in his pillow and made some sort of loud noise into it. I thought he might be yelling as he hit the bed beside it with his fist. I stood there, watching with amusement as he attacked the pillow around his face. Seconds passed, and he finally became still and slowly looked up at me. He composed himself, propped his head up with his hand, and stared over at me.

"Okay, I'm ready," he said, trying to sound normal again, and I couldn't help but giggle at him. "But in my defense, if a hand slips to some nefarious place on your body later, it was you that gave me too much credit."

I laughed again. "Duly noted," I said with a stern nod. "Are you ready now?" I asked, my hands on the bottom of the shirt.

"Ready," he said, and I lifted the shirt up over my head and threw it behind me on the floor.

Robert was so still as he stared at me I wasn't even sure he was breathing. He definitely wasn't blinking or moving in any way. I smiled over at him, waiting for him to have some sort of reaction. I started feeling so self-conscious, thinking he was hating the view I'd given him, so I worked up the nerve to ask, "Well?"

Robert finally blinked and with a long sigh said, "Beautiful. You're completely beautiful, Jen."

I smiled and came over to the bed, crawling in beside him. When I turned off the lamp and rolled over to look at him, his eyes were shut, and he wasn't moving again. I grabbed one of his hands and put it on my side, just above the gauze he had put on for me, and he stiffened.

"What's wrong?" I asked.

He opened his eyes, barely visible in the dark room, and said, "You're gonna be the death of me, do you know that?"

I giggled and kissed him, feeling him finally relax into me, and I was glad to have shared myself with Robert like this. It was a big step for me, and he made it so effortless.

"Ready for sleep?" I asked as the kissing stopped.

"I can try, but I'm not promising anything," he said, and I smiled again.

I turned over to face the bathroom, putting my back to Robert, who still wasn't moving, and grabbed his arm to drape it across my stomach. He was reluctant about it, but he let me do it. Just as I had settled into my spot on the bed and was getting comfortable, Robert's arm disappeared from my waist, and the bed started shaking as he moved around under the covers. Before I could ask what he was doing, I felt him stuffing a pillow between my bare butt and the boxers he was wearing. Once the pillow was in place, Robert moved back over to me, throwing his arm around me and pulling me in close.

"Better?" I asked him, holding in a laugh.

"Safer," he said, and I could feel his smile against the back of my neck.

I couldn't help but giggle that time, and he nipped the back of my neck, causing cold chills down my spine. I laughed out loud, and he pulled me in tight against him, smooshing the pillow between us, and I smiled, knowing no matter how nervous I was about things with Robert sometimes, he could always make me feel at ease after I let him in.

I got comfortable as we lay there and the warmth from his body enveloped me. I knew it wouldn't be long before I went to sleep so before I dozed off I made sure to say, "Good night, Robert."

"Good night, my sweet girl," he replied and gave me a chaste kiss on the back of my neck.

I lay there feeling warm and protected, relishing this moment with Robert and thinking about all the time we'd been spending together, then I suddenly heard noises coming from behind me. I held my breath listening and realized I was being sang to sleep. I smiled and listened as the sweet sound filled my ears and soothed my heart. The words in the song, which were "You're the closest to heaven that I'll ever be" and "I don't want to go home right now," made my eyes water, and I wondered when I became so sappy that a song could affect me in such a way. Maybe it was Robert's deep, Southern voice that made it sound so wonderful or how he seemed to put so much feeling behind every word. I wasn't for sure, but by the next part of the song when Robert sang, "I just don't wanna miss you tonight," I had tears running down my face and onto my pillow. Right here, in this one moment, my life was perfect, and I never wanted to lose what I had with Robert. I waited until he finished the song before I said to him, "You just made 'Iris' my new favorite song."

He gave me a squeeze and said, "Sweet dreams, darlin'."

"Sweet dreams, Robert," I replied and hoped that we were both right tonight.

Robert and I woke up the next morning tangled in each other's arms, and I smiled as our eyes met. Robert leaned his head down and gave me a kiss, which only served as a reminder to brush my teeth. I really hoped I didn't have terrible morning breath.

"How'd you sleep?" Robert asked, rolling to his back and stretching his limbs.

"Really good, actually. You?" I asked, sitting up.

"Great. I could get used to sleeping next to you every night," he said, grinning.

"How's my eye look today?" I asked, changing the subject, not sure if I was ready to entertain the idea of something so serious so soon.

Robert studied my face then said, "Not too bad. A lot of the swelling has gone down."

"That's good," I said, standing slowly to see how my hip was.

"How is it?" Robert asked, knowing I was checking on my hip.

"It's stiff, but it doesn't really hurt," I told him and was glad it was feeling better. If today went well, I could return to work tomorrow.

"Really?" Robert asked, walking around the bed to me as I slipped his shirt back on.

"Really," I said, putting my arms around him.

"Good. I'm going to fix us something for breakfast," he said, giving me a quick kiss.

"Thank you. I'll see you in there in just a few minutes," I told him and left him to go to the bathroom, brush my teeth, and get dressed for the day.

I felt really good after being up and moving around for a little while. When I was ready, I walked into the kitchen and found Robert sitting at the kitchen island on one of the stools. He had a bowl of cereal in front of him and another next to him for me. He briefly looked up from the cereal box he was reading to watch me walk around the island and take a seat beside him.

"No bacon and eggs this morning?" I asked, taking the cereal box from him and pouring some into my bowl.

"This is your kitchen, remember? We had a choice of cereal or yogurt. I chose cereal," he grumbled, wishing I had real food in the house.

I laughed and asked, "Did you at least make coffee?"

Robert's head shot up, and he looked at me. "There's coffee?" he asked.

"Yes," I answered and laughed at the expression on his face. "I'll make some," I offered, going over to the cabinet.

"I'm so glad there's coffee," Robert joked over his cereal bowl.

A few minutes later we put our cereal bowls up and took our coffee to the front porch. The bright morning sun felt amazing on my skin as it rose higher over the surrounding fields. It was quiet and peaceful this morning, and I loved it. Robert had me tell him all about the fight and getting attacked at the hospital. He had heard bits and pieces of the story at the hospital but wanted the whole story from me. I knew he wouldn't like what I had to tell him, but I put everything out there that happened that day. Robert had a million questions about the hospital, patients, staff, and our safety procedures. I did my best to answer them all, and he tried once more to talk me out of working there, but he soon realized I'd never quit no matter what he said.

I couldn't do a lot. It was doctor's orders, so most of the morning was spent either talking with Robert or watching TV together. At one point, I got him to explain what cold-water jumping was and found out that it was a big deal in our small town. Every year in the fall, when raging waters of the Ohio river a few miles away got cold, everyone would meet at the river's edges and take turns diving in. Supposedly, it was a big adrenaline rush, and they made a whole day of it, bringing out chairs and coolers. They'd grill out and drink around a bonfire while everyone splashed around and hung out. Robert said he hadn't been in a long time but promised to take me once I was all healed up. I liked the idea of us doing something fun together like that, and it gave me something to look forward to. When lunchtime rolled around, we heard a car pull up in the driveway, and we both went to the window to see who had come by.

"Who's that?" Robert asked as a blond girl in nursing scrubs came bouncing up the porch steps.

"Kara!" I yelled as I ran to the door, opening it for her.

"Hey, girl!" Kara squealed as soon as she saw me.

"What are you doing here?" I asked, moving so she could come in.

"I'm feeding you," she said, carrying in tote bags of covered dishes.

"Hey, Kara," Robert said, taking the bags from her. "I didn't recognize you in your work clothes." I watched the two them, just realizing how small this town really was. Everyone knew everyone around here.

"Hey, Robert," she said, handing over all the bags and giving him a quick hug.

"You didn't have to do all this," I exclaimed as I watched Robert take dish after dish from the tote bags.

"Sure I did. We're friends, and someone's gotta make sure you're eating," she said as she started opening lids from the dishes.

"Your grandma really did a good job with you," I said, half-teasing.

"You know she did," Kara said with a proud smile on her beautiful face.

When her and Robert were finished opening every dish, I looked over the kitchen counter and was shocked by all the food she had prepared for us. There was fried chicken, finger sandwiches, coleslaw, green beans, potato salad, biscuits, baked beans, corn on the cob, a cobbler, and even plastic silverware, napkins, and paper plates. My jaw dropped, and I couldn't have been more surprised or more in awe of her.

"Damn, Kara, how many people were you planning to feed?" Robert asked, looking at all the food.

"I'm not sure. I just wanted to make sure we had enough," she said as she put a little bit of everything on a plate and handed it to me.

"I can't eat all that," I said, staring at all the food she'd piled high on the plate.

"Well, you can try," she said then handed a second plate, stacked even higher than mine, to Robert.

"When did you have time to cook all this?" I asked.

"Last night and this morning. Now sit and eat. You're going to need your strength if you're ever going to feel better," Kara bossed, pushing me into a chair at the kitchen table.

I sat as I was told and looked up to see Kara running out the front door, just as Robert took a seat beside me at the table. We traded looks, then glanced over to the door again.

"Did she just leave?" I asked.

"I have no clue," Robert said with a mouth full of food, and I looked to see he had already started eating. "This is so good," he continued, taking another bite, and I giggled at him before taking a bite off my own plate.

Everything tasted so good, and I was jealous of how good Kara could cook. The front door closed, and I turned to see her walking back into the house, this time carrying a pitcher of tea with her.

"You have tea too?" I asked, surprised.

"Of course I do. Who wants some? It's good and sweet like my granny makes it," she said smiling as she poured some of the tea into a glass and held it up to us. We both raised our hands, and Kara looked pleased that we were happy with what she had brought us.

After we were all set, Kara fixed her own plate and came to sit with us at the table. The three of us talked and laughed like we'd known one another for years. Even though I was the newbie here, they made me feel loved and welcome. I didn't feel like an outsider at all as we sat there laughing and eating together. An hour went by in a flash, and Kara had already cleaned up the kitchen and stocked my fridge with all the leftovers.

"Do you really have to go?" I asked, disappointed that she said she had to go back to work.

"Yeah, I'm sorry. I really have to get back, but everyone at the hospital said to tell you hi, Jenny. You saving that nurse is all anyone is talking about. You're a hero," Kara said as she headed for the door.

"I can't wait to be back tomorrow," I exclaimed.

"Tomorrow?" Kara asked, sounding surprised.

"Doc said Friday on light duty. Tomorrow is Friday," I told her.

"I just didn't think it would be so soon," she said.

"Me either," Robert chimed in.

"Well, take good care of her, and I'll see you at work tomorrow, Jen," she said, leaving for her car.

"I will," Robert said as he held the door open for her.

"Thanks, Kara!" I yelled as she got into her car.

She smiled and waved before pulling out onto the highway. Robert and I retreated to the couch, and I lay against him as he wrapped an arm around me.

"What are you laying there thinking about, darlin'?" Robert asked as he played with my hair.

"Just stuff," I said as I let out a contented sigh.

"Wanna talk about it?"

"I think I'm really going to love it here in Indiana."

Robert gave me an approving squeeze, and I couldn't imagine my life being any other way, now that I had him and Kara in it.

Friday morning came sooner than I had expected, and after a long goodbye kiss from Robert, I was on my way to the hospital. The talk Robert had given me during breakfast replayed in my mind, and I smiled as I drove toward the hospital for my first day back to work.

"Please take it easy today and be safe," he had pleaded with me.

"I will, I promise," I told him as I ate my yogurt.

"If you need me to come get you today, I will. If it gets hard or you start hurting again, I can be there in five minutes," Robert told me as he dared to hold my keys hostage.

"Something you need to know about me, Robert, is that I'm no quitter. If it gets hard, that's just going to push me to do better," I said, then jumped up, snatching my keys from Robert's hand as he held them above his head.

"You're so frustrating," he snapped.

"That's why you like me," I said, teasing him.

"Love you," he corrected me.

I dropped my stuff on the table and looked at him. Sure I hadn't heard him right.

"Huh?" I asked, even though I wasn't ready for the answer.

Robert smiled and walked over to me, placing his hands on my shoulders. "I love you, Jenny," he said as he stared down into my eyes.

"You just met me," I stammered out.

"I know that, but there's no doubt in my mind. I love you with all my heart, Jenny. More than I've ever loved anyone in my life. You're it for me," he said and continued looking at me for a response.

I just stared at him, replaying everything in my mind since we'd met. A minute passed before I looked back up into his beautiful green eyes and confessed, "I love you too, Robert."

The smile Robert gave me was worth every word I'd just said. He was glowing as he leaned down and kissed me hard. I threw my arms around him and let myself get smothered in his affection for me. My heart soared, and butterflies danced in my stomach. I was so unbelievably happy.

We pulled apart, both of us gasping for air, and we both smiled at each other like a couple fools, but it was incredible to know we felt the same for each other.

"You better get to work," Robert said, and I turned, picking up all the stuff I had dropped on the table, then headed for the door.

Robert caught my arm and turned me around to face him before I could get out the door and kissed me again. I kissed him back, but never stopped smiling through the entire kiss.

"I love you," I said again as soon as our mouths pulled apart.

"I love you too, darlin'. Be safe today," Robert said.

I smiled wide at him and turned to go. I got a hard swat on the butt before I could get out the door, and I squealed, making Robert chuckle.

I was almost to the hospital now and, as I looked in the rearview mirror, noticed that I was still smiling. My cheeks were starting to hurt, but I didn't care. I parked in the employee parking lot today since I had my badge now and used it to buzz myself through the thick metal door that was labeled employee entrance. Security guards a few feet from the door checked my ID and let me pass, so my next stop was my locker to put my stuff up. As I passed other employees coming in this morning, I noticed that I was getting a lot of stares, but figured it was due to my black eye, which was now more of a yucky yellow color. I entered the employee lounge for the hand-off meeting and found Blake waiting for me.

"What's wrong with you, princess?" he asked, scowling at me.

"What are you talking about?" I asked.

"You have a goofy grin on your face, and you usually look pissed off most of the time," he told me, and I smiled even wider.

"He loves me," I blurted out.

"Robert?" he asked dryly.

I shook my head more than a little enthusiastically, causing Blake to roll his eyes.

"You're such a girl," he said, taking a seat at the table and then patted the chair next to him.

"Me?" I asked, surprised.

"Yes, you," he said and huffed in exasperation.

I practically skipped around the table and sat down next to him.

"Are you going to be like this all day?" he asked, sounding irritated.

"Probably," I said, looking around the room.

"You're annoying when you're happy," Blake snapped at me.

"Well, you're a crabby ass all the damn time," I snapped back.

Blake laughed and said, "It's good to have you back, princess."

"Thanks," I said, still smiling and loving the fact that it annoyed him.

Several of the nurses walking in made a point to stop and talk to me about the other day, wanting to know my side of the story and how I was feeling. Some of the other nurses, those close to the nurse that had been attacked, made sure to thank me for saving their friend. I was touched by all their nice words. Then it died down as everyone started taking their seats. My attention returned to the orderlies sitting at the table and was immediately drawn into the conversation they were having with Blake.

Chapter 10

"Tonight's the night," Zack said, seeming to be excited over it.

"Bet you can't wait," another orderly at the table said.

"It's just like any other Friday night," Blake said, nowhere near as excited as the other guys.

"What's tonight?" I asked, and they all froze.

"How much of that did you hear?" Zack asked me.

"Not much really," I confessed.

"It's nothing," Blake snapped.

"Then just tell me," I told him, but he wouldn't look at me, let alone talk to me.

"Hey, cupcake. Why don't you come sit with me?" Blake asked a cute nurse walking by, driving home that he was not going to tell me anything about their conversation.

She smiled, and an orderly sitting next to Blake got up, giving her his seat. She giggled and flirted as Blake ran his fingers across her hand and whispered dirty suggestions in her ear.

"Sorry," Zack mouthed to me when I looked over at him. I smiled and shrugged, letting him know it was no big deal, and it really wasn't.

In the few days I'd worked at the hospital, Blake was constantly flirting with the nurses, and they ate it up. They were always waving at him and saying hi as we walked down the halls. On one of our breaks, I'd found him hiding in a dark corner of a hallway, making out with a nurse. Not the nurse sitting at our table now. He was shameless in his pursuit, and although everyone knew of his one-night-stand reputation, it didn't stop the females of the hospital from giving themselves to him every chance they got. I found it disgusting but was glad he'd never been dumb enough to hit on me like that. He'd probably end up with a black eye to match the one I had now. Blake could be a rude ass to me all he wanted this morning, he still had to work with me the rest of the day, and I wasn't letting him, or anyone else, ruin the good mood I had this morning.

Kara came running into the lounge right before the meeting started and sat down beside me, giving me a quick squeeze before she got comfortable in her chair. I was glad to have her next to me and couldn't wait till the meeting was over to tell her all about the morning I'd had with Robert. Tom and Kelly gave long speeches about the importance of teamwork, reliability, being accountable, and safety measures to help avoid instances like the one that happened the other day with the nurse. I was recognized during their speech, and people applauded, but the entire room went quiet when Kelly started giving us an update on the injured nurse. She was going to be okay, but she was recovering at home and would have to go through counseling before she could return to work since her attack was so traumatic. It could be weeks before she came back to the hospital. My heart ached for Joanne, the nurse that I had saved. What she went through was hell, and I hoped she would be all right.

When the meeting was over a little while later, I took a minute to pull Kara to the side and told her all about my morning with Robert, our confessions to each other, and how incredible our relationship was becoming. Kara smiled the entire time, nodding and giggling along with my story, and never interrupted me once. She was so fun to talk to, and when I got to the part where Robert told me he loved me, Kara and I actually jumped up and down together as we squealed like schoolgirls. Everyone who walked by stared at us like we had lost our minds, and I loved it. Having a girlfriend was so damn fun!

"Okay, girls. Time to break it up," Blake said, walking over to us.

"You're such a party pooper," Kara told him, smacking at his shoulder, and I inwardly groaned, realizing that she was another nurse riding the Blake train.

"You know better," Blake said, smiling wickedly at her, and she blushed fiercely.

"You two are going to make me throw up," I said as I watched their shameless flirting.

Kara just giggled and ran off to follow some of the other nurses from her ward up to their floor. I turned to face Blake, who was watching Kara's ass as she ran off, and I rolled my eyes, turning to go to the elevators.

"What's wrong, princess?" Blake asked when he realized I wasn't standing next to him anymore. "You aren't jealous, are you?"

"Are you kidding me?" I asked as I looked over my shoulder. I watched as he caught up, standing beside me as we waited on the elevator.

"You sound jealous. You can just admit it if you are. I wouldn't think less of you," he said and nudged me in the side without thinking.

I grabbed my hip and tried not to make a face, but I failed when the pain hit me hard.

"Oh shit. I am so sorry. Are you okay, princess?" Blake asked, moving quickly to look at my hip.

"Get off me!" I yelled when he tried to look at my hip.

"Dammit, Jenny, I'm just trying to make sure I didn't pop your stitches," he said, scowling at me.

"You didn't hit it that hard. I'm fine," I said, gritting my teeth to avoid punching him in the face.

"I can still look at it if you want," he said, and I looked over at him to see the cocky grin that was stretched across his face. When he saw me looking, he wagged his eyebrows, and I couldn't help but laugh out loud.

"You're an idiot," I said as the elevator doors opened, and we both stepped on.

"I think you like that about me," he said, pushing the 5 button on the panel.

“You can save your efforts. I know you like to sleep with every female in the building, but you won’t be adding my name to that list, ever,” I assured him.

“Never say never,” Blake said wistfully in my ear, and I couldn’t help but grin even though I was trying to be serious.

“See, you like me, or you wouldn’t be smiling about it,” he said, confidence oozing from him.

“You’re an ass,” I said, wishing the elevator would hurry up and get to five.

“What’s your proof?” he asked, egging me on.

“What’s happening tonight that you wouldn’t tell me earlier?” I asked.

“Nothing,” he said matter-of-factly, without hesitation.

“See, you’re an ass,” I said just as the doors opened and I was free.

For the rest of the day, Blake had me glued to his side. I wasn’t allowed to assist with any patients, and I wasn’t allowed to go anywhere alone. I was basically his shadow for the day, and every time I tried to help with anything, he was quick to shoot me down and put me in my place. Zack gave me pitiful looks more than once, knowing I was more than capable of helping out. After lunch, Blake instructed Zack to escort me to the medical wing for a follow-up appointment with my doctor, who was supposed to check out my stab wound today. The walk was a quiet one as we went from hall to hall on the walk over. Zack didn’t have much to say to me except comments about the weather, and he was glad to see I was feeling better. I was worried that the doctor wouldn’t take me off light duty, so I really wasn’t all that talkative either.

Zack sat in the waiting area as a nurse took me back to an exam room, and I was glad he wasn’t coming with me. I put on a gown, removing my pants as instructed, so the doc could get a good look at my hip, and I prayed everything was all right with it. A few minutes later the doctor came in and laid me back on the table. He poked at my side, my head, and had the nurse take me to get x-rays done to make sure everything was healing good on the inside as well as the out. My doctor’s visit ended up taking most of my afternoon, and

I was impatient to hear if I was going to get back to work or not. Finally, after I was dressed and had been waiting forever, the doctor came into the room one last time and told me everything was looking great, and if I promised to watch my weekend activities, give myself a couple more days of healing, then I could be released to full duty work when I came back Monday morning. I agreed to take it easy and was ecstatic by the time I came bouncing out into the waiting area, where Zack was still sitting, watching *Dr. Phil* on the flat screen that hung on the wall.

"Good news?" he asked, noticing my bubbly attitude.

"Great news!" I exclaimed as we hit the hallway. I was practically jumping up and down, knowing I'd finally get to get back to work soon.

"Full duty?" he asked.

"Full duty as of Monday," I told him. "Man, I really needed to hear that."

"Settle down, Lil' Firecracker," Zack said, and it made me giggle.

"I'm trying. I've just been so bored, following Blake around today and not being able to do anything, that I was really glad to hear I can actually do something on Monday," I explained.

"You deserve some good news. You earned it," Zack said, but the smile on his face didn't touch his eyes.

"Are you upset about the way everyone has been thanking me for saving the nurse? I noticed that I hadn't heard anyone say too much to you, but you were there. You helped," I offered.

"Oh, that doesn't bother me. Besides, you did all the work. I just held a crying nurse as she freaked out," Zack said with a light chuckle.

"I was still glad to have you there, Zack. If you ever need me for anything, you can count on me," I told him and meant what I said.

"Thanks. Same for you, okay?" he said, and I was glad to have made another friend.

I smiled at him and took the opportunity to ask him as we walked, "So what are your plans this weekend?"

Zack looked surprised and slowly answered, "Nothing much. Why?"

"I was just wondering if there was anything to do around here. I'm still getting familiar with the area," I told him, hoping he'd give in and tell me what was happening tonight.

"Oh, I forgot that you just moved here. Yeah, I guess you wouldn't know..." he trailed off.

"Know what?" I asked as we continued walking. We were getting close to our ward, and I knew I was running out of time to get all the details. If we got back to our ward, there'd be no way Zack would tell me anything in front of Blake. The guys worshipped Blake, so he wouldn't do anything to get on his bad side.

Zack looked troubled as he glanced around the hallway. I didn't press, as I waited for him to debate on telling me what I wanted to know or not. Finally he sighed and asked, "I guess you were wanting to know what was happening tonight, right?"

"I was curious, but I wasn't going to ask about that specifically," I told him, glad he knew what I was getting at.

"I'm sorry, I just can't tell you, but if I were really curious about it, I might be prone to wait in the parking lot after work," he said low so that no one passing in the halls could hear him.

"Why would I wait in the parking lot after work?" I asked, having no clue what he was getting at.

"Get in your car and follow Blake when he leaves. Don't let him know, just follow him. You'll end up where the crowd will be tonight. That's all I'm gonna tell you, and when you show up, you have to put it all on yourself. None of this came from me," Zack said, and I could tell he was going to get in a lot of trouble if anyone found out.

"I promise, I won't say anything to anyone," I told him.

Neither of us said anything else as we entered the ward, and Zack buzzed us through with his badge. I told Blake I was cleared for full duty on Monday, and he actually acted happy for me. My day was shot, having stayed so long in the medical wing, so there wasn't much to do before we headed to the hand-off meeting. After we let out, I ran to the locker room, changing my clothes, and then hurried out to my truck, trying not to tip anyone off that I was up to something. I sat in Ol' Red and looked around the parking lot for Blake, not knowing what he drove. My phone buzzed in my pocket, and I pulled it out seeing that Robert had text me.

Crap, he knew I was off work. No doubt that he was checking on me. I was getting ready to text him when a tap came at my driver's side window and scared me half to death. I practically jumped out of my seat and heard laughter outside my window before I could look over. When I did turn my head, I found Blake standing there. He gave me a small wave and motioned for me to roll my window down.

"What?" I snapped at him.

"You're hilarious, princess," he said as he leaned in, resting his arm on the door.

"What do you want, Blake?" I asked again, irritated that he was bugging me. I wasn't on the clock.

"Just seen that you were sitting out here, I thought I'd check to see if you were having car troubles. You're usually gone when I leave," he said and almost sounded sincere, making me look over at him. He was out of his orderly uniform and in his regular street clothes. The long sleeves of his black shirt were rolled up to his elbows, and his forearms were surprisingly hard and muscular beneath his tattooed skin.

"I'm fine," I said, turning the key in the ignition. Ol' Red roared to life, and I smiled over at Blake. "See. All good here."

"Good to know. Have a good night, princess. I'll see you Monday," he said walking away.

I rolled the window back up and watched as Blake walked over to a black Jeep Wrangler and climbed in. The doors had been removed, ready for summer, no doubt, and music blared from the oversized speakers as Blake started his Jeep and turned on the radio. He pulled out of his parking spot in seconds, and I had no choice but to throw my phone into the passenger seat and press my foot down on the accelerator if I had any hope of keeping up with him. He sped down the highway, going the opposite direction of my house, and I had to do at least ten miles over the speed limit the entire way to stay close to him. We pulled off the highway a few miles up and turned onto a gravel road in the middle of nowhere. There were no houses out here, no farms that I could see, and the sun started to set casting dark shadows over the road ahead. I was nervous about where we were headed and almost talked myself into turning around and heading home, but my curiosity got the best of me, and I continued forward, trying to stay close enough to Blake that I didn't get lost, but far enough behind him that he didn't notice me. I was hoping wherever we were heading, we arrived before the sun set, and I was forced to turn my headlights on.

We drove another fifteen minutes further into the country than I'd ever been before. Even the cows out here looked lost. The sun was almost completely gone now, and I was just getting ready to turn on the headlights when Blake's jeep took a quick turn to the right, and I slowed down, trying to figure out why he would suddenly pull into a field. I reached the spot where Blake had turned and could plainly see why he'd done it. I just couldn't believe the number of people out here.

I pulled over, giving Blake time to get far enough ahead that he wouldn't see me pulling in behind him. Whatever it was he had going on out here, it didn't matter. I knew if he saw me, he'd surely send me home. Once I thought it was safe to go on, I pulled the truck back onto the road and continued driving until the cornfields ended, and a massive, open pasture came into sight. In the middle of it ran an old, heavily used dirt road. I turned onto it, following it until a huge red barn came into view. There wasn't a parking lot, only bumpy fields where more than fifty cars were parked. I happened to see Blake as he walked through the large wooden doors of the barn and was thankful when he didn't notice me. No one was outside as I parked next to an old brown truck that was so rusted it looked like the mounds of mud that were caked onto it were the only things holding it together. I took a deep breath and gathered up the courage to walk in, not really having any clue of what I was getting myself into.

As soon as I got out of the truck and closed the door, I could hear a roaring hum coming from inside the barn. I quickly walked to the entrance of the barn, and the closer I got to it, the louder the shouting came from inside. I inched my way in, relieved that all the men around me had their backs to me, so no one noticed me sneak by. I looked around the old barn, and a loud thud from up ahead boomed, echoing off the rotting barn wood around me. The massive crowd roared to life, causing me to jump, then the men around me cheered while others shouted various obscenities as they all looked ahead, and I was determined to get a closer look.

Everything about this place screamed that I didn't belong. There wasn't one other woman besides me as far as I could see, and the place was falling apart. The air was a mix of blood, sweat, and fertilizer as sweaty men moved around me. Arms swung about in the air, exchanging money and gestures to communicate over the noise. I caught the attention of some of the men that were close by, and dirty looks were thrown my way. I ignored them, determined to get a better look at the action. I squeezed through the crowd, going in the direction where the most noise was centered. Halfway there I felt someone tap me on my shoulder from behind, and I turned around, startled to see that Blake had found me already.

"What the hell are you doing here, cupcake?" he asked, clearly irritated to see me.

I winced and shrugged my shoulders, having no real answer for him.

"You don't know?" he asked in surprise. "Do you even know what we do here?"

"I'm guessing you fight here. That's what's going on, right?" I asked, trying to raise my voice above the screaming crowd.

"You guessed right, and it's no place for a cupcake to be. Let's go," he said, pulling my arm to lead me to the exit.

I planted my feet and refused to budge, causing Blake to stumble before he turned to look back at me.

"What are you doing?" he yelled at me.

"I'm staying!" I yelled back and crossed my arms over my chest. "I love a good fight."

Blake's face faded from irritation to amusement as he said, "You don't know what you're getting yourself into, princess. Do you see any other women here?"

I looked around and saw only men and shook my head no.

"That's because there's a rule here, princess. Anyone that comes here can be challenged to a fight. You can't refuse, and you can't leave if that happens. You're taking a big risk by being here."

I hesitated for a moment, letting what Blake said sink in, then I looked from the floor back up into his icy-blue eyes and couldn't help but smile when I told him, "I'm cool with that."

Blake looked shocked, already thinking he had me convinced to leave. "You're really staying?" he asked with raised eyebrows.

"Of course. This looks great!" I yelled.

"So if I challenged you to a fight right now, what would you do?" he asked sarcastically.

"I'd kick your ass all over this old barn," I snapped, causing Blake to laugh, but he didn't know how serious I really was.

"You're insane, princess." He chuckled.

I just shrugged, moving to start pressing through the crowd again, but Blake stopped me.

"If you're not leaving, you stay close and follow me," he said, turning to move in another direction.

A wide grin spread across my face, and I happily followed him through the crowd, ignoring my cell phone when it buzzed again. I knew if Robert found out where I was, he'd be livid. So for now, I'd just leave my cell phone where it was, safely tucked away in my back pocket.

When Blake and I stopped, we were in front of a sea of people who were all surrounding a dirt floor circle, lined with old, junky tractor tires as its border. My eyes widened at how many people had shown up tonight and the fact that I recognized several of them from the hospital. Two men were already fighting, and blood splattered on the floor at my feet. Blake reached back and took my hand, more out of protection than plain ol' flirting, so I let him. My heart pounded with adrenaline as the two burly men in the circle threw more punches and screams erupted again when someone's tooth was knocked out and went flying into the crowd. It wasn't long after that when one man knocked the other unconscious and the fight was won.

Money changed hands quickly, and as I watched, more and more of the nearby patrons were noticing a girl was in the building. I quickly looked away, hoping no one would start any shit about me being here. After the circle had been cleared, one man, who was tall and as broad as a house, came dragging a chair out into the middle of the circle. His head was shaved bald, and years of fighting had left multiple scars along his face. As he stood on top of the chair, people started to quiet down, and I was amazed at how easily he had gotten the attention of so many at once.

Holding a wad of cash in one hand, he yelled, "Welcome to my circle. My name is Brett. I take the cash, and I call the fights. If you're here, that means you're willing to fight, and if you're challenged to a fight, you cannot refuse. Robert Shaw and Blake Jaxson started this three years ago, and I would lay down my life before letting any of you shit stains ruin it, so understand this: if you break any rules tonight, you will have your ass beat, then thrown from a moving truck doing sixty miles an hour down the highway. I kid you not."

Laughter erupted from the crowd and cheers sounded while Brett patiently waited for it to quiet before continuing. I was standing there in disbelief. Robert and Blake had started this madness. It was insane to think my sweet Robert had been a fighter like Blake. Maybe the two of them were more alike than I really wanted to know.

Brett removed the chair from the circle and was standing in the center of the circle again when he started to speak over the men who were finally starting to quiet down. "I am greatly honored to give you our next fighter of the night, Blake Jaxson!" Brett announced over the crowd and everyone cheered, excited to see Blake fight.

My mouth dropped open, and I looked over at Blake, who had a cocky grin stretched across his handsome face. "This won't take long," Blake said, looking at his opponent. "Jeremy's a punk. He probably won't even get a hit in on me."

I shook my head, smiling at his overly confident attitude, and watched as he took his shirt off and handed it to me. "Stay close to the circle," he said as he looked back at me one last time, giving me a wink, before walking out into the circle.

The volume in the barn exploded when Blake crossed to stand by Brett, who was already announcing Jeremy's name. I watched as the men on the other side of the circle parted to let Jeremy through. There were both boos and cheers for the contender. Blake's eyes were on Jeremy, and watching Blake's muscles flex from across the circle had my full, undivided attention.

Blake watched Jeremy, looking completely relaxed even though he was a lot taller than Blake. The guy was young, though, just a kid, and I was surprised that Blake was going to fight him. I watched Jeremy laugh and celebrate with his friends in the crowd, proud of himself for actually entering the circle to fight the legendary Blake Jaxson. Blake walked up to Jeremy, looking unaffected. Lean muscles stretched under Blake's tattooed skin as he nodded to Jeremy and gave him a taunting grin. It wasn't until this moment that I realized how many tattoos Blake had covering his sculpted body, including the one on his bicep that perfectly matched Robert's, representing their band and the best times of their life.

Brett left the circle, and the two men took a few steps back from each other. Then Brett screamed over the roaring crowd, "Fight!"

Jeremy went on the defensive as Blake attacked. Everyone around me moved in tighter, all of them wanting a closer look at the fight. I got shoved back, and I couldn't see the fight anymore. I inched back through the chaotic crowd and reached the circle just in time to see Blake ram his knee into Jeremy's face. Jeremy hit the floor hard and was just getting up when someone brushed my hand so lightly with theirs that it caught my attention. I looked over to find the man it belonged to, smiling at me.

"Hey there, sweetie. Enjoying yourself tonight?" he asked.

"I was," I snapped, pulling my hand away.

"Did I see you here with Blake?" he asked, now running his hand down my arm.

"Yes. What's it to you?" I snapped and pulled my hand away again.

"Ooh, you're a feisty one. I like that. What's your name, sexy?" he asked, still finding small ways to brush against my skin, and it was really starting to freak me out.

"What's your name?" I barked at him, but he didn't care.

"I'm Chase. You want to get out of here?"

"You're Chase?" I asked, letting the words ooze distain.

"You know me?" he asked, his eyes lighting up.

"Are you the guy that had to take Blake down while his back was turned to you because you were too pathetic to finish the fight any other way?" I asked, remembering the guys at work talking about it.

Chase wasn't smiling anymore, and I was glad that I'd pissed him off. Maybe he'd get the hint and leave me alone now. I laughed out loud at his obvious embarrassment, but before I could enjoy my victory, I got a hard slap across the face.

"Now who's laughing, you little bitch?" he yelled over the crowd.

I brought my knee up quick and hard as I held my lip, which he'd cut during the slap and was greeted with a loud groan from Chase as my knee made contact with his groin. "I am, you bitch!" I yelled and kicked dirt at him as he kneeled down on the dirt floor, holding his private. He glared up at me, preparing to stand, and I readied myself for a fight, but before Chase could retaliate, Blake stepped between us, cutting him off. I could see his hands were clenched into fists and his tendons were standing out under his tattooed skin.

"What the hell is going on?" Blake snapped at Chase, and I looked over at the circle just in time to see two men picking Jeremy up off the floor, covered in his own blood and sweat. He seemed disoriented as they carried him away, and I glanced back to Blake and Chase, who were now standing toe to toe. Brett came over and handed Blake a large wad of cash, interrupting the argument he was having with Chase.

"Guys, enough," Brett snapped. "If you want to fight, do it in the circle."

"That's a good idea," Chase said with a grin.

"Are you seriously challenging me again?" Blake asked as he rolled his eyes at Chase.

"No," Chase said, surprising us all. "I'm challenging her."

All three men looked over at me as Chase's finger pointed in my direction.

"A woman?" Brett asked, his eyebrows raising in surprise.

"Oh, hell no!" Blake shouted.

"Anyone here can be challenged, and if you're challenged, you fight. Isn't that right, Brett?" Chase seethed.

Brett turned back to Blake with a sympathetic look on his face.

"You've got to be fucking with me, Brett. There's no way you're going to let him fight her. She's the size of a child, for fuck's sake!" Blake yelled.

"Fuck you!" I yelled, catching their attention. "If he wants to fight, then I'll fight."

"I'm sorry, Blake," Brett said, shrugging. "You shouldn't have brought her if you didn't want her fighting."

"I didn't bring her!" Blake yelled, but it fell on deaf ears as Brett grabbed me, pulling me to the circle with him.

"You sure you can take him, kid?" Brett asked so that only I could hear. "I could always let you slip out the back."

Chapter 11

I SMILED UP at him and then looked over my shoulder at Chase who was lagging behind. "I've got this," I said back up to Brett, who gave me a big smile and a squeeze before leaving me next to the circle alone. I wasn't standing there long when Blake came up to me looking worried.

"What's with you?" I asked, nudging his arm.

"This is insane," he said, still looking mopey.

"Quit worrying. You're not my big protector, and this isn't your fault. I came here uninvited and got myself into this fight, not you. I can handle this, I promise."

Blake looked surprised by my willingness to fight Chase and smiled softly at me.

"Watch his right hook. It's his best move, and it comes out of nowhere," Blake said, rubbing his face as he remembered their last fight.

"Thanks," I said and heard Brett announcing my fight.

I turned to walk into the circle and felt Blake grab my arm, spinning me around to look at him. He had a worried look of concern on his face, but he wasn't saying anything.

I took his hand off my arm, smiled, and said, "Stay close to the circle. This won't take long." Blake's frown turned into a grin as he got his words thrown back to him. I took a step toward the ring then stopped, took my shirt off, and threw it to Blake. His mouth gaped open, and he was speechless as I turned and entered the circle.

I'd fought many times back home in a sports bra, so this was no different to me, and I was thankful now to have taken all those classes back in Kansas. Chase and I stepped up to each other, and the crowd was a mix of boos and cheers. Some of the men even whistled, but I was too focused to feel embarrassed. I tried to imagine myself in one of my classes, imagining in my head the moves before they would happen.

I stared into Chase's hate-filled eyes and replayed our scuffle back in my mind, letting the anger fuel me as Brett yelled fight and we began. I moved in fast, faked a right hook, then came in, surprising Chase with my left. He dodged my right, but my left caught him right at the jawline, and he stumbled back. My left had never been to strong, so it didn't do much damage, then Chase came at me fast. In my hurry to get away from him, I lost my footing in the dirt. He saw my slip and caught me right across the cheek as I fell back. Loud boos came from the crowd as I sat there, trying to shake off the pain. I was not a crier, and I was not going to start now no matter how much it hurt.

I got back on my feet and put my hands back up, ready to go again. I heard Blake shouting over the intense noise of the crowd, "You've got this, J! You got this!"

I smiled at Chase, and he looked confused. I went in directly at him like I'd done before, knowing he'd anticipate the move, but before I could do any more than that, Chase hit me hard in the stomach, and I doubled over, taking a direct hit to my right eye from Chase's knee. I fell on the ground, groaning in pain as I held my stomach. Chase walked over, leaning down to whisper in my ear, "Had enough yet, you little cunt?"

I closed my eyes until I felt the dirt shift, and when I looked up again, I saw that Chase had turned his back to me and was laughing with his friends. I twisted on the floor, brought my legs around, and kicked as hard as I could, knocking Chase's feet out from under him. Chase yelled as he fell to the ground. I jumped to my feet and kicked him hard in the ribs. He moaned and rolled to his side, grabbing his ribs. I kicked him again, this time across the face, but my third kick was blocked as Chase grabbed my foot, causing me to fall back on my ass.

We were both up and on our feet in seconds. The look on Chase's face was murderous as he stared me down. He came at me, hitting me hard across the cheek, but I blocked a second hit and came back, hitting him over and over again. Chase failed to get his arms up in time, and my right hook connected with such force that it threw Chase down on his back. I ran over and straddled him, hitting him again and again as he tried blocking my punches. He brought his arm around, knocking me off him with a blow to the side of my head. I had too much adrenaline coursing through me to slow down now, so I was up and on my feet before Chase could even push up from the floor. I came over and gave him another kick to the ribs, but this time there was a loud crack, and everyone around us yelled and winced, knowing I'd just broken some of Chase's ribs.

"I'm out!" Chase screamed as he rolled on the floor, groaning with pain.

Brett ran into the circle and pulled me back before I could do any more damage. To Chase, he asked, "You're done?"

Chase nodded, and Brett came over to me, grabbing my wrist and thrusting my arm high into the air. "Winner!" Brett shouted, and the men went nuts around us.

Blake was at my side in seconds and had the smile of a proud father on his face. I couldn't help but laugh. "See, no big deal," I said, grabbing my shirt from Blake to wipe off the sweat and blood running down my face.

Blake smiled wide and grabbed me hard, pulling me into him for a hug. I patted his bare back, feeling his tight skin under my hands, and the smile on my face faded away. The air around us changed, and although the room was filled with cheers and congratulations for my victory, I couldn't hear any of it. As I stood there, in that tight embrace with Blake, the only sound filling my ears was our two heartbeats, which seemed to be in perfect sync as they beat hard in our chests. Blake pulled back, leaving his hands on my shoulders, as he looked down at me, and I noticed neither of us were smiling any more. He smirked a little as he ran his hand across my cheek, wiping some of the blood away, and I watched as he quickly wiped it across his jeans before looking back up at me.

"That was a great fight," he said, low and seductive.

"Thanks," I said, watching his mouth and wishing it was on mine.

Whoa, my mind suddenly screamed, *He's not Robert!* I went to pull away and was saved from an awkward moment by Brett, who came over and pulled me from Blake, putting an arm around my shoulders.

"That was fucking amazing, kid!" he said and flashed a wad of cash in front of me.

"For me?" I asked, more than surprised.

"Hell yes it's for you. The winner always gets a percentage of the take," he said, waving the stack of money at me like a fan.

I smiled and took it from him, guessing there to be at least a few hundred in there.

"You're the first and only female we've ever had out here in the three years we've been doing this. I love that you kicked Chase's ass and won the money," Brett said, looking proud of me.

"Thanks!" I said and looked over at Blake, who was staring at me. "What?" I snapped.

"That was sexy as fuck, J," he finally said, causing me and Brett both to burst out laughing.

"You two are a perfect match," Brett said, still laughing. "You're both fucking insane."

Blake and I shared a look but didn't say anything as Brett walked off, getting the next two guys ready to fight.

"What do you say we get out of here?" Blake asked as he took my hand again and pulled me toward the exit.

It was a madhouse in the barn, and everyone stopped us as we tried to leave. They wanted to meet me and congratulate me on my fight. When we finally reached the field and started over to Blake's Jeep, I noticed he still had my hand in his, and for whatever reason, I let him keep it.

Blake pulled down the small tailgate of his Jeep and motioned for me to hop on, so I did, letting my short legs dangle over the edge.

He reached into the back seat, where a red cooler sat, and grabbed two beers, handing me one and keeping the other for himself. I cracked it open and let the cool liquid pour down my throat, enjoying how cold it was.

Blake sat his down and walked over to me, standing between my legs as he studied my face. At first, I was afraid that he was going to kiss me, but then I realized what he was doing.

"We're going to have to get you cleaned up. If you go home like this, Robert will kill us both," he said as he took out a small first aid kit from the Jeep.

"Is it bad?" I asked, taking another drink of my beer.

"You have one yellow eye where it's been healing, and now you have a black eye to go with it. Your cheek is swollen, and both it and your lip have been split open, so there's that, and when we get done with your face, I want to look at your stomach and side," he reported, and with every injury he listed, I winced even more, knowing I'd have to explain all this to Robert somehow.

Blake patched and doctored my face up the best he could, and I let the adrenaline in my veins run its course, feeling no pain at all until several minutes later when I started to relax. My body hummed with a pain that seemed to radiate from my head down to my toes. I was sure there wasn't anything on me that didn't hurt. Blake was patient and let me finish my beer before making me stand to look at my side and stomach. There were some bruises on my stomach and ribs that weren't too bad, but that wasn't the part we were both worried about.

"Shit," Blake snapped as I pulled my pants and underwear down enough for him to look at my stab wound.

"What is it?" I asked. I couldn't see anything out here in the dark. The only light we had was coming from the inside of the barn and the dim light the moon cast over the field.

Blake shined the light from his cell phone screen over my hip as he bent down and looked closer, assessing the damage. "You definitely popped your stitches, J. The bleeding has just about stopped, but your underwear are soaked and stained red," he said, standing back up.

I let go of my clothes, letting them fall back to my waist with a snap and winced as they made contact. "Well, there isn't anything we can do about it now," I said, taking my seat back on the tailgate. Blake got two more beers from the cooler, and I gladly accepted.

"So what's up with you calling me J now?" I asked when Blake took a seat beside me.

"Suits you better than Jenny," he said, opening his beer.

"I like it better than cupcake or princess," I teased.

"Yeah, sorry about that. Now that I'm starting to know you better, I can see that you're definitely neither of those," he offered with an apologetic smile.

"Thanks," I said, smiling, and couldn't help staring at his shirtless body. His finely chiseled abs and bare, tattooed chest were still covered in sweat, and I liked it.

Blake chuckled as he took another drink of beer.

"What?" I asked, looking up to meet his eyes.

"I've never seen a girl fight like that. You're a badass, Jenny," he said, looking at me in awe.

I felt it again, that quick charge in the atmosphere, a sudden intake of breath, and we both froze as we stared at each other. I wanted to protest when Blake started to lean toward me. I stared at his smooth pink lips, his square jawline, and his perfect face. My mind went from screaming a million reasons into the air at why this shouldn't happen to complete silence as it turned off. My eyes closed, and my body readied itself as I felt Blake's lips reach mine. At first I felt how soft, how sweet they were, as they melted against mine, but two seconds later my mind woke up and screamed Robert's name at me. I snapped my eyes open and jumped off the tailgate, looking around to see if anyone had seen us. Luckily, no one was around.

I looked over at Blake, who was frozen on the tailgate, looking shocked and confused, but he didn't say a word. "Robert!" I shouted, and Blake's face went white.

"Robert," he mouthed. The realization of what we'd just done crashing in on him. "I'm sorry, J," he said quickly.

"We can't. I mean I can't…" I stammered, my mind racing as it tried to form words.

"It was the adrenaline and the alcohol," Blake claimed, and I was quick to jump on the train.

"That's right. We weren't thinking. It was the rush of the fight, then we were drinking," I said as I paced back and forth in front of Blake's Jeep.

"Exactly," Blake said, following me with his eyes.

"It didn't mean anything. It was just the alcohol," I said and looked to Blake for confirmation.

Blake stared at me for a moment, furrowing his brow at my words. When he finally spoke, he quietly said, "Right, J. It didn't mean anything."

I nodded and didn't miss the fact that there wasn't any conviction in his voice as he mindlessly agreed with me before taking another drink of his beer.

"Okay then. No need to tell him, right? I mean if it was nothing, then why hurt him?" I asked, more to myself then to Blake.

Blake slowly nodded, continuing to drink his beer, and I stopped my pacing to study him for a moment. I walked over to stand in front of him and asked, "I don't have to tell Robert because it'll never happen again, right, Blake?" I watched Blake as he studied my face then slowly sat his beer down on the tailgate and looked directly into my eyes.

"Right, J. It won't happen again," he said and picked up my beer, handing it out to me.

I sighed with relief and took my beer from him. He picked up his own, and I returned to my spot beside him on the tailgate, feeling my heart relax again.

Just as I took a drink of my beer, Blake said in a mischievous tone, "Unless you ask me to do it again, then no promises."

I almost dropped my beer, shocked that he'd just been so bold as to say that to me. I looked over at him, eyes wide, processing what he'd just said.

Blake laughed when saw my expression then said, "Drink your beer and shut up, J."

I smiled, smacking him on the arm before returning to my beer.

After that, Blake and I sat there for the next few hours talking and drinking as patrons from the barn came and went around us. Sometimes we had company, but mostly it was just us. Blake opened up about his family, and I learned about the crappy childhood he'd had growing up. Abusive dad, absent mom, fighting all the time, until him and Robert got close. Robert's dad had practically raised Blake, and it shattered Blake when the old man had died. I felt so bad for him but found the connection in our stories to be so similar that it was easy to start opening up, and I sat there telling Blake everything that I'd been holding back from Robert. Blake was actually a great listener, and he understood what it felt like to have a parent that didn't want you, abused you, and forced you to be someone you weren't proud of. I saw Blake in a whole new light, and I was glad I had someone here I could relate to, that really got me. I let it all out, and Blake understood now why I was such a good fighter. It was my only outlet for the emotions raging inside me all the time.

A case of beer later had us giggling and making fun of the way Chase had looked when he realized that he'd had his ass handed to him by a girl. The grass rustled next to the Jeep, and we both turned to see Robert walking up out of nowhere. The laughter stopped abruptly when we saw the look on Robert's face. His face was set in unfamiliar lines of outrage as he came around the back of the Jeep and took my face in his hands, turning it side to side to get a better look at all the damage.

"Oh my god, Jenny! Are you okay?" he exclaimed, worry flooding his voice.

"I'm fine," I told him, worried more about losing my buzz than what Robert thought about my face.

"Did you fight tonight?" he shouted.

"Yeah, and I kicked his ass too," I reported, feeling proud of myself.

Robert wasn't impressed at all as he scowled over at Blake.

"Hey, don't look at me, man. This was all her," Blake said smiling.

"Who the hell brought her here?" Robert demanded.

"I came on my own," I said, going in for another drink of beer.

"You just got out of the hospital two days ago," he said, and when I didn't respond, he snatched the beer can from my hand and threw it into the weeds of the field.

"Hey, I was drinking that," I whined as I watched my beer can fly through the air and disappear into the night.

"I guess the party's over, J," Blake said, tossing his empty can into the back of his Jeep and jumping off the tailgate.

"Why'd you let her do this?" Robert asked, getting in Blake's face.

"I'm drunk, Robert, but I'm not that drunk. You need to take a step back," Blake said low and menacing as he and Robert stared each other down.

Robert took a small step back before repeating his question to Blake.

"Man, I'm not her dad. I tried to get her to leave, and she wouldn't. Then she got challenged to a fight, so—" Blake was saying until Robert cut him off.

"Who the fuck would challenge her to a fight? She's the size of a child," Robert snapped.

Blake laughed. "That's what I said."

"It was Chase!" I yelled over them both.

"Chase?" Robert spat his name, and I could tell he knew him.

"Yeah, that asshole. But J surprised us all when she got out there and completely whooped his ass," Blake said, still sounding very proud of me.

"J?" Robert snapped.

"Jenny," Blake said, pointing over at me.

"Yeah, he calls me J now," I said, slurring a little.

Robert stopped then, looking at us both, studying us like we were a puzzle.

Lights turned off as the barn shut down, leaving the three of us to stand there in the dark. Those that were left came walking out to their vehicles to leave, and soon, the only three vehicles left in the field were mine, Robert's, and Blake's. We all looked at one another, watching as the moonlight cast shadows from the tall trees at the edge of the field, and in the far distance a coyote called to its pack.

"Let's go," Robert said, sighing as he walked over to me.

"Bye, Blake," I said a little too cheerfully.

"See ya, J," Blake said, sounding defeated as he jumped into his Jeep.

He was out of the field and heading home before we even reached Robert's truck. Robert kept wincing at me every time he touched a cut or bruise on my body. I just rolled my eyes at him and let him buckle me into the passenger seat of his truck like he had the night we'd left the airport together. He closed my door and walked around, getting into the driver's seat of the truck. When he just sat there, I looked over at him. He had his hand on the key, ready to start the truck, but only sat there staring out the windshield into the empty field surrounding us.

"What's wrong?" I asked, trying to lower my voice to sound sincere. I always got a little high-pitched when I drank.

"Can I ask you something?" he asked softly.

"Sure," I said, almost afraid of his question.

"Did you mean what you said when you told me you loved me?" he asked, still staring out the window.

"Of course I did," I answered quickly.

"Then why did you come out here with Blake tonight, do something so stupid as to fight with someone twice your size, then ignore all my texts and calls? I had to hunt you down, and I find you drinking and laughing with Blake when you should've been home with me."

"I'm sorry," I said, looking away from him.

"Are you?" he snapped, and it surprised me.

"I said I was, Robert. What do you want from me?" I asked, feeling angry at his outburst.

"You can start with the truth," he snapped again.

"What do you want to know? And I'll tell you the truth," I said, feeling the last of my buzz fade away. I was completely sober now, and the anger inside of me was boiling over.

Robert huffed and waited for a long moment before asking, "Do you like Blake?"

"What?" I blurted out as a flash went through my mind of Blake's lips on mine.

"It's okay if you do. You can just tell me. Most girls fall for Blake at some point, and I'd rather know now than later if you like him," Robert said, looking so sad as he continued to stare outside.

I felt like a complete ass. I wanted to tell him about the kiss and the talk I'd had with Blake, and just put it all out there, but I didn't. I was too scared I'd lose Robert, and I did love him. The kiss I'd had with Blake meant nothing. My heart belonged to Robert.

"I love you, Robert. Not Blake. Blake and I are just friends, I promise. And the reason I didn't return your calls is because my phone got busted up and broken during the fight," I said and took my phone from my back pocket, showing him the shattered mess it was. Robert smiled, weakly taking in the appearance of my phone, then finally looked up at me. I smiled at him, and he took my hand in his as he laid my phone aside.

"Jenny, I love you more than you'll ever know, and I worry about you. Especially after what happened this week. I can't help it, but if we're going to make this work, you have to talk to me. You can't run off like you did tonight and scare me half to death. Just be honest, please," he said, but it sounded more like begging, and I felt so horrible to have hurt him like this.

"I promise I'll tell you next time," I said.

"Will there be a next time?" he asked, making a face as he gestured at the barn.

I couldn't stop the smile that stretched across my face. "Oh yeah," I said, and Robert closed his eyes as he talked himself out of starting up a whole new fight with me.

I giggled, and he opened his eyes, looking me over. He slowly shook his head and turned back to start the truck. With a promise that he'd bring me back the next day for Ol' Red, Robert drove me home.

Saturday was miserable, and I spent the day on the couch with ice packs all over my aching body. Robert was there, taking care of me as he always did, and I promised myself that I wouldn't give him attitude about it today like I had after my hospital stay. Robert was sweet and caring. He couldn't be faulted for trying to be there for me.

Chapter 12

SATURDAY NIGHT WAS the night Blake was supposed to come over, so after checking to see if Robert was still okay with it, I tried both calling and texting him, but Blake never responded to any of it. I even sent a text to Blake telling him Robert wasn't mad anymore and both of us wanted him to come hang out, but even that text went unanswered. Robert rolled his eyes at my tenth time trying to call Blake and only shook his head when I told him, again, that there was still no answer. I didn't give up till around eight o'clock that night, feeling my body ache worse as the sun went down. I sent Robert home, wanting the bed to myself so I could relax and stretch out. He caved after he realized I wasn't going to change my mind and went home saying he would call me to check on me tomorrow.

Sunday morning was too nice not to be outside, so I decided I didn't want to be in the empty house any longer and a walk would do me some good. I went out the back door, and the warm sun shining down on me felt wonderful. I headed out into the tall wheat field that surrounded the back of my home and took my time, not really knowing where I was headed yet. I suddenly remembered the pond in the back of the field, and the large trees shadowing one edge of the pond's shoreline gave me the location of the water, which was well hidden by the tall wheat.

I took my time getting there, soaking up the sun's warmth, listening to the birds' chirp, and watching as little bugs hopped about. It all made me smile, giving me the feeling of security that my empty house did not. I was usually very comfortable on my own, but something felt off today. I reached the shores of the pond, and little frogs jumped into the water, sending tiny ripples out from their splashes. I stared across the pond's still water. It looked like a flat mirror, without the wind blowing, casting perfect reflections of the nearby trees. No one was around for miles, so I decided to lie back, enjoy the sun's hot rays, and sunbath to try to put some color into my pale skin. I picked a spot a little way from the water, where the earth looked flatter, and there was no debris from the nearby trees. I sat down, put my arms behind my head, and leaned back, turning my face up to meet the sun.

"Jenny," I heard in the distance. It was very faint, but clear enough I knew someone had said my name. My eyes snapped open, and I looked around, but all I could see around me was the tall wheat. I held my breath and listened intently, but I couldn't hear anything. Must have been my imagination, I decided, and went back to soaking up the sun's rays. The sun was amazing, but it had lost its luster now. I had an uneasy feeling, and I kept opening my eyes and looking around me. I couldn't shake the feeling that I wasn't alone anymore. I got up on my knees and slowly moved up to peer over the wheat and look around the large field. There wasn't a soul around, even toward the house, and I started to feel silly about the uneasiness I'd felt.

I took one last look around the field to appease myself and could swear that I saw someone walking. I tried to blink the bright sun out of my eyes to focus on who it was, but as soon as I blinked and looked again, they were gone. This didn't seem right, and I could feel the hair on the back of my neck stand on edge. A cold breeze whipped through the field, swaying the tall wheat like something was moving through it, directly at me. I got to my feet, backing away, even though it was only the wind that moved harmlessly past me. Something caught my eye, and I looked toward the house. Moving through the wheat, at an unhuman pace, was a short female figure. She was too far away to pick out any details accept for the color of her hair, which whipped around behind her as she ran. It was red, like fire, over the tall stems of wheat. Stumbling in panic, I ran head long into the trees. I heard my name again, more deliberate this time. It floated on the wind that grazed my body, and I knew this time it was Laura's voice. A scream threatened to escape my throat, but I managed to hold on to it.

At first, I paid no attention to where I was headed, focused only on whom I was running from. By the time I gathered enough courage to look back again, I was deep into the woods. I finally stopped, turned around, and squatted to the ground. My hands were shaking violently as I placed them on the cool, muddy ground to help steady myself. The quiet whisper of unseen things moving among the leaves sent my heart beating wildly in my chest. The sudden rush of a squirrel moving up a nearby tree made me scream, and I lost my balance, falling back into a briar bush. Thorns tore at my bear arms and legs and the long, viney branches tangled in my hair. I tried pushing myself up, cutting my hands in the process, but the vines refused to let go of my hair. I pulled hard and yelled in pain as a chunk of my hair ripped from my scalp, freeing me from the grasp of the bush. I was too scared to cry and looked around everywhere for what I had thought I'd seen in the field, but there was nothing. I put my back against a nearby tree and watched in every direction I could see for anyone that moved. It seemed like hours that I sat there.

Small droplets of blood trickled from open wounds, and my head ached where my hair had been yanked out. I rubbed at it, but it only made it feel worse, so I quit. I slowly got to my feet and started walking toward the field. I probably walked for an hour, trying to find my way out of the thick woods. Through a break in the trees, I could see sunlight and wheat. I instantly started for it, moving faster now. The exhaustion my body was feeling was pushed aside now that I knew I'd soon be home. I couldn't wait to get back to the safety of the house. Twigs broke, and leaves rustled under my fast, determined footsteps, but I didn't care. I hadn't seen or heard anything since I had fled from the field hours ago. Anything or anyone that had been lurking in the field earlier would be long gone by now. When I got to the edge of the tree line, where it gave way to the fields, I stopped just long enough to take a quick look around. There wasn't anyone or anything as far as I could see. I got my house in sight and stepped out into the field, determined to make it without incident.

I walked fast and kept very aware of my surroundings. I still didn't see anything, then my traitorous mind broke through and said if someone was waiting on you to go home, they wouldn't give themselves away by walking or running out in front of you. If they're smart, they'd be lying next to the hot soil, below the tall wheat stems, waiting for you to approach them. When you walked by, they'd just take you. I stopped dead in my tracks and surveyed the ground all around me. It was scary how true that thought had been. I looked around me again and then at the house. I was only halfway there, and that left a lot of field to walk through. Anyone could be out there waiting for me. A shiver ran through me, my heart rate skyrocketed, and adrenaline kicked in as I started to run as fast as I could. *Let them grab me like this*, I thought almost smugly, but my attitude was no match for my imagination. Every time one of my feet touched the soil beneath them, I could picture a hand jotting out from the wheat, grabbing at me to pull me down. I almost screamed in panic and pushed myself to run even faster. My hair whipped around in the wind behind me. My heart felt like it could explode, it was beating so hard, but I kept running and running. I was only focusing on my house, which got closer with every step.

The sun was starting to set, and I could see fireflies hovering over the wheat. My kitchen light was still on and became my beacon, bringing me in like a lighthouse for a ship. I finally took my last step out of the wheat and onto my flat, open green yard. I slowed to a walk, fighting to catch my breath. I bent over, placing my hands on my knees, and made myself take in slow, steadying breaths. When I started feeling better, I stood up and headed for the stairs on my back porch. Just when I lifted my foot up to take the first step, cold fingers grasped my arm tightly, spinning me around. I was face-to-face with Laura. I went to scream but found my throat was so dry that I had no voice. When I really looked at her, standing there staring at me, I wasn't frightened anymore. She was young and beautiful, and her long red hair fell in waves down her back. We stood there staring into each other's eyes until she started to speak.

"Moo…" she struggled to get out, and I furrowed my brows at her.

"Moooo…" she tried again, looking frustrated.

"What is it, Laura?" I asked.

"Moon," she said, then her face shifted, and she looked so frightened, just like I remembered her looking in the hospital.

"Laura, are you okay?" I asked, realizing as I said it that it was a dumb question.

Her hair started falling out, and I watched as large handfuls of it fell onto my lawn at our feet. When I met Laura's gaze again, I stumbled back and gasped at her appearance. She was a standing corpse. Her face was mangled, her skin was rotting away from her bones, and her lips were only partially there as she opened them again to speak.

"Moon!" she screamed at me in such a menacing voice that I couldn't help but throw my hands up over my ears, not wanting to hear this evil sound escape my sister.

Laura flung herself at me, knocking me back onto the porch steps, and I groaned when my back made contact with the wood. I looked up and saw the most pained expression on Laura's face. She was inches away when she said again, "Mooney." Then her pained expression became something twisted and grotesque. I couldn't move, and before I knew what was happening, Laura threw up blood all over me. Gallons of warm crimson liquid covered me and soaked my clothes. I screamed, and Laura vanished before the sound of my scream echoing in the distance had time to fade.

Between the fear and the exhaustion, my body had too much, and I started to hurl, but it wasn't blood that escaped my system. My entire lunch from that afternoon lay next to my feet, and I suddenly felt like I could pass out at any minute. I had to get to my phone to get help in case I did pass out, or in case Laura came back again. I got to my feet and ran into the living room, snatched up my phone, and called Robert.

"I can't explain over the phone, but I need you!" I quickly shouted when Robert picked up.

"I'll be right there," Robert said, hanging up.

I walked into the bathroom to get a towel and strip off my bloody clothes, but when I looked in the mirror at myself, I couldn't see any blood at all besides the little that had spread when the thorns on the briar bush had cut into me. I stared at myself in shock. My eyes were wide, my mouth hung open, and I stood there staring at my clean clothes, not believing or even comprehending what had just happened to me. Did I just imagine all of it? Was I like Laura, having hallucinations? What would I tell Robert when he got here? He'd definitely think I was crazy. Maybe I was crazy. Maybe, just like Laura, I was schizophrenic too.

I grabbed my phone, catching Robert before he could leave, and made up some ridiculous story that I couldn't find my cold ice packs for my hip, but I had just found one. Took some convincing before Robert was satisfied enough not to come over. I hung up the phone and walked around the house, locking all the doors and windows before crawling into my bed and pulling the covers up to my eyes.

I kept picturing Laura. I could smell her rancid, hot breath when she spoke. I felt the warm blood as it poured all over me. My ears burned as she screamed the word Mooney at me. I knew she had really been here, but now I had to figure out why. What, or who, was Mooney? It sounded like a name, but I'd never heard it before and had no clue why she'd made sure I heard it now. I picked up the phone three different times with the intention of calling Patty but talked myself out of it each time. I hadn't been in Indiana long, and I didn't want to call her so soon with problems about Laura. I doubled up on my meds that night, determined not to see Laura again, and let the drugs take me under so that I'd be rested enough to start work Monday morning.

I walked into the employee lounge the next morning feeling hungover from all the drugs and sat at one of the far tables, hoping no one would ask about my new injuries from the fight with Chase Friday night. First-shift employees filtered in, and the chairs started to fill up quickly. I looked at the door as Blake walked in with two beautiful nurses, one under each arm. When Blake got closer, he spotted me and quickly looked away, avoiding eye contact, which I didn't understand. Blake and his two nurses took a seat in front of me, putting their back to me as they sat down in their chairs. I noticed the nurse sitting on Blake's right placed her hand on his thigh, and I quickly got the message Blake was sending. He'd avoided me all weekend, and now he was making a show in front of me with his fan club. *Yes, Blake, I get that we're just friends.* I never thought he was really interested in me anyway. Our kiss Friday had been a huge mistake, and only happened because one, we were drinking, and two, Blake was a total player. I knew there wasn't one woman that Blake considered to be off limits, and I should've known better Friday night than to give in to his good looks and charm.

The nurse massaging the inside of Blake's leg glanced over her shoulder at me and noticed I was staring. I hadn't even meant to, but that didn't stop her from snapping at me. "What's your problem?"

I shook my head, looking around, as I realized after a moment she was talking to me.

"Nothing," I said and looked away, not wanting a fight this morning. She could do whatever she wanted with Blake's leg. I didn't care.

"Leave her alone, Mia," Kara snapped as she took the seat next to me.

"She needs to mind her own business," Mia barked at Kara.

Blake visibly stiffened for a moment before turning around and looking at both of us. "Leave her alone, Mia," Blake said in a bored tone.

I ignored her dirty stare and tried to talk to Kara, but as Mia continued to talk about me to Blake, it became harder and harder to concentrate on anything Kara was saying.

"Who is she to you?" Mia asked Blake, and it got my attention.

"That's J. She started here last week, while you were on vacation," Blake told her, and I got a small smile from him.

"J?" she asked, oozing distain over my nickname.

"Jenny. She's my new recruit on five," Blake explained.

"You mean she's an orderly?" Mia asked and looked me over top to bottom.

"She sure is, cupcake," Blake said and gave me a wink. I couldn't help but giggle hearing the nickname for her that used to be mine.

Mia caught our exchange, and she made it obvious that she was mad. "I've never known a female orderly. Are you a dike or something?" she asked.

"No." I spat, starting to get mad now.

"Shut your mouth, Mia," Kara snapped, and I smiled at her having my back like that.

Blake smiled at the two of us and stood up. To Mia, he said, "You better watch it. She's an orderly because she's such a badass. I wouldn't mess with her."

Mia's mouth turned to a pout as she watched Blake move around to my table and sit next to me.

Kara and I exchanged a look, then Kara looked around me to Blake and asked, "What are you doing?"

"What?" Blake asked with a shrug. "J's my best friend. Can't a guy sit next to his best friend?"

"I guess so," Kara said, drawing out the words, and we both looked dumbfounded as she returned her attention back to me.

Blake got situated at the table, and that was when we all noticed Mia glaring hard at him.

"What, Mia?" he asked, sounding irritated.

"We always sit together," she whined.

"Ashley's sitting there. Hey, Ashley, take my spot and keep Mia company," Blake said to the other nurse he had brought in with him.

Ashley blushed at the mention of her name and did as Blake had asked, changing seats to be next to Mia. Blake quickly leaned forward and gave Ashley's butt a smack before she took his seat next to Mia. Ashley giggled, but Mia only looked more upset as she continued to pout at Blake.

"Oh, Mia. You know you're still my best girl. Now cheer up, and I'll see you tonight, cupcake," Blake said with a wink and his cocky grin that drove all the women crazy for him.

I rolled my eyes and waited for him to look over at me as Mia returned her attention to Ashley.

"What?" Blake asked, still grinning.

"Get hit with many sexual harassment claims?" I asked, teasing.

"No, never. Why?" he asked, looking amused.

"Just curious," I said, and Blake's smile turned into something genuine as he looked at me.

We were still staring at each other when Tom and Kelly came in and started the meeting, tearing our attention away from each other. When the meeting ended, Kara gave me a quick hug as she ran off to the stairs, and Blake led the way to the front of the room.

"Hey, you two. I need to talk to you for a minute," Tom said, pulling me and Blake to the side.

"What's up, Tom?" Blake asked as we moved over to an abandoned table.

"We have someone new being admitted to the hospital this morning, and he'll be on your floor, so I wanted to make sure you both knew."

"Is there a problem? You don't usually give me a heads-up about new patients," Blake asked, looking concerned.

"Yeah, this one's going to be a real handful, Blake. I didn't even want him at our hospital, but the state facility is at capacity, so we didn't have a choice but to take him," Tom said, looking through a manila file folder he held in his hands.

"You've never turned anyone away before. What the hell is so wrong with the guy that you didn't want him here?" Blake asked, leaning in closer to Tom.

"The guy was found criminally insane at his trial. According to his file, he's killed over twenty kids in the last year," Tom said, wincing at the pages in the file folder.

"So he's a serial killer. That shouldn't make him difficult to handle," Blake said, confident he was right.

"It's not how many he killed. It's how he killed them. I've never seen anything like it. I wish I could unsee it," Tom said, shaking his head as he closed the file.

Blake held his hand out for it, and Tom pulled back, refusing to let Blake have the file. Blake was mad when he looked back up at Tom.

"You don't want to know what he did to all those little kids, Blake. Trust me when I tell you that. His file is going straight to the therapist assigned to him," Tom said, looking apologetic.

“Well, the guy is obviously sick. Is there anything else we need to know?” Blake asked.

“He’s a flight risk,” Tom said.

“Are you kidding me?” Blake snapped.

Tom winced. “No, he’s broken out of two facilities prior to coming here.”

“We have a juvenile center on the grounds,” Blake said, raising his voice. “We have kids here!”

“I know. You aren’t telling me anything I haven’t thought of,” Tom said, placing a hand on Blake’s arm to try to calm him down.

At first, I was clueless about the kids, until I remembered Diane telling me on my first day of working here to stay to the left when the lane split coming in. Left would take you to the hospital, but staying right would take you back to the juvenile center, a mental health facility for kids under the age of eighteen. They weren’t going to be in the same building as the patient we were getting, but the children’s facility wasn’t that far away either. You could look out any of the southside windows here and see not only the juvenile center but the large playground behind it as well.

I gasped, realizing why Blake had been so upset. All the windows in the fifth-floor commons area faced the juvenile center. Anyone seeing the playground behind it would know it housed children.

“Isn’t there anywhere else they can take him?” I asked, interrupting their conversation.

Tom looked sad as he shook his head and answered, “No, I’m afraid they’ve exhausted all other options but here. That’s why I’m telling the two of you so you can prepare the staff on five and do what you need to do to make sure this guy doesn’t do anyone any harm or escape while under our care.”

“We’ll do what we can, Tom,” Blake assured him, and I nodded.

As soon as we got upstairs, Blake grabbed everyone for a private meeting at the guard’s desk. Blake gave the information to Zack and the three guards, and I watched their faces change as they to became outraged that Tom would agree to house such a high-risk patient. We all would have to work together to ensure everyone’s safety and to make damn sure the patient wouldn’t escape.

"I'd never forgive myself if one of our patients escaped on my watch and hurt those little kids," I told Blake later when we were headed to break.

"I know, J. Me either," he said as we rounded a corner and stopped to wait for the elevator.

As soon as we stepped on to the elevator, I turned to Blake and asked, "Can I ask you a question?"

"I think you just did," he teased.

I made a face, and he gestured for me to go ahead. "Am I really your best friend, or was that all bullshit for Mia this morning?"

"Damn, J, you're not gonna be all girly about it, are you?" Blake asked as he scowled at me.

"No, I just want to know," I said.

"Why?"

"'Cause, I would think, if I was your best friend and all, that you would've returned at least one of my calls or texts Saturday," I said, turning to watch his face.

Blake sighed and looked over at me. "I didn't talk to you because Robert needed time to cool down, and I don't care what he told you, he did *not* want me over there Saturday night."

"Yes, he did," I said, knowing I was right.

"No, he didn't, and if I had come over, all we would've done is fight. It happens every time we're together for longer than five minutes, and don't ask me why because I don't know," Blake confessed, and the elevator doors opened, letting staff members on from the third floor, causing me and Blake to squeeze into the back corner together.

"It doesn't matter," I whispered to avoid the stares of those in the elevator with us. "You should've stopped by to see me anyway."

"I knew you were sore and hurting Saturday. You didn't need the drama. Besides…" he trailed off.

"Besides what?" I asked.

"Besides…" he whispered seductively, and I felt his fingers run across the skin of my hand. I involuntarily quivered at his touch and was instantly covered in goosebumps, making Blake smile. "Besides, there's that," he said as the elevator doors opened, and we stepped out as a massive blush spread across my cheeks and I was happy to have Blake walking in front of me. With every step, my knees felt shaky, and butterflies danced in my stomach. As much as I loved the sensation, I hated it too, knowing he could affect me like that.

We sat at different tables in the lounge. I was pretending to be extremely interested in the magazine I had in front of me, and Blake stared at his phone, refusing to look my way. Every few seconds I'd see movement in the corner of my eye and glance up at Blake, only to find him still staring at his phone. I huffed after the fifth time, knowing I was going to catch him staring at me, and felt disappointed when I didn't. Dammit, why did I have to be so attracted to him and his gorgeous body? I knew Blake was a cocky, confident womanizer, and there'd be no way I could ever be in a steady relationship with him. That just wasn't Blake, and a relationship was all I'd ever be interested in. The thought made me smile, but it wasn't because of Blake. It was because it made me think of Robert and how reliable he was. I knew I could always count on Robert and he'd always be there for me no matter what.

Blake's cell phone chimed and he jumped, making me laugh out loud. He gave me a goofy smile before answering it. "Hey, Aunt Patty."

I smiled, knowing it was her calling Blake and was glad they were so close. I missed seeing her every week for our therapy sessions and knew I'd have to call her soon to check in. I went back to reading the magazine in front of me, not wanting to be rude and eavesdrop on Blake's conversation, but a few minutes later Blake walked over to me and held his phone out to me.

"What?" I asked, confused.

"It's Aunt Patty. She wants to ask you something," Blake said, taking the seat across from me.

Patty had called Blake to tell him she was getting married in June and wanted him to fly out to Kansas to be in the wedding. As they talked, she let it slip that she was planning on asking me as well, so Blake gave me the phone to save her an extra call.

"You've always felt like a daughter and a friend to me, Jenny. Would you please consider being one of my bridesmaids?" Patty pleaded into the phone. I was so touched that I couldn't tell her no and explained that I'd always felt close to her to.

"Can I bring Robert?" I asked, hoping she'd be okay with me bringing a date. Blake made a face, but I ignored it.

"Is that your boyfriend, dear?" Patty asked, and I remembered that I hadn't bothered calling her once since I'd been in Indiana. I sat there telling her all about him and the time we'd spent together. I told her about Kara and how well it was going for me here. Patty was ecstatic to hear the move had been an easy one for me.

"Of course, bring him," she said, and after our goodbyes, I gave the phone back to Blake.

Our break was well over by the time he finished his call, and we went back to the elevators. As we stepped on to the open elevator, Blake threw my words back at me and asked, "Jenny, can I ask you a question?"

The fact that he'd used my actual first name wasn't lost on me as I took in the seriousness of his tone. "I guess so," I said, nervous about what it was.

"Why Robert?" he asked, and he sounded sad.

I thought for a moment and then turned to Blake, making him face me as well. "I could explain why Robert in a million different ways, but after our talk Friday night, I think you'll get it when I tell you that the special thing about Robert is that he makes the empty hole and the pain easier to bare."

Blake's eyes widened and then saddened as he got my meaning all too well. He gave me a small smile and pulled me into him softly, wrapping his arms around me as we both thought about everything each of us had been through. It was enough to last a lifetime. We stood like that for a moment, and it didn't upset me. It was comforting. It didn't feel like when Robert embraced me this way. This was friendship.

He let me go as the doors opened, and we continued onto the ward, as if nothing ever happened. I was glad there weren't any secrets between me and Blake, and I looked forward to being in his aunt's wedding with him in June. A couple hours later, Blake left me and Zack to watch over the floor as him and two of the guards headed down to meet Tom on the first floor. Our new patient, whom nobody wanted, had arrived, and they had to go through the admittance process with Tom. Everyone in the hospital had been abuzz with rumors and gossip over the man. They speculated on how he came to be a serial killer, talked about how he'd been caught by the police, and some gave court details from what they'd remembered seeing on the news last year.

I was nervous about having him on our ward, and with the news that he'd arrived at the hospital, even our patients seemed to be on edge. Everyone was extra quiet today as Zack and I watched over the patients in the commons area. Most of the men on our floor had already gotten used to dealing with me every day, so the problems up here were kept to a minimum. When Blake called the floor phone sometime later, he instructed me and Zack to get everyone to their rooms for some quiet time, making it easier for him and the guards to bring up the new patient. We did as we were told and had just shut the last door when the main door to the ward opened. Tom came in first, followed by Blake, and I held my breath in anticipation as I imagined how hideous and terrifying a child murderer must look.

I was quickly disappointed when a short thin man who looked like he was in his sixties stepped through the door behind Blake. If it hadn't been for the black uniform, I would've been sure they'd had the wrong man. He looked sweet and polite as he gave me and Zack a tight-lipped smile. His gray hair shined under the florescent lighting in the room, and little dimples formed at the corners of his mouth. He looked like someone's sweet, old grandpa as they walked along, following Blake without incident.

Zack and I shared a look before we glanced back at the man. As he was led down the hall, he passed us, and Zack smiled at the patient. He turned his head to look straight at Zack and gave him a manic smile, causing Zack to drop his goofy grin. He then passed me, and I got a good close look at him. His eyes, where color should've been, were completely black and cold. There was no spark or light in his eyes as we stared each other down. No doubt he was sizing us all up, as we were him. Tom and Blake finished up in the patient's room and met us in the commons area as Richard, our fifth-floor guard, locked the patient in for the night.

"How'd it go?" I asked when they reached us.

"Better than we thought it would," Blake said, looking to Tom for confirmation.

"Yeah, he really wasn't any trouble," Tom agreed.

"But don't let that make you comfortable with him," Blake said to me and Zack both.

"He's smart, and I wouldn't put anything past him just yet."

"You never told us his name," Zack said. "What do I put on his nameplate at his door?"

"Dylan something," Blake said, trying to remember the guy's full name.

"Mooney," Tom chimed in.

My ears sparked, and I turned to Tom, wide-eyed. Surely I hadn't heard him right.

"What's his name?" I asked to make sure.

"Dylan Mooney," Tom confirmed, and my heart stopped.

"What is it?" Blake asked quickly, and I grabbed one of the chairs next to me, sitting in it before I fell.

Everything that happened with Laura yesterday came flooding back, and it hit me hard as I remembered the terrifying look on her face as she screamed one word at me, Mooney.

Chapter 13

Weeks went by with us all on edge around Mooney, waiting for him to act out or try to escape, but so far he'd been the model patient. Eventually nerves settled, and things seemed to return to normal on our floor. No one was fooled, though, and we all watched him like a hawk. Laura hadn't returned yet, although I kept waiting to see her again. The dreams—the dreams, however, came every night. Laura's sad and haunting voice was on repeat in my head as her warning screams about being in danger seemed to be on replay with no further explanation. I yearned for more information about Mooney and why he was so important to her, but after a couple weeks went by with no appearances, I gave up on seeing her again except for in my dreams. Those damn dreams were keeping me from getting a full night's sleep, and I had to call Patty about doubling up on my medication to keep the nightmares at bay.

Patty suggested that I keep myself busy to help keep my mind occupied, and I did just that. For three weeks straight now, I'd went nonstop. During the week I worked at the hospital and even stayed for a double shift a few times when Tom needed someone to fill in on another shift. On Friday nights, I was with Blake at the fights. Sometimes I fought, when one of the assholes there would challenge me, and other times I was just there to cheer on Blake. We had both asked Robert to come with us, but he always refused. His only explanation was to say that fighting wasn't a part of his life anymore. He wasn't crazy about me going with Blake, but after a couple fights, he had either given up arguing with me about it or just decided he didn't really mind me going. Either way, I was happy to spend my Friday nights at the barn.

Saturdays we all hung out. Usually me, Robert, and Blake, but sometimes Kara would make it over too. I was rarely at Robert's house anymore, even though I loved it there. He was always at my house now, and that seemed to be the hangout spot for all of us. It was great to see Robert and Blake getting close again, although at times they could get pretty annoying together.

"Oh shit, do you remember that one time with Bobby?" Blake asked Robert as we all sat around my kitchen, eating and talking.

Robert burst out laughing. "Yes! And do you remember when he—"

"Oh my god, that was some funny shit," Blake finished for him.

"Then there was that girl," Robert said, going to the fridge.

"Jessica! Man, she was hot," Blake said as he caught the beer Robert threw to him.

This was what they did every weekend. They talked and told stories of the good old days and continuously finished each other's sentences. I'd always sit there smiling as I enjoyed the show they put on, but I could rarely keep up with whatever it was they were talking about. On the weekends Kara came over, we usually talked and giggled about the guys having a secret bromance no one knew about. Our nights almost always ended with the guys making a bonfire out back. We'd bring the lawn chairs around and sit there enjoying the warmth from the fire as we continued to drink and talk the night away. Sometimes Blake stayed the night and crashed on my couch, while Robert and I took the bedroom, and sometimes he went home.

Blake and I never kissed again after that first night, but he was always finding ways to touch me. A brush of his hand against mine, sweeping a stray hair from my face, or if we were at the barn, he'd hold my hand. On Saturdays, when we were all together like this, I felt whole. Any other day I always seemed to feel a pull on my heart, like a piece of me was missing. I had to have both Blake and Robert in my life. They each had half my heart, and unless the three of us were together, things just didn't feel complete. Robert babied me as if I were a porcelain doll, delicate and breakable. Blake treated me all rough and pushy, making me feel like he thought I could take it, like I was unbreakable, even if I didn't feel that way all the time. Of course I'd never tell anyone how I felt. No one would understand, because I didn't even understand it. Together, Blake and Robert were the perfect man for me, and I had to have both of them in my life.

I hugged Blake good night as he went to crash on the couch. The sun was almost over the horizon, and the three of us had spent the entire night at the bonfire. I heard about old girlfriends and crazy adventures, and the guys even sang me a couple songs from their days when they still had the band. Robert took my hand as Blake disappeared into the living room and led me into the bedroom, closing the door behind us.

"Robert," I giggled against his mouth as he picked me up and carried me to the bed. "Blake will hear us and think we're doing something," I whined as Robert ran a trail of kisses down my neck.

"I don't care what he thinks," he breathed out in raspy tones.

"Well, I do," I said, stopping him to look in his eyes.

Robert brought his face up to mine and stuck his lower lip out in an exaggerated pout, making me giggle again. He smiled and pressed his lips to mine. His mouth was soft and his kiss gentle as I let my arms wrap around his neck. Soon, our bodies were pressed together, and he kissed me more urgently. I let it continue, feeling his hands roam over me, and when I felt him press his erection into me, I knew our time on the bed together was done. I stopped kissing him and pulled away. He knew the lines I had drawn for our physical relationship. He seemed to always be in agreement with those lines until we kissed, then he somehow forgot where the lines were.

"Be good," I said, still catching my breath.

"Do you think I'll ever get better at this?" he asked, grinning at me wickedly.

"I think the problem is we're both to good at it," I said, blushing.

He rolled closer to me and put a hand on my hip as he said, "Well, I know you are."

His deep, husky voice was intoxicating, and I had to make myself stand my ground.

"Good night, Robert," I said sweetly and gave him a quick peck on the lips.

"Good night, darlin'," he said, still grinning as he reached over and turned off the light.

When we got up, which wasn't until Sunday afternoon, Blake was nowhere to be found. I looked out the front window and noticed the Jeep was missing from its usual spot in my driveway. I frowned and sent a text to Blake, making sure everything was okay. The only reply I got was a short message saying he was fine. I knew right then he was mad. After weeks of hanging out together, some days I felt like I knew Blake and Robert better than I knew myself. I didn't bother Blake anymore that evening, knowing I wouldn't get anywhere with him by phone. I'd just talk to him at work in the morning.

"How's my sweet girl today?" Robert asked as he walked up behind me, letting his arms slide around to the front of my waist as he buried his face in my neck.

I smiled, letting his warmth envelope me. "Tired after you and Blake kept me up half the night," I said, teasing him.

"I hope you aren't too tired. I have a surprise for you," Robert said, nuzzling my neck with his nose until I tilted my head, giving him better access to what he wanted.

My whole body tensed in the most delicious way as Robert left a trail of kisses from my collarbone all the way to my ear. "What surprise?" I asked, barely able to get the words out.

Robert stopped kissing me, but he left his mouth on my ear, giving me chills as his warm breath danced across my earlobe as he spoke. "I called my uncle Ron. He's the one I told you has the car lot in Salem. I'm finally taking you to get your own car."

I spun in his arms and threw my hands around his neck before planting a hard kiss on his lips. When we pulled apart, I couldn't stop the smile that spread across my face, and I loved that Robert seemed just as excited as I was. "Really?" I squealed.

"Really. So go get your cute butt ready to go," he said, and I wasted no time getting ready to leave.

On the way to Salem, Robert was very insistent that I should get a truck even though the only one I'd ever driven was Ol' Red, so the pros and cons were still under debate with me. I watched out my window as farmhouses, one lone gas station, a small post office, Jerry's Bar and Grill, and a general store all went by. That was the extent of Pekin, my new hometown and the place that had quickly turned into home. Sure, it was small, but it hadn't taken long to fall in love with the place. I knew it all had to do with my current company sitting next to me in the driver's seat. Robert was always smiling, always so sure and steady. That, combined with the warmth he seemed to always be radiating, was like having my own personal sun. I smiled and continued to stare out my window. Robert had said that Salem was only about twenty minutes from Pekin, as long as you didn't get stuck behind a tractor, then the ride could take you a good hour. I wasn't sure I wanted to know why a tractor would be on the highway, so I let that one go. As I watched, the cornfields gave way to streets and stores as we made our way into town. Salem wasn't a city, hell, they didn't even have a Walmart, but they had their fair share of restaurants, banks, car lots, and grocery stores. We went through the square that sat in the middle of town, and coming out on the other side I saw a large car lot with rows and rows of shiny vehicles.

"This is it," Robert said as he slowed the truck down to turn into the car lot.

I looked up at a giant sign sitting next to the road that read Ron's New and Used Autos. Robert pulled into a parking spot at the main building, and we both got out and went inside. When I walked through the door, I could really tell how small the place was. There was one office with a desk and two chairs sitting in front of it for customers, and outside of that office was a TV and a couch for people who were waiting. Beside the TV on the left was a table with magazines stacked high on it, and to the right of the TV was a gray metal door that led into a garage, where they worked on and cleaned up vehicles on their lot. There were no pictures on the walls or decor of any kind. It was very plain and simple, just a place to sit down and fill out paperwork, I supposed. When we came in the door, a bell sounded, and seconds later a tall, chunky man with salt-and-pepper hair came through the door from the garage. He wore tan dress slacks, a white button-down dress shirt, and a tie.

"Robert!" he yelled as he made his way over to us. A smile stretched across his face from ear to ear. When he got closer, and leaned in to give his nephew a hug, I could see how tall he actually was. Robert towered over me at over six feet tall, but his uncle was even taller than him. He was a good-looking older man even though he was packing on a little more weight than he should be. He was clean-shaven, and his hair was cut short. The joy in his face when he saw Robert was contagious, and I found that by the time he had walked over and given Robert a hug, we were all smiling like fools.

"Now, is this the pretty young lady you were calling me about?" Ron asked Robert, looking over at me and continuing to wear his goofy smile.

"Yeah, this is my friend Jenny. Jenny, this is my uncle Ron, my mom's brother," Robert said, introducing us to each other. I smiled and shook Ron's hand as he extended it out to me.

"Well, Jenny, what brings such a pretty girl to my little ol' car lot?" Ron asked me.

"I just moved here from Kansas, and I don't have a vehicle yet, so I was hoping you could help me out, Ron," I said, plastering on my biggest, brightest smile for him.

"Jenny, Jenny, Jenny," Ron said, shaking his head at me and smiling. "I am deeply flattered that you thought so much of me that you hopped on a plane from Kansas to Indiana, kidnapped my nephew here, stole his truck, outran the cops, and probably knocked over a liquor store to get the money for the car just so you could come to my fabulous car lot. My reputation must have reached all over the country for you to have heard about me all the way out in Kansas. I must say, though, we do have some mighty fine vehicles sitting on our lot. Come with me and we'll start looking around. If the cops show up, you duck down behind a car, and I'll distract them so you can make your getaway." And with that funny and loud performance, he put an arm around my shoulders like he had known me for years and started leading me out onto the lot. I couldn't help but smile at him and the bold speech he had made. He was a funny man, and I thought this car-buying experience would be a most memorable one for sure. As we continued out onto the lot and Ron started telling me about the vehicles he had for sale, I glanced behind me to look at Robert, who was walking a couple steps behind us. He looked at me, grinned, and then shrugged his shoulders. I could imagine him thinking, *Sorry for my uncle, but you just gotta love him anyway.* I smiled at the thought and returned my attention to Ron.

"Now what are we looking for exactly?" Ron asked me, looking out over his selection of cars, trucks, SUVs, and mini vans. "I have a car that was given to me by the Queen of the Nile, a minivan that Elvis was sure to have rode in once or twice, a truck that the pope himself handpicked and delivered to me, and I think I still have the Escalade that Tupac passed out in when he was shooting his last rap video."

"Wow, Ron, you really have a lot of good choices here," I said, giggling at him.

He grinned down at me and said, "Oh, yes, young lady, we surely do. You know, I take pride in my rare collection of new and used vehicles. Well, they couldn't be any better if they were made of gold. I handpicked all of them because they were the best, well, all but the one from the pope. I even went through them myself with a fine-toothed comb to make sure they were good and ready for the next driver that walked through my door, and that, my dear friend Jenny, is you today, you lucky, lucky girl. Now you just walk around, and if something grabs your attention, you let me know, and I'll get the keys for you to take her on a test drive."

"Thanks, Ron," I said as I watched him walk over to the small concrete porch in front of his office building and sit down on a bench. He sat back on the bench, arms outstretched across the back of it, and his legs crossed wide like he was the coolest man on the planet. He was absolutely wonderful, and I found myself a little jealous of Robert to not have had family like this myself. Turning my attention back to the task at hand, I started walking through the rows of vehicles surrounding me. Robert came to my side to look with me, and we talked about the colors I liked and what really interested me. I told him I was leaning toward an SUV of some sort. I thought Robert was right about not really needing a car during the winter months here, but I wasn't quite ready for a big truck yet, so I thought an SUV was a good compromise between the two. Some of them came in four-wheel drive, and that would be great if we had a bad snow this winter.

"Or if we decide to go muddin' in the back field," Robert said, grinning at me.

"Mudding?" I asked, not understanding.

"You've never been muddin'?" he asked me, raising his eyebrows in surprise.

"Nope, never have," I said, smiling at him.

"There is plenty of country in Kansas. How could you not go muddin' in it?"

"I grew up in Lawrence, in the city. There wasn't a lot open land there, and I lived in an apartment on the sixth floor of a large apartment building. I didn't even know anyone who used the word *mudding*," I said and giggled at him as a shocked expression washed over his face.

"Wow, Jen. We have got to get you living right," Robert joked.

I didn't say anything, just raised an eyebrow at him and crossed my arms over my chest.

"I think what you need, next time you're off work, is a tractor ride by my home, taking your SUV that you pick out muddin' in the back field, and follow it up with a good old-fashioned camping trip in the woods. If you can survive all that, there might be hope for you after all," Robert said in a scolding tone.

"Listen here, Mr. Country Boy," I said, walking up and standing so close to him that our bodies were almost touching. "I can handle any challenge you throw my way."

"Oh really?" he asked with the sexiest smile I had ever seen.

"Yes," I answered, feeling confident I could do country with the best of them.

"Good. By the end of it, you'll either love or hate country living. There won't be no in-between, and I promise either way, you'll have the city all out of your system," he said, adding in a little more of his natural country, Southern drawl to his words, and I loved it.

"I'm sure I'll love it," I said, giving him a long, suggestive stare from the tips of his cowboys boots, all the way up to his ridiculously handsome face.

"Why do I get the feeling that the subject just changed?" he asked, grinning, and then, with no warning, he gave me a little push.

It caught me off guard, and I stumbled back a little. I couldn't believe he pushed me. I ran up and pushed him back, but he was ready for it, and it was like pushing against a brick wall. He didn't budge at all. He reached out and grabbed both my arms with his hands and pulled me against him. I was breathing hard from laughing, and our body contact made it that much harder to catch my breath. My chest was just above his stomach, and my arms were around his back where he had put them. His arms were around me too, and we were standing still, breathing hard and staring into each other's eyes. He smiled down at me, and I smiled back up at him. My heart skipped a beat, and I found that I was now holding my breath. Robert started to lean down to me, and I closed my eyes. When his mouth found mine, everything in me caught on fire. The kiss wasn't hard or all-consuming, but it didn't have to be for it to have such an effect on me. When he pulled back, I found myself wanting more, and that scared me for some reason. I wanted everything with Robert, and that was something so new, so unexpected. I didn't know how to react to it.

I turned and started babbling on about the SUV sitting in front of me. I knew I was an idiot, but hopefully Robert wouldn't hold it against me for too long. Robert watched me, listening as I went on and on, and he never said a word. Instead he just kept this funny little smirk on his face as we walked around the lot and I continued to talk. When I finally settled on a bright-white Chevy Tahoe, Robert went over to get Ron. I was both relieved to have a second to breathe and disappointed to watch him go. I took in a deep breath and turned back to the Tahoe I'd picked out. The sunlight glared off the tinted driver's side window, and I had to shield my eyes as it suddenly blinded me. Keeping my hand at my forehead to shield my eyes, I slowly, carefully, looked back at the tinted window, while trying to keep the sun at bay. When I found my reflection staring back at me, it wasn't my eyes, and I gasped to see as my eyes focused that it was Laura's image in the window, not mine. She was staring at me with such purpose, such intensity, that it scared me. I took a step back and looked around the car lot, trying to find Robert. This had gone on long enough. I needed him to look, to see if what I was seeing was actually there, because I felt like I was going crazy. When Robert came walking back over with his uncle Ron, I pointed at the window. Just as Robert reached me, I glanced back over, and all that I could see was him. Frowning, I walked closer and looked again, but the only thing looking back at me in the dark tint of the window was me. I shook my head. This wasn't right, but I couldn't say anything to Robert. I'd have to talk to Patty, and soon.

Without a second's hesitation, Robert pointed at the Tahoe and smiled over at his uncle Ron. "This is the one," he said, smiling.

"Oh, my dear Jenny, Robert has informed me that you have found a prize-worthy Tahoe. This is a good choice. I remember the day I got it. Madonna was here on vacation, driving this beauty down the road, when she saw me from afar and pulled in to ask me to run away with her and live happily ever after. Of course I couldn't, I was already married to the most beautiful woman in the world, so obviously no one else could compare. She left her Tahoe with me as a token of her affection, which I have cherished every day," Ron said to me, looking very fondly at the white Tahoe in front of us, his arm around my shoulders again.

"If it means so much to you, are you sure you want to get rid of it?" I asked, smiling at him.

"Oh, yes, she must go. Once I told the wife my story of love with the fair Madonna, she told me I was on the couch until I sold the vehicle Madonna had so affectionately bestowed upon me, and to tell you the truth, dear Jenny, my back is really starting to hurt." He groaned terribly and stretched his body, holding his hand to his back like an old man would.

I laughed at his performance and told him I'd be glad to take it off his hands. Robert was happy because I hadn't gotten a car and I was happy to. When I test-drove it, the height and width of it made me feel like I owned the road. It drove so smoothly, and the sound system was amazing. Robert had me cranking the radio up to someone named George Jones. I had never heard of him, but the song we were listening to about a rocking chair was pretty catchy. When we got back to the lot, Robert haggled with Ron over the price of the Tahoe, and when the two men were satisfied, they shook hands, and I wrote Ron out a check. He was surprised I wasn't going to need financing since the vehicle was practically brand-new, but I explained to him that my dad had passed away, leaving me a good chunk of money, and Ron never said another word about it. He looked momentarily sad, and I really expected him to go into another dramatic story of some sort, but he just sat there at his desk smiling a sweet smile at me and continued filling out all the documents for the sale. With a full tank of gas, we headed back to Pekin, to home, and the whole way home all I could think about was Laura's face staring back at me in the window. Two weeks went by, owning the new Tahoe, before I could walk out to the car and not stare at the windows expecting a ghost to be looking back at me. When Laura's face didn't appear again, I finally relaxed down enough to enjoy my new car.

May brought warmer temperatures, and I rode to work that Monday morning with the windows down. My long brown hair beat against the back of my neck as it fought against the wind, trying to break free from the ponytail holder that held it in place. I smiled, smelling the hay from the nearby fields, and waved when a farmer caught my attention from the cab of his tractor. I smiled even wider when he returned my wave, and I felt glad to live out in the country.

I didn't see Blake in our hand-off meeting at work, so I waited by the elevators for him. I wanted to talk to him this morning about why he was so upset. When a few minutes passed, and he never rounded the corner, I decided I better get upstairs before my shift started. Richard, Wayne, and Jerry were in their usual spots behind the monitors and made a point to smile and nod at me as I walked past them and into the ward. I was shocked when I walked in to find Blake already on the floor and talking to Zack.

"Hey, guys," I said as I walked over.

"You're late," Blake snapped as he looked down at his watch.

"I was waiting for you downstairs," I said, noticing he already had a shitty attitude this morning.

"Well, no one asked you to do that. Now you've put us behind by fifteen minutes," he shot back and walked away, heading to a patient's room down the hall.

I looked at Zack, who only shrugged and whispered, "I don't know."

We followed Blake, and he purposely avoided any eye contact with me as we started our morning routine with the patients. Several times throughout the morning, I tried talking to him or joking around, and each time I was given a cold shoulder or quick response. When it was time to go to break, Blake and I were scheduled to go together, so I waited for him in the hallway, but he purposely stayed five steps behind me all the way to the elevator. When the doors dinged, and we stepped on, I knew this was my chance to find out what the hell was going on.

Knowing I had him cornered for the next few minutes, I asked, "Would you tell me what your problem is with me today?"

Blake laughed sarcastically at his phone he'd been playing with but didn't answer.

"What?" I almost shouted. "Would you please just talk to me?"

Blake snapped his face up to glare at me, and I was taken aback. Blake had never looked at me like that before. I took a step back, and he noticed, but it didn't detour him.

"Could you please do me a favor, princess? The next time I'm at your house, could you wait till after I leave to fuck your boyfriend? I don't want to hear that shit."

"You're an asshole," I said, letting the hurt fill my words.

"Why, because I'm honest?" he asked, lowering his voice as he said it.

The elevator dinged as tears welled in my eyes, and as the doors opened, I stepped up to Blake. In his face, I said so that only he could hear, "I'm a virgin." Then before he could say anything, I stormed out of the elevator and down the hallway.

We didn't sit next to each other or even look at each other during our entire break in the lounge. I glanced at the clock, seeing we had one minute left on our break, and said fuck it, getting up from the table to go back upstairs. Blake reached out for me as I passed him, but I jerked my arm away and kept walking. Wishing the elevator would hurry up so I could ride up alone did me no good, and just as I hit the 5 button on the panel, Blake jumped in before the doors could close.

"J, I'm sorry," he said from beside me.

"I thought I was back to princess," I snapped.

"I'm really sorry. Please look at me," he begged, and because we were connected in an odd way, I couldn't stand to hurt him, but I only turned my head, and that's all he was getting.

"Please don't be mad at me. I didn't know," he said.

"You didn't have to know. You know me. And you should know I wouldn't do that when you're ten feet away, laying on my couch," I barked.

"I know, and I'm sorry. You're right, and I should've given you more credit than that. It's just that I heard you giggling and what I assumed was you two falling on the bed together and I couldn't take it. I got in the Jeep and left," he explained, and I was hurt seeing the pain in his eyes. I didn't know why, but his pain seemed to set off little stabs of my own.

"You could've knocked on the door or, at the very least, called me on Sunday, and I would've explained. Nothing happened, I promise," I said and wondered why I felt the need to explain any of this to Blake. I could do whatever I wanted to do with Robert. He was my boyfriend, not Blake.

"Were you serious when you said that you're a virgin?" he asked, and fire burst through my cheeks as I looked at the floor.

"Hey," he said sweetly as he lifted my chin to look me in the eyes. "Tough girls don't blush, and you're the toughest girl I know."

I smiled, still blushing, and said, "Well, this one does."

"Well, it's pretty adorable on you," he said playfully. Then his smile faded, and he asked, "Can you do me a favor, please?"

"Sure," I said, staring at his full lips, ignoring thoughts I should not be thinking.

"If that ever changes, if you ever sleep with Robert, I mean, please do it when I'm not around, and don't tell me about it. I don't want to know," he said, dropping his hand from my face.

"Why?" I asked, staring into his electric-blue eyes.

"J," he said, putting a hand on my cheek. "You know why, don't you?" he asked, running a finger down my jawline.

I watched him, studying his sad expression, and I knew. Just like I knew Blake had fallen in love with me, I had fallen for him too. I never meant to love him, but I needed him. He was my best friend, but I knew that would never be enough for him, and the thought of losing him over that made me ill.

"Yeah, I know," I said, putting my hand over his. Tears welled in the corners of my eyes, and Blake pulled me into him.

"Don't do that. You're tough, remember?" he said, trying to soothe me.

I refused to cry over the possibility of Blake when I already had someone as great as Robert. I pulled back, dried my eyes, and steadied myself just as the doors to the elevator opened on our floor. I got out, never looking over my shoulder at Blake. I stepped into the commons area and came face-to-face with Mooney, who was sitting at a table, idly looking me over. When he saw me look at him, he smiled, revealing two rows of brown rotting teeth. I winced, only making him smile wider as I walked past him and over to Zack.

My morning went by in a daze. I couldn't concentrate on anything after what had been said between me and Blake in the elevator. We were short-staffed today, so lunchtimes among the staff members had to be taken individually, and I was glad to get away from Blake for a while to clear my head. I meandered through the halls, which were filling up quick with the cafeteria-goers, either headed to or coming back from lunch. I wasn't paying as much attention to where I was going as I should have been. I was trying so hard not to think about him. More than anything, I was trying to beat down my guilt. I didn't even know why I was feeling that way. I hadn't done or said anything to feel guilty about. I stomped along, heading past the cafeteria toward the rear of the building. I needed to get outside and let my head clear. I had plenty of time before I would need to get back upstairs, and I definitely needed to get my mood in hand before I saw Blake again. I ran my hands through my hair and took a couple of deep breaths before I continued around a corner.

Four of the part-time orderlies, who only filled in when we were understaffed, came around the corner I was headed for, talking casually as they approached me. They were joking loudly among themselves and laughing vigorously as I scooted next to the wall, giving them room to pass me. I walked softly, looking past them to the corner.

"Hey there," one of the taller of the four men said. It had to be to me, because no one else was around. I looked up automatically to see all four men had stopped. The one closest to me was a very tall, broad, muscular man in his early twenties and was the one who had spoken. He took half a step toward me.

"Hello," I mumbled, an automatic reaction.

"You work on the fifth floor, right?" he asked me, and something about the way he looked at me made me feel uneasy.

"Yeah, with Blake and Zack," I answered then quickly turned and walked around the corner, out of sight of the men. I could hear them laughing at full volume again as it echoed through the hallway.

I found myself at the rear of the building and punched my code into the keypad. When the door chirped, I pushed my way through fast, and as soon as the bright sun hit my face, I instantly felt relieved. I walked down the stone pathway that led out to the orchard behind the hospital. This area was off limits to the patients, but it was rare to see any staff back here either. In fact, Blake was the only one I knew of that ever came out here to get away, and I was glad he had shown it to me. The apple trees smelled wonderful heating up under the warm sun, and the birds singing made me feel even more sad. I walked and walked, passing rows of trees. When I got a pretty good distance from the hospital, I glanced over my shoulder to look at the sun glistening off the hospital windows when I realized, with a shock, that two men were walking quietly about twenty feet behind me. They were from the same group of orderlies I had passed in the hallway, although neither was the tall one that had spoken to me. I quickly turned my head forward and quickened my pace. I listened to their quiet footsteps, which were way to low in comparison to all the noise they had been making in the hospital.

As I walked faster, they didn't seem to be moving any faster, or getting any closer to me, and part of me said that my nervousness about the men was stupid. Maybe they wanted to enjoy the warm day too. I didn't slow down, but I did try to steady my nerves, telling myself, *You don't know they're following you.* I looked at the path and the rows of trees in front of me. In a few feet, the path would end in a *T*. The left side circled you back to the hospital, and the right side took you further into the orchard. I decided I'd wait till I got to the split in the path then turn left and head back to the hospital. If they turned right, I could slow down and actually enjoy my walk back.

I listened intently and could hear that they were still a good distance behind me. When I turned left, I walked a little, then hesitated, listening to see which way the two men were going to turn. When I heard their footsteps again, I knew they had followed me, and I debated as I swiftly walked toward the hospital, if I should break out into a run or not. The men still sounded a good distance back, so I kept my pace, not wanting to look stupid if they were just out for a walk. Halfway back to the hospital, and in the thickest part of the orchard, I risked a quick glance over my shoulder and saw the men were even further back now. I should have been relieved at this, but both men were staring at me. I turned back around and was almost sprinting now. The men never quickened their pace, but just before I could get past the tall lush trees towering over this part of the path, two more men stepped out from the trees and onto the path about forty feet ahead of me. I skidded to a stop, looking at them, seeing they were the two orderlies from the group I had passed. Both men stood there with excited smiles as I froze dead on the stone path.

Chapter 14

I REALIZED THEN that I wasn't being followed. I was being herded. I paused, only for a second, but as my brain processed what was happening too late, the two men behind me were coming up fast, their footsteps were echoing off the stones, and I put my game face on, remembering my self-defense training. With nowhere to go but forward, I tried to look unaffected as I walked up to the two men in front of me and tried to push past them, keeping my gaze to the ground.

"Don't be that way, baby," the tall man said, breaking the silence in the orchard, and he turned into a stone wall that I couldn't get past. The other three men, all close now, laughed.

"Let me through," I demanded, looking him in the eyes.

"And why should I do that?" he said in a low, threatening voice.

I backed up a little as he took a step forward.

"Because if you don't, Blake will have your ass," I said sternly.

"I don't think he would, sweetheart. Everyone in the hospital knows about you, the only female orderly on staff. We all know you're a dike, trying to sneak a peek at the hot little nurses. Even Blake knows, but I'm going to do you a favor," he said, brushing his hand on my face, and I smacked it away, which only made him smile more as he moved right in front of me. The cologne he was wearing invaded my nostrils, and I braced myself, trying to think of what to do next.

"What are you going to do?" I asked, but my mouth had become so dry with nervousness that my voice sounded weak instead of strong like I wanted it to.

"Oh, baby, I'm going to show you exactly what you've been missing," he said down at me, and everything I had been scared of suddenly became real.

I should've been fighting him off by now, but panic was taking over, and I couldn't think straight.

"Please don't," I whispered, but he didn't seem to hear me anymore as two of his buddies ran up behind me, grabbing my arms as they held me in place so I couldn't move.

He leaned down, smelling my hair, and his mouth brushed against my neck.

"Let me go," I begged, and tears started to fall.

"I'll let you go down on me. How about that?" he asked and licked my neck.

His friends were laughing again. I was suddenly fueled with rage as his trail of spit dripped down my neck, and from somewhere deep inside me, I got up enough courage to fight back. I kicked my knee up as hard as I could and made contact right between the tall man's legs. He groaned and went down, sinking to his knees. I tugged as hard as I could against the two men that held my arms. My right arm came free, and I brought it around, hitting the man holding my left arm right across his cheek. He yelled out in pain and dropped my other arm. I turned to run, and that was when two of the men tackled me to the ground from behind. I hit hard on the stone path, and it bit into my cheek, tearing away the flesh. I screamed as loud as I could for help, still struggling to get free.

"Turn that stupid bitch over," I heard the man I'd taken down say to his friends.

The two men flipped me onto my back, and the tall man straddled me, pinning me down with his weight.

"Let go of me!" I screamed, finding my voice had fully returned.

"You like it rough, don't you, sweetheart?" he snarled down at me and ripped open my uniform shirt. My white bra was all that was left to keep me from being fully exposed to these assholes, and all three men cheered on this maniac, whom I knew was going to rape me.

I screamed again for help and in midscream was hit hard right across the face, and the metallic taste of blood filled my mouth from my lip the man had just split open. I pulled and struggled, determined to give a good fight, even if I couldn't get free.

"Let her go," a low, growling voice came from behind me. I couldn't see him, even as I angled my head up to try to look at who was there, but I didn't have to see his face to recognize his voice. I was just glad this was all going to be over soon now that he was here.

"What are you going to do about it, Blake?" the tall man asked, moving away from me to ready himself for a fight.

"I'll kill you," Blake growled, and the two men holding me down traded glances before releasing me. I shot up off the ground and ran to Blake, who engulfed me in his strong arms.

"The four of you have two choices. You can either leave right now and pray that I don't see you off hospital grounds and I'll tell Tom you quit. Or you can stay here, and I'll have Zack take Jenny inside while we finish this here and now," Blake said, staring down all four men. I glanced over Blake's shoulder to see Zack standing behind him, and he gave me an apologetic smile when our eyes met. I just buried my face back into Blake's shoulder, holding on to his shirt with both hands.

"Fuck this shit. Little dike isn't worth the trouble," the tall man said, more to his three friends than to Blake, and they all nodded.

"So you're leaving then?" Blake asked, never once cowering as he met their hard glares.

"Yeah, we're leaving," the tall man answered.

"Shame," Blake teased. "If you're ever up for a real fight, you know where to find me."

The man just gave Blake a look like, "Yeah right," then the four of them walked off in the direction of the employee parking lot. I didn't look up till Blake spoke again.

"J," he said, in a soft, soothing tone. "You ready to go in?"

I looked up and nodded, tears still streaming down my face as I silently cried. Blake looked down at my shirt, and I realized it was open. I crossed my arms over my breasts, ashamed that he'd seen me like this, and looked at the ground.

"Here, J, put this on," Blake said, taking his shirt off and handing it to me.

Zack quickly turned around, being the nice guy that he was, and I removed my torn shirt and slipped Blake's on. I no more had it pulled down when Blake scooped me up in his arms and started carrying me back to the hospital.

"I'm so sorry this happened to you," Blake said, still mad, and gave me a light kiss on the top of my head.

"Where are you taking her?" I heard Zack ask.

"Let's get her up to the medical ward so they can check her out. She's got to have that cheek looked at," Blake said, reaching the hospital.

"Okay," Zack replied as he opened the door for us.

When we got on the fourth floor, the ward was divided up, and everything to our right was devoted to the medical wing of the hospital, set up like a regular physician's office. Zack ran ahead of us to the window and told the medical assistant behind the glass that an orderly had been attacked and needed checked out right away. I looked over at the lady behind the glass and saw that she didn't look fazed at all by his words. This was a common thing in a mental hospital. When she opened a door for us to go on back, she took in the scene in front of her and gasped. I could just imagine how we looked to her with Blake half-naked, carrying me in his arms, and blood trickling down us both from my face. We were a complete mess.

"Oh my god, what happened to her?" the lady asked Zack.

"Some part-time, asshole orderlies attacked her out back," Zack said and anger flooded his voice.

"Orderlies?" the lady asked in surprise.

"Where do you want us to take her?" Blake snapped, not having any patience to explain to her what was going on right now.

"Take her back to room three, straight down to your left," she answered, shutting the door behind us and effectively closing off the curious stares of those sitting in the waiting area.

We were almost to room three when I heard Mia's high-pitched, flirtatious voice call, "Hi, Blake."

He turned to face her, with me still in his arms. Her tone changed from flirtatious airhead to knowledgeable nurse in the instant it took her to see I was hurt and bleeding.

"Jenny," she gasped. "Get her in there on the bed," she ordered Blake.

Blake laid me down gently on the hospital bed, and I almost started crying again when he pulled away, but in an instant, he was back, pulling the doctor's stool over to sit next to the bed. He reached out and took my hand in his and gave it a little squeeze, making me feel better. Mia busied herself around me, looking me over, accessing my injuries, and cleaning me up.

"Are you hurt too?" she asked Blake, seeing the blood on him as well.

"No, this is hers," he answered, looking down at the blood.

I could feel myself getting more and more angry by the minute. I was angry that those jerks attacked me. I was angry that I hadn't used my training to take them down. I was angry for letting fear shut me down like that. I was angry that Blake and Zack had to save me and seen me cry. I was even angrier now that I was being babied all over again and Mia was the one taking care of me. She couldn't stand me. It was no secret, and we both knew it. I waved Mia away from my face, let go of Blake's hand, and sat up straight in the bed, forcing myself to be strong.

"You can both stop. I'm fine," I said, but still sounded shaky.

Mia looked shocked. "Jenny, you aren't fine. That gash on your face is going to need stitches," Mia snapped.

"Just let her work," Blake said, trying to sound soothing.

"I'm going to be out in the waiting area," Zack said from the doorway.

"Hey, man, can you track down Tom and get him up here? He's going to have to know about this," Blake asked, and Zack nodded, looking thankful to have something to do.

Mia took out a hospital gown and laid it on the bed. "Put this on, and Dr. Baker will be in soon," she instructed me and left the room.

Blake stood up, grabbed the gown, and opened it up for me to slip into. I didn't move, just looked at him skeptically and raised an eyebrow at him.

"What?" he asked at my hesitation.

"I'm not changing in front of you," I said and couldn't help but blush even though it was ridiculous too after what had just happened. After all, I was wearing Blake's shirt.

"I promise you don't have anything new. Now quit being a baby and let's go. I'll turn my head if you want."

I rolled my eyes and let out a sigh of exasperation but did as I was told, removing Blake's shirt carefully so that it didn't rake across the wounds on my face. When I looked back at Blake to put my arms into the sleeves of the gown, his head was turned just as he'd promised. I smiled until my lip pulled, and the pain radiated through me, making me quickly relax my face. Once my arms were in, Blake had me turn around, and he tied the back of it for me, and I noticed how careful he was not to touch my skin. I was glad he was being so thoughtful, because as much as I usually welcomed his touch, right now I probably would've smacked him.

"What about your pants?" Blake asked seriously.

"I'm not taking them off unless the doctor says I have to," I told him and sat back down on the bed, almost missing it completely, causing Blake to rush over to grab me.

"Did you hit your head?" he asked, lowering me back down onto the bed.

I pointed sarcastically at my cheek and asked, "What do you think?"

"Damn, you're feisty when you're hurting," he said, grinning at me.

I wanted to smile, but I refused to let myself, not wanting to feel the pain from my busted lip again. I leaned my head back on the pillow and closed my eyes.

A few minutes later Dr. Baker came in. He was a big man, both in height and weight, and would have been very intimidating to look at if it hadn't been for his warm smile and sparkling eyes, which sat under a pair of wire-frame glasses.

"Hey, sweetie," he cooed at me. "Can you tell me how this happened?"

As I spoke, he sat about examining me and all my scrapes, bruises, and cuts. He seemed to be hanging on to my every word, and Blake, sitting next to me, looked pissed all over again as he listened to me tell all the details of my attack in the orchard.

"Blake, how did you and Zack know she was out there?" Dr. Baker asked when I was finished.

"We had to take turns going to lunch today because we're short-staffed. When Jenny wasn't back in thirty minutes, I knew that wasn't like her, and I started to pace across the corridor upstairs. One of the windows overlooks the orchard, and I happened to look out just in time to see Jenny get confronted by the men. I told the guards so they could watch the floor for us, and then I grabbed Zack for back up as we ran out back," Blake reported.

Dr. Baker nodded like he was satisfied with both our accounts of what had happened then turned to me. "Based on your examination and your symptoms, I think it would be wise to get a CAT scan done to check for a concussion, and then you'll need stitches in that cheek. Should I go ahead and have Mia bring you in something for the pain?" he asked as he filled out a sheet of paper in my newly started medical file.

My head, body, and especially my face all throbbed, so I nodded for the painkillers.

"Very well. I'll let her know. You try to relax. Someone will be in shortly to take you for the CAT scan," he said then exited the room.

"How are you doing?" Blake asked once Dr. Baker was gone.

"I'm hanging in there," I said, but it wasn't convincing either of us.

Blake raised an eyebrow at me then asked again, "No, really?"

"I'm hurting, scared, mad, and embarrassed. Just about every emotion I could possibly have right now. They're all swimming around in my head," I told him and stared at the little dots on the bedsheets so I wouldn't have to look into his piercing blue eyes.

"I'm so sorry I didn't get down there any sooner," Blake said, squeezing my hand.

"Blake, this isn't your fault," I said, looking at him again.

"I just feel like if I had moved faster and had gotten to you sooner, the worst part of all this could've been avoided."

"Please don't feel that way. I'm grateful you and Zack got there when you did. I'll be okay," I told him and squeezed his hand this time.

Blake opened his mouth to speak, but Mia walked in carrying a cup of water and some pills. "Here, Jenny. These are very strong pain pills. You'll be feeling good in no time," she said, smiling, and her kindness caught me so off guard that I was hesitant about taking the pills until she practically shoved them in my face.

I swallowed them and handed the water back to her.

"Blake, Zack wanted me to tell you that he and Tom are waiting for you in the waiting room," Mia informed him as she sat my water on a nearby table.

"Thanks, Mia," he said to her but never took his eyes off me. "J, you okay if I leave for a bit?"

"Yeah," I replied, but really didn't want to be alone.

"Oh, she'll be asleep in just a few minutes, once those pills kick in," Mia chimed in.

"I'll be back soon," Blake said, smiling.

"Okay," I whispered and watched as both Blake and Mia left the room. I noticed right before they shut the door that Blake was still shirtless and covered in my dry blood. I winced and turned to my side, pulling my knees up to my chest and replaying everything in my mind, becoming even more mad at myself. I felt my eyelids becoming heavy, and I tried to fight the sleepiness taking me over, but I lost, and just a few minutes later I was out.

I could hear voices talking, and I felt a slight movement, but I couldn't make my eyes open. I heard a man's voice say, "Make sure you give me her chart before you go in with her." Then a woman said, “I will.” I was sure it was Mia, but then I was out again. I don’t know how long it had been when I started hearing voices again.

“How’s she doing?” a young voice asked.

“Doctor said the worst part of it was the gash on her face,” Blake’s cool voice responded.

“That’s good, I guess,” the young voice responded.

“No, it’s not. None of it should’ve happened,” Blake snapped.

“Tom fired them and said if Jenny wants to file charges, he’d back her up,” the guy informed Blake, and I could finally comprehend enough that I knew it was Zack’s voice.

“That’s not enough,” Blake said, raising his voice.

“What are you going to do, Blake?” Zack asked, sounding concerned.

“I’m going to catch them fuckers off hospital grounds and make them pay for this,” Blake growled.

“Man, you’re going to get yourself hurt or in a lot of trouble,” Zack warned.

“I don’t want to hear it, not now,” Blake said, still sounding mad.

“I’m just looking out for you,” Zack said, and you could hear the worry in his voice.

“Well, who’s looking out for her?” Blake snapped once more.

“What’s your deal, man?” Zack asked, sounding fed up with Blake.

“What do you mean?” Blake asked, letting his anger fade into annoyance.

“Blake, look, I like Jenny, we all do, but I’ve never seen you get all worked up like this over a girl. She’s not even your girlfriend. She’s dating Robert, and he’ll be here soon. Tom already called him. Why don’t you let him deal with this?” Zack asked in a pleading tone.

“You don’t get it,” Blake said, sounding low and defeated.

“Get what?” Zack snapped.

“I’ve never met anyone like J. I’ve never felt anything like this before. It was always about having a good time and getting a piece of ass. You know that,” Blake said, almost sounding embarrassed.

“Yeah, I know,” Zack said, sounding less irritated now.

"I can't explain it exactly, but it's not like that with her. You're going to think I'm so fucking stupid when I tell you this, but I think I'm in love with her," Blake blurted, and even though I couldn't open my eyes or saying anything, I was freaking out on the inside.

"Yeah," Zack said, no feeling in his voice.

"What do you mean 'Yeah'?" Blake asked, sounding confused.

"Anyone who knows you already knew you had fallen in love with Jenny. Why do you think Mia can't stand her? It's not because Jenny isn't likable," Zack explained like it should've been obvious.

"Oh," Blake said, sounding a little surprised.

"Yeah, oh. So have you told Jenny any of this?" Zack asked.

"No, not in those words exactly," Blake confessed.

"Really, Blake?" Zack said, sounding irritated again.

"I couldn't just say, 'Hey, I'm in love with you.' We've never even gone out on a date, plus, she's with Robert," Blake said, sounding fed up.

"What are you going to do about that?" Zack asked.

"What can I do? Me and Robert were like brothers. We may not be as close now, but he's still a good guy, and Jenny is crazy about him. I don't want to hurt either of them by stepping in," Blake explained, and the way his voice kept shifting it sounded like he was walking around the room as he talked.

"So you wait till they have problems then jump in and sweep her off her feet?" Zack said and laughed a little.

"Right now that's my only plan." Blake said and sounded so sad that Zack didn't laugh after that.

"Well, I'm out of here, man. I'm going to check in with second shift, see if they need anything, and then head home for the night. I'm glad she's all right."

"Thanks, Zack, see you tomorrow," Blake said, and I could hear the door to my room close.

Blake let out a long sigh, and with that I was back asleep.

The next time I woke up, I was able to open my eyes, and the lights were so bright that I had to squint. "Hey, sweet girl," Robert's soothing voice came from beside the bed. "How are you feeling?"

I moaned and tried to focus on his face, but everything seemed blurry.

"That good, huh?" he asked, moving my hair back from my face.

"Mm-hmm," I hummed, feeling how fat my lip felt.

"Darlin', I'm so sorry this happened to you. I met with Tom and Blake. They told me everything, and I'm just so sorry."

"Please don't," I said, not wanting to think about any of it.

"Okay, sweet girl. Is there anything I can get you?" he asked sweetly.

"Just you," I said, trying to give him a weak smile.

"Well, I can definitely provide you with that," he said and leaned up, giving me a kiss on the forehead, and I winced with pain.

"Are you okay?" he asked, pulling away to look at me.

"Oh, she's fine," Mia answered for me. "She's still healing, is all," she continued as she walked over to look at the monitors, which were hooked to me.

"How bad is the damage?" Robert asked, moving to the foot of the bed to give Mia room to work.

Mia looked down at me when she answered, "Just what you can see. A busted lip and split cheek with a couple stitches."

"No concussion?" I asked.

"Nope. We're already putting your discharge papers together," she said, writing down my blood pressure reading before removing the cuff. I studied her as she worked and could see why Blake was attracted to her. Mia was a dark, beautiful woman. Her tanned skin made the caramel highlights in her long brown hair pop. She had her makeup perfectly applied on her flawless face, and her nails were painted a dark red, standing out against her gold jewelry. She had long lashes and big brown eyes. Her posture was perfect, and she had a small, firm body other than her breasts, which made me sad to notice that they were at least two sizes bigger than mine. She could've easily been a model rather than a nurse, and I had to give her a little respect for choosing to be a nurse over the other. It showed that she wasn't just gorgeous—she was smart too.

Robert smiled, and we watched Mia remove all the wires and pads from me.

"You can go ahead and get dressed," Mia said, leaving us alone in the room.

I was still a little loopy from the pain meds, so Robert helped me get dressed. I noticed he had brought me clean clothes from the house, and I was thankful someone had asked him to do it. Once I was ready to go, I looked at myself in the small mirror above the sink in my room. One whole side of my face was swollen, and I looked horrible.

"I'm gonna have to stop fighting," I said in the mirror.

"What?" Robert looked up, hoping he'd heard me right.

"I look like Frankenstein. I can't be in Patty's wedding next month if I look like this," I said, turning to him as I pointed to the gash on my face, combined with aging bruises from previous fights.

"You're beautiful no matter what, darlin', but do you really mean it?" he asked, pulling me over to sit on his lap.

I ran my hands over Robert's handsome face and smiled as best I could before reassuring him that I was done with the fighting, at least until after Patty's wedding.

"You have no idea how happy that makes me," Robert said, wrapping his arm around my waist. "Every time I see you with another injury, it kills me. I worry about you all the time."

"I'm sorry," I said, kissing him lightly on the mouth.

"But not sorry enough to quit it for good, right?" he asked as he studied my face.

"I'm not sure," I said, being as honest as I could.

Robert sighed, wishing I'd given him more, but I didn't know what I'd be doing a month from now when the wedding was over.

"At least I'm stopping for now and you won't have to go to the wedding with Frankenstein as your date," I said, trying my best to get a smile from him, but the lines on his face only deepened as he frowned at me even more.

"About that," he said, sounding nervous.

"What?" I asked, watching him fidget with the hem of my shirt.

"I know Patty's wedding isn't for another few weeks, but it looks like I'm not going to be able to make it," he said, barely meeting my eyes.

"Why not?" I asked.

"Ginger, one of the horses, is due to have her colt soon. I have to be there when she does."

"Why can't someone look after her for you?" I asked, feeling my heart sink with disappointment.

"If she gives birth and everything is okay by the time you leave, I can go, but if she's still holding on, I'll have to stay. I'm sorry. I know with everything you went through today, that's the last thing you need to hear, but at least Blake will be there with you, so you won't be alone," he said, trying to reassure me, but the thought of spending three days alone in a hotel with Blake did little to reassure me.

I smiled and nodded so Robert wouldn't think I was mad at him, but on the inside I was freaking out, hoping Robert would be able to go after all. I didn't know if I could trust Blake to behave for three unsupervised days together, and what was even scarier was that I didn't know if I wanted him to.

Chapter 15

EVERYTHING HAD BEEN a mess after the attack on me at the hospital. There were reports to file and statements to give. Officers from our local sheriff's office were able to arrest the four men involved after viewing footage from the security cameras overlooking the orchard. I had gone back to work the next day since my wounds were so minor. Everyone acted like I was going to fall apart or freak out since I'd come so close to being raped, but honestly, I'd been through closer calls. I shook it off and tried my best to act normal, even if Blake was making it damn near impossible. He hovered all the time, and it got on my nerves. Finally, one day at break, I had enough and told him to back off. He smiled and said he was glad to see I was back. It didn't stop there, though. At home, Robert was the same way. He acted as if we were fused together at the hips, and I couldn't go anywhere without him right by my side.

Blake was disappointed when I told him I wasn't going to the barn with him for fights anymore. At least not until after we were through with the wedding. Since I wasn't going to the fights anymore, neither was Blake, and the last two weekends in a row had him and Robert spending two nights at my house on the weekends instead of one.

It was Friday night again, the third Friday since my attack, and I left the guys sitting around the bonfire to run in the house for more snacks. The screen door closed, and I rummaged through my kitchen cabinets for anything Robert and Blake hadn't already eaten. I had just grabbed the last can of Pringles that I had in the house when elevated voices carried in through the screen door. I stopped moving, trying to hear what had them so upset.

"So I'm not welcome any more? Is that what you're saying?" Blake asked, almost yelling at Robert.

"That's not what I said. I just asked for one damn night alone with my girl when you're not around. Is that so bad?" Robert asked, raising his voice back at Blake.

"I don't see what the problem is. J obviously likes me being around," Blake snapped.

"I'm not stupid, Blake. I see the connection you and Jenny have, but you need to remember who her boyfriend is!" Robert yelled again.

"I haven't forgotten, Robert. You rub it in my face every chance you get."

"I do not! I don't say anything about you two spending so much time together, even when it bugs the shit out of me. So don't act like I'm the bad guy when I ask you for one night alone with her."

"So you can fuck her? Is that it?" Blake shouted, and I gasped as my hand flew to my open mouth, waiting for the fall out of his words. Seconds ticked by, and I couldn't hear either of them anymore.

I creeped over to the door and looked past the back porch to the bonfire where they had been sitting. Both men were up and in each other's faces. Even though I could tell they were pissed, neither spoke above a whisper, and that seemed so much worse to me than when they'd been shouting. Not knowing how bad it was scared me more than the yelling had. I debated if I should stay put and give them a chance to work it out or head back out there and break it up. I stared at the two of them, and when Robert poked Blake's chest hard enough that Blake's body rocked, I grabbed the Pringles can and ran out the back door.

"Found us something," I called as cheerfully as I could, holding up the can for them both to see. They quickly stepped apart and gave me fake smiles as I approached.

"Thanks, darlin'," Robert said, taking the can and sitting back down in his lawn chair.

I sat beside him and noticed Blake was still standing, his hands in fists at his sides.

"What's wrong?" I asked, standing back up to look into his eyes.

Blake wouldn't look at me, and he was breathing hard, still trying to calm down after his altercation with Robert. I gently touched his arm and patiently waited.

"Nothing," he finally said.

I looked back at Robert and made a face at him when he only shrugged and stuffed a chip in his mouth. "Are you sure?" I asked in a low voice as I tried to comfort him.

"I'm going to head home, J," Blake said, finally looking over at me.

"You sure?" I asked.

"Yeah, I'm ready to call it a night," he said, staring into the fire.

"Will we see you tomorrow night?" I asked, hoping we would. Hoping *I* would.

Blake glared at Robert and, when I turned around, found Robert glaring right back.

"No, I think I'll let you two have tomorrow night to yourselves," he said, with every word slow and laced with acid.

"We leave at the end of the week, though. This will be our last bonfire for a couple weeks at least," I said, and realized I was almost begging.

Blake broke eye contact with Robert to smile over at me. "I know. That's okay, though. A weekend out in Kansas will be all the fun we need."

I smiled, having no clue what he was talking about, and reached up, wrapping my arms around his neck. I stood on my tippy toes to be able to reach that far and felt his hands slide to the small of my back as he hugged me back. I felt his cheek press against my ear and knew he was smiling at Robert behind my back. "Behave," I whispered in his ear.

"I'm trying," he whispered back, and I could tell he was holding in a laugh.

I pulled away, shaking my head as we looked at each other and couldn't stop myself from returning Blake's goofy smile.

"Get out of here," I said, swatting at him when his smile turned into his signature cocky grin I both loved and hated.

He was almost to the porch when Robert called over his shoulder, "Bye, Blake," in a mocking, girly tone.

"Fuck you," Blake called back then walked into the house to get his things before leaving.

Robert chuckled, and I took my seat beside him again, grabbing the Pringles can out of his hand.

"What?" he asked, feigning innocence when he caught my glare.

"I will never understand you two," I said.

With only a week to go before I left to go to Patty's wedding, I wanted to get my hair cut and my nails done. Saturday morning, I called Kara, and an hour later, we were riding together in her yellow bug with the top down and our hair whipping in the wind.

"I'm so glad you called me!" she yelled over the wind and the music blaring from her car speakers.

"Me too!" I yelled back, and we both laughed.

"I have something for you," she said and reached behind my seat, pulling a box out and handing it to me.

"For me?" I asked, surprised by the gift in the pretty bright-pink box.

"Yes, it's for you," she said, laughing. "Open it."

I took my time opening the box, thinking about the last time someone got me a gift like this and couldn't think of one. I pulled the zebra-striped bow and black ribbons off carefully and set them aside and could hear Kara's sigh as she wished I'd just rip the box open. I smiled even more when I opened the pink box and found zebra-print tissue paper covering my present, which completely matched the bow I'd taken off. Under the tissue paper was the most beautiful wooden frame. It was a split frame, curving between each of the three pictures it held. The first picture was me wearing my orderly scrubs, and I looked like I was pretty nervous. It was kind of funny to look at now since that had been so long ago. With an arm wrapped around my shoulders was Kara looking as gorgeous as always, wearing her nursing scrubs. The two of us, still in Kansas when it was taken. On the opposite side of the frame was another picture, and that one was me and Blake standing next to his Jeep in the parking lot at work. Kara had asked the two of us to pose for a quick picture out of nowhere, and I'd wondered what she'd been up to. I couldn't remember what Blake had said to make me laugh in the picture, but my smile was wide as I stared at the camera. Blake, however, was looking straight over at me. He looked oblivious to the fact that Kara had been standing there trying to snap a pic of us as he smiled down at me. I stared at the picture longer than I probably should have before looking at the center and final photo in the beautiful frame.

The middle photo was of me and Robert standing in front of the tree line that bordered the gravel lane next to my house. Robert was shirtless and had an arm wrapped around me as I stood next to him with my arm around his waist. I was beaming in the picture as I stared up at Robert, and he smiled for Kara as she took the photo. God, Robert was so damn handsome. I finally looked away from his gorgeous body and sexy smile to look over at Kara. I was smiling so hard that it hurt my cheeks, and I had to stop myself from crying as I told her thanks for the gift.

"Are you crying?" Kara asked when she glanced over at me.

"No," I said quickly and made sure I wasn't.

"I noticed you don't have any pictures anywhere in your house. I had to make this one extra special for you. I hope you like it," Kara said as she drove down the road.

"I love it. Thank you so much," I said and hoped she could tell how true that was.

I put the picture and the beautiful pink box away so that it wouldn't get messed up, and we continued our drive down to Clarksville. We talked about the guys, the hospital, and all about Kansas, which, for us, was the good old days. Once we got to Clarksville, Kara took me to all her favorite places. We shopped and got our hair and nails done, and I was waxed in places I'd never been waxed before, but Kara insisted I get it done.

After a late lunch at her favorite restaurant, she took me to a little boutique on the main strip, where Kara assured me I would find something completely gorgeous to wear to the wedding. Every time I tried on a dress, Kara would make me step out and model it for her.

I felt ridiculous turning, stopping, spinning again, and posing for her at all the stops in between. She finally settled on a short, strapless black dress that barely covered anything and showed every curve I had. Paired with some red high heels, adding three inches to my height, I felt like a movie star. If Kara hadn't picked this for me, I'd never bought anything as short or as tight as this dress was. I insisted on buying Kara a dress too, even if she never knew when she'd wear it, and found that she was so much more picky about her own dress. It took us forever to get out of the store because Kara tried on almost every dress they had. When she was sure about a little black dress of her own, she insisted we had to wear them home.

We drove back to my house with the top up so we didn't mess up our hair after we'd gone through the trouble of having it styled. Kara kept me talking the entire way back, and I loved every minute I spent with her. When we pulled into my driveway, Kara turned off the music and pulled to my steps, dropping me off instead of parking to come in.

"Aren't you coming in?" I asked.

Kara smiled wide at me then nodded to the house as she said, "I don't think I'm invited."

I looked up the porch steps, which were lined with rose petals, to see Robert standing in the open door of my house. He was wearing a black tux and holding a bouquet of red roses as he waited for me to get out of the car.

I couldn't speak. I opened the door of the car and stepped out, careful not to fall in my new red heels. I walked up to the bottom step and looked at the masterpiece Robert had turned my simple porch into.

"Wow," Robert said as he looked me over, and I couldn't help but blush.

"Wow yourself," I said, gesturing to his tux.

"Oh, this old thing?" he said, and I giggled.

I heard Kara honk before turning onto the road, but I didn't look back. I couldn't take my eyes off Robert. He quickly came down the steps when he saw my hesitation and offered his arm out to me.

"Thank you," I said, taking it as we walked over the hundreds of rose petals under our feet.

Robert took my shopping bags, and the little pink box from me, laying them on the couch. Then he stepped back in front of me, holding out a dozen red roses. I took them, smiling up at him, and couldn't get over the lengths he'd taken to make tonight special for us.

"You know this is our last night together before you leave for Kansas?" he asked.

"I know," I said, feeling a stab of pain in my chest.

"It had to be special, because you're special," he said, and turned, leading me into the kitchen.

My country-style dining table had been turned into a grand five-star restaurant setting. Fancy linens, tableware, goblets, and candles adorned the table.

"This is amazing," I said, sitting as Robert pulled my chair out for me. He came around and lifted the cover of my dish, revealing a heart-shaped pancake with strawberries lining the outside of the plate. I laughed, covering my mouth, as I gazed down at the plate.

"Pancakes are your favorite," he said, grinning down at my shocked expression.

"They are," I squealed, impressed that he'd remembered.

Robert took his seat across the table, and we sat there eating as soft, romantic tunes played from a nearby radio. I couldn't stop smiling, and every time we made eye contact, I'd blush and giggle. "I love your blush," Robert said in admiration, and it only made me blush more, causing Robert to stifle a laugh at my embarrassment.

Robert finished before me and got up, taking his plate to the kitchen sink. I played with the last strawberry on the plate for a moment, soaking it all in. The music, the meal, the roses and candles that were everywhere, and Robert's sexy-looking tux. I stiffened as I thought about it and was suddenly so nervous. If he'd done all this for me, what was he expecting in return? At first, I thought, *Oh my god, he's going to propose*, but then I thought there was no way because we'd only been seeing each other for a few months. Then I knew. Robert had done all this to get me into bed with him. He knew it was my first time, so he was trying to make it special for me. A ton of pressure hit me all at once, and my heart started beating out of control. I stood, ready to voice my objections to Robert, and he quickly ran from the kitchen over to me.

"I'll get that, darlin'," he said as he picked up my plate and silverware.

All I could do was smile, and I felt queasy, like I was going to throw up all over his damn vanilla-scented candles. Robert came back, smiling at me, flashing me his most gorgeous smile. It didn't feel right. It wasn't time. I wasn't ready, dammit.

Robert led me by the hand to the living room, where the music played louder, and pulled me into him. I stared into his eyes as we started to sway with the music, and I tried to force a smile. I knew I must feel stiff and rigid in his arms, but I couldn't help it. The song ended a minute later, and we stopped dancing. Robert let go of me and took both my hands in his as he looked uneasy and nervous.

"Robert…" I started to say, to voice all the objections in my head, but he stopped me.

"I need to tell you something. Could you give me just a moment, please?" he asked, and his voice had become shaky.

I shook my head for him to continue, but inwardly groaned as I waited for him to say…

I didn't get to finish the thought. Robert pulled a black box from his tuxedo and started to get down on one knee as he said, "Would you make me the happiest man in the world and—"

"What?" I yelled, and we both jumped at my outburst as I cut him off midquestion.

Robert composed himself again and slowly opened the little black box he held, exposing the biggest, brightest diamond I'd ever seen. It sparkled under the light, and the white-gold band it was attached to shined beneath it.

"Jenny, darlin', you are beautiful and smart. You're tough as nails, and I have loved every minute of every day since you've been in my life. You would make me the happiest man in the world if—"

"Wait!" I shouted, cutting him off again, sounding hysterical, but I couldn't let him finish.

Robert stopped midquestion, looking at me like I'd lost my mind, then slowly stood up in front of me, still holding out the ring.

"What are you doing?" I exclaimed, running my hands through my hair.

"I'm trying to ask you a question," he said patiently.

"That's what all this was for?" I shouted, spinning around the room like a crazy person.

"What did you think I did it for?" Robert asked, slowly closing the ring box and staring at me.

"I thought you were going to try to sleep with me," I blurted before I could stop myself.

"Sleep with you?" he asked as he looked around the room. When he finally realized why I'd thought that, he slowly smiled at me then asked, "So you were going to sleep with me?"

"No," I said. Then quickly blurted, "I don't know, okay? I don't know." I picked up my pacing again, and Robert came over, grabbing my wrist and pulling me around to face him.

"What's wrong?" he asked, his voice a soothing tone.

"What's wrong?" I repeated. "I'm not ready to get married. I don't know if I'm ready for sex. Two months ago I was barely ready for a boyfriend, and yet here we are."

"You're scared," he stated, still calm.

"I guess," I said, feeling like my emotions were out of control. This whole night was out of control.

His sensual lips curled in amusement, and I hit his arm with my hand. He stifled a laugh and asked, "Do you know you can always count on me, Jenny? For anything you need."

"I already count on you more than you know," I told him, trusting him with such a big piece of myself.

Robert played with an end of my hair as he looked down at me and asked, "Then what are your reservations about taking the next step with me? We're perfect together."

"I don't know. I just feel like there should be way more steps between a first kiss and marriage," I said, looking into his green eyes.

"Okay, then let's make more steps," he suggested.

"What steps?" I asked. He had my attention now, and my heartbeat settled a little.

"What about moving in together first? That could be a step," he offered.

"That's a pretty big step." I exclaimed.

Robert smiled. "I know, but it's a smaller step that we can work toward."

"You have got to be the most patient man in the world," I said, smiling up at him.

"For you, always. I'm not going to take anything from you that you aren't ready to give me, darlin'. That's how love works," Robert said and gave me a light kiss on the forehead.

I closed my eyes and melted into him, letting his warmth and security envelope me. He pulled me tightly against him and held me like that as minutes ticked away on the clock.

"So what do you think about it?" he quietly asked.

"About moving in together?" I checked.

"Yes," he said, and I felt his chest tighten as he held his breath in anticipation of my answer.

"Can I think about it?" I asked, feeling terrible that I couldn't go ahead and give him an answer. He let out the breath he'd been holding and pushed back, holding me at arm's length to look into my eyes.

"You can take all the time you need," he said, making sure I knew he meant those words.

I smiled as I said, "Thank you for not being upset or trying to pressure me into anything."

"Jenny, I'll wait till the end of time for you as long as you promise me you're considering it. That's all I want, is to know we're heading toward something more with each other. I'll never pressure you into anything, and I'll always be here to talk about it if you want. Whatever you need me to be, I'll be that for you."

"I feel like I ruined your entire night," I said, looking around the room.

"You didn't ruin anything, sweet girl," he said and laughed.

"What's so funny?" I asked.

"Were you really going to sleep with me tonight?" he asked and wagged his eyebrows at me.

"Robert!" I squealed, and we both started laughing, feeling the pressure drain from the room.

The rest of the night was spent talking, drinking the expensive wine Robert had bought, and holding each other as we got ridiculously drunk on the wine. Everything Robert said was hilarious to me, and neither of us could stop laughing. We finally passed out in the living room floor together sometime before dawn, me still wearing my little black dress and Robert still in his tux.

The workweek rolled by quickly, and in the blink of an eye, I was standing in the airport with Robert and Blake. Robert's damn horse never had her colt, so he refused to leave her to go to Kansas, leaving just Blake to make the trip with me. Blake held my bags as Robert pulled me to the side for a big goodbye. Families bustled through the airport entrance and moved around us, making it hard to find the romance in the moment, but Robert was determined to.

A huge smile spread across Robert's face before I pressed my lips to his. "Damn, Jenny, I love you so much," he growled against my mouth.

God, I was going to miss his husky voice and Southern drawl.

"I'm leaving something with you," I whispered as we pulled apart.

"What?" he asked, never letting go of me.

"My heart. Take care of it please," I said, and he kissed me again.

Blake cleared his throat, and we looked over at him. "It's only three days, guys," he said, giving us an inpatient glare.

I smiled at Blake and held up a finger, asking for another minute. He rolled his eyes, and I turned back to Robert.

"I love you," I said into his green eyes.

"Say it again," he said, kissing the tip of my nose.

I giggled and said, "I love you, Robert."

"I love you too, darlin'," he said and kissed me hard on the mouth.

"Comes on, guys. It's not war," Blake said sarcastically.

We both smiled and went back where we'd left Blake standing.

"Take care of my girl," Robert said and reached a hand out to Blake.

"I will," Blake said with a little too much enthusiasm, then reached out, shaking Robert's hand.

I got one last chaste kiss before Robert ran out to his truck that he'd parked in a no-parking zone. I smiled as I watched him go and already missed his warmth. I reached for my bags, and Blake jerked them back, picking them all up as we continued further into the airport.

We reached our seats on the plane and got comfortable in our chairs as other passengers filed in around us.

"You smell good, J. New perfume?" Blake asked.

"Don't start," I said, smacking his arm.

"What?" he asked, grinning wickedly at me.

"Just because Robert isn't with us doesn't mean you don't have to behave this weekend," I scolded.

"That's right. Robert isn't here. You're mine for three whole days. You should just get used to the fact now that for three days, I'm going to be flirting with you nonstop," he said and winked.

"As long as that's all it is," I said, looking him in the eyes so he knew I was serious. He smiled wide, and I laughed as I squealed, "I'm serious, Blake. I'm not sleeping with you."

Blake looked me over, still smiling, and when his eyes reached my face again said, "But you're clearly dressed to seduce me."

I quickly looked down at my outfit. A short blue-jean skirt and a white tank top were clearly not going to seduce anyone. Blake laughed before I could look up, and I elbowed him hard.

He laughed out loud, causing me to laugh with him, and I felt myself settling into another version of myself, the self I usually was when it was just me and him. I was a little less responsible. Someone who might, on occasion, do something really stupid for no good reason. Blake reached out and took my hand in his. I stared at our fingers as they intertwined and felt my heart skip, even though I tried to fight against it. The lines with Blake were becoming blurred again, and I fumbled to try to think of something to make the boundaries clear again. They seemed to get blurred a lot with Blake. I noticed from the corner of my eye that he was watching me again, closely, intently, and it was unnerving.

"I have a bad feeling about Mooney," I said out of nowhere.

Blake stiffened beside me, but I didn't dare look over at him. I continued looking out my window. I never talked about the dreams I'd had or the visit from Laura. I'd never once said anything to him about the uneasiness Mooney left me with, but knowing we had an entire plane ride to get through made me want to tell him everything.

"I do too," he confessed. "I don't like him being in our hospital."

Blake's serious tone wasn't lost on me, and I turned to face him. His normally bright-blue eyes were dark and full of concern. "I'm worried something terrible is going to happen."

"He's not like the other patients on our ward, is he?" he asked, watching me, and I shook my head. "I keep watching him, waiting for him to try something, and I thought after he'd been there for a while, the feeling might go away."

"I thought so too. He's been on the floor for weeks, but no matter how quiet or how compliant he is with all us up there, I just can't shake the feeling that at some point, all that's going to change," I confessed, and as those words were spoken out loud, a cold chill ran up my spine. It didn't make me feel any better knowing Blake felt the same way about the patient. It only made me worry more that maybe there was more trouble ahead of us, and we wouldn't be ready any of it.

Blake watched me in silence for a long moment before he forced a smile onto his face. "Don't worry about anything, J. I've always got your back up there," he said, trying to lighten the mood.

"And I've always got yours," I said. Blake's smile turned genuine as he brushed one finger down the length of my hand that was resting between our seats. New shivers ran up my spine, but they had nothing to do with the hospital or the patients in it.

Trying to hide my blush that was spreading across my cheeks like wildfire, I quickly turned to look out my window once more. No matter how much I wished for it, my feelings for Blake never seemed to go away. The sexual tension between us seemed to grow each time we saw each other rather than dwindle into nothing like I wanted.

Sitting so close to him now had my body reacting in ways that I didn't want to acknowledge. I didn't understand all the unwanted feelings for Blake when I was sure I was in love with Robert, yet here I was wishing he'd lean over and kiss me.

The passengers around us buckled in, and the plane started to gather speed as we prepared to take off. Blake squeezed my hand, and I looked over at him. He was smiling at me, staring into my eyes, but this was a look of longing, not his usual cocky grin. My stomach flipped, and I was terrified. I tried to tell myself that the fear was pointless, but my stomach wasn't buying it. The plane lifted into the air as Blake and I concentrated on each other, and I wasn't just worried about making it through the flight. I was worried about how I was going to spend the next three days with Blake and neither of us act on this feeling building between us.

About the Author

Shannon Everhart has generated new interest in the wild tales surrounding mental asylums, something people have been fascinated with for decades, and has brought renewed life to the age-old concept of love at first sight. This first installment of *Moments at McBride* has us on the edge of our seats as we anxiously await books two and three of the series.

Shannon and her husband, Chris, live with their children just outside of Scottsburg, Indiana, with the cats who adopted them and the crazy dog who won't stop chasing the cats. They spend their time having family and friends over to their place where they enjoy having parties and get-togethers on their seven-acre mini farm. When Shannon isn't writing or spending time with the family, she often enjoys reading good books, watching bad zombie or shark movies, and eating pizza.

For more information, visit https://shannoneverhartbooks.wixsite.com/mysite or follow her on Facebook.

CPSIA information can be obtained
at www.ICGtesting.com
Printed in the USA
BVHW032252020321
601492BV00006B/471

9 781662 417313